She fascinated him,

and Max was tempted to break down all her defenses. She had a large arsenal—she could spear him with a flashing violet look, pierce him with a laugh. Perhaps some battles were better left unfought.

Still, the moonlight made her look so enticing. . . .

He reached for her and his mouth captured hers. Susan didn't fight. The heat of passion melted her armor and, with a sigh of surrender, she opened her mouth to his.

He could taste sweet victory. He moaned, plunging deeper. And his heart sang with triumph. She had been conquered. . . .

Dear Reader,

Welcome to Silhouette **Special Edition** ... welcome to romance. Each month, Silhouette **Special Edition** publishes six novels with you in mind—stories of love and life, tales that you can identify with—romance with that little "something special" added in.

July is a wonderful month—full of sizzling stories packed with emotion. Don't miss Debbie Macomber's warm and witty *Bride on the Loose*—the concluding tale of her series, THOSE MANNING MEN. And *Heartbreak Hank* is also in store for you—Myrna Temte's third COWBOY COUNTRY tale. Starting this month, as well, is Linda Lael Miller's new duo BEYOND THE THRESHOLD. The initial book is entitled *There and Now*.

Rounding out this month are more stories by some of your favorite authors: Bevlyn Marshall, Victoria Pade and Laurie Paige.

In each Silhouette **Special Edition** novel, we're dedicated to bringing you the romances that you dream about— stories that will delight as well as bring a tear to the eye. For me, good romance novels have always contained an element of hope, of optimism that life can be, and often is, very beautiful. I find a great deal of inspiration in that thought.

Why do you read romances? I'd really like to hear your opinions on the books that we publish and on the romance genre in general. Please write to me c/o Silhouette Books, 300 East 42nd Street, 6th floor, New York, NY 10017.

I hope that you enjoy this book and all of the stories to come. Looking forward to hearing from you!

Sincerely,

Tara Gavin
Senior Editor
Silhouette Books

BEVLYN MARSHALL
Swiss Bliss

Silhouette Special Edition

Published by Silhouette Books New York

America's Publisher of Contemporary Romance

SILHOUETTE BOOKS
300 East 42nd St., New York, N.Y. 10017

SWISS BLISS

Copyright © 1992 by Bevlyn Marshall Kaukas

ISBN: 0-373-09753-0

First Silhouette Books printing July 1992

All the characters in this book have no existence outside the
imagination of the author and have no relation whatsoever to
anyone bearing the same name or names. They are not even
distantly inspired by any individual known or unknown to the
author, and all incidents are pure invention.

®: Trademark used under license and registered in the United
States Patent and Trademark Office and in other countries.

Printed in the U.S.A.

Books by Bevlyn Marshall

Silhouette Special Edition

Lonely at the Top #407
The Pride of His Life #441
Grady's Lady #506
Radio Daze #544
Goddess of Joy #562
Treasure Deep #598
Thunderbolt #665
Above the Clouds #704
Swiss Bliss #753

BEVLYN MARSHALL,

a Connecticut resident, has had a varied career in fashion, public relations and marketing, but finds writing the most challenging and satisfying occupation. When she's not at her typewriter, she enjoys tennis, needlepoint, long walks with her husband and toy spaniel, and reading. She believes that people who read are rarely bored or lonely because "the private pleasure of a good book is one of life's most rewarding pastimes."

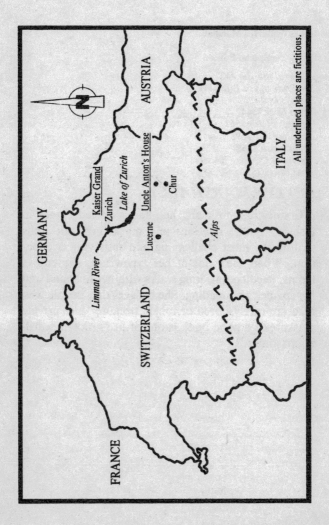

All underlined places are fictitious.

Chapter One

Susan didn't know the name of the man sleeping beside her. It didn't matter. She would be parting with him soon enough. She'd been relieved when his last drink had done him in and he'd fallen into silent oblivion. Now he shifted restlessly until his shoulder pressed against hers. Resenting this invasion of her space, Susan considered giving him a hard jab with her elbow but thought better of it. Let sleeping bores lie.

Alas, he opened his bleary eyes. "Oh, excuse me," he said, moving his body away from hers. "Was I leaning against you the whole time I was asleep?"

"No, just now," Susan replied coolly.

"I hope I didn't snore."

"Well, you did," she informed him.

He rubbed his eyes, straightened his bow tie, and sat up straighter in his airplane seat. Susan went back to studying her book of German phrases, hoping he would get the hint that she didn't want to chat with him.

He didn't. "I started flirting with you after my third drink, didn't I, miss?"

"Your second," Susan corrected. "You fell asleep after your third."

Her traveling companion exhaled a stale whiff of whiskey. "Liquor goes straight to my head, I'm afraid."

"Then don't drink," Susan curtly advised, not looking up from her book.

"I don't usually. But I have a tremendous fear of flying."

Susan had her own deep-seated fears and although flying wasn't one of them, she felt a twinge of compassion for the man beside her. She gave him a sympathetic smile.

"I don't usually flirt with young ladies, either," he added, then laughed sheepishly. "Why, you're young enough to be my granddaughter. I apologize if I offended you."

She noticed that he studiously avoided looking at her chest, although he'd certainly ogled that part of her anatomy enough before he fell asleep. But now he looked so embarrassed that she forgave him his past transgressions.

"Apology accepted." She offered her hand.

"My name is John Morgan," he said, shaking it.

"Susan Barnes."

"I promise you I won't get out of line again, Susan. But I could surely use a little friendly conversation to get me through the rest of this flight."

She closed her book, willing to accommodate him now that he was sober. "You must not fly often if you find it so upsetting."

"This is my first time ever." He swallowed hard.

"Well, it's almost over. We should be landing in Zürich in less than an hour."

"If we don't crash into the Swiss Alps before then!"

"I'm sure the pilot knows exactly where they are and how to avoid them."

"Yes, silly of me to worry about that. But I'll feel so much better when I'm on solid ground again. I hear Switzerland is beautiful. I suppose you've been there before. You look like a seasoned world traveler to me.''

Susan was happy to hear it. She had dressed carefully for this journey, wanting to look as sophisticated as possible when she met her new employer, Maximilian Kaiser, at the Zürich airport. She had bought her beige silk dress on sale for less than half price, but had still paid more for it than any dress she'd ever owned.

''Actually, I have traveled quite a lot because of my work,'' she told John. ''But only in America. I've never left the States before.''

She'd never flown first-class before, either, but Mr. Kaiser had sent her the ticket. Her last boss had cut corners whenever possible, which had been fine with Susan. She didn't need or expect luxuries. Although she appreciated her new employer's generous gesture, she considered it an unnecessary one. The way she saw it, you got where you wanted to go just as fast sitting in the Economy seats.

''What sort of work do you do?'' John asked her.

''I'm a hotel consultant.''

''That sounds important.''

Susan laughed. ''Not really.'' She didn't want to talk about herself. ''What's your line of work, John?''

''I'm a botanist,'' he said. ''The University of Zürich invited me to give a lecture on the propagation of ornamental plants, all expenses paid. I was so flattered by the invitation that I couldn't refuse, despite my reluctance to travel by plane.''

''I can understand why. That's quite an honor.''

''I only wish my dear wife could share it with me. She passed away three years ago.''

''I'm sorry to hear that.'' Susan knew all about the pain of loss. Her childhood had been filled with it. She'd resolved, long ago, to depend on only herself and had avoided deep attachments ever since. At first that had been difficult to do because it went against her nature. But she believed it had enabled her to survive plenty of rough times.

"Becky and I were together for almost fifty years," John went on. "Half a century of companionship and love. My wife looked very much like you when she was young, Susan. Same dark hair and pale skin and ... uh ... charming figure, if you don't mind my saying so. I was struck by the likeness when you took your seat. I even started pretending to myself that you *were* Becky, and that I was still young, too, and we were taking our first trip to Europe together. That's why I behaved like such an old fool with you."

Tears welled into Susan's eyes. For all her determination to remain detached in her dealings with people, her emotions were always too close to the surface. She patted John's arm. "Well, now that I know why, I'll take it as a compliment."

"You're a very understanding young lady. I notice you're not wearing a wedding ring. Is there someone special waiting for you in Switzerland? Some lucky fellow?"

Susan shook her head. "The only thing waiting for me there is a new job."

She tried to sound blasé about it even though this new venture frightened her a little. She'd been so excited and nervous during the trip to the airport that she'd left her raincoat behind in the taxi. That wasn't like her. She usually took great care of her possessions. She'd had so few of them growing up.

"Will you be working in Zürich?" John asked her.

Susan nodded but volunteered no additional information. She figured Maximilian Kaiser would appreciate discretion. Although she had never seen or spoken to him, the stilted letter he had sent her to formalize their agreement had left her with the impression that the man was just as stiff and formal.

And old. Very old. Almost as old as the hotel he owned and managed, perhaps. The Kaiser Grand had been in business for over a hundred years and was considered one of the finest in the world. European royalty had patronized it in its illustrious heyday. And now that royalty had grown scarce, the luxurious Kaiser Grand depended on rich tourists to keep it going. But apparently it wasn't going all that well if Mr. Kaiser needed *her* expertise, which had more to do with no-nonsense efficiency than luxury.

The pilot's voice came over the intercom, announcing that the plane would be landing exactly on schedule.

John paled. "I'm getting nervous all over again," he told Susan. "The landing is probably going to be scarier than the takeoff was."

"Everything will be fine, John. Flying is one of the safest ways to travel. We'd be more at risk in a car now."

"I know the statistics are in our favor. But I still can't get used to the idea of something as heavy as an airplane actually flying through the air. I've devoted my life to the study of nature. Aeronautics, however, remains a mystery to me."

"So tell me about your work," Susan said, attempting to distract him from his anxiety. "Botany must be fascinating."

"Oh, it is," he replied, but without much enthusiasm. A steward wheeling a beverage cart had caught his attention. "A double bourbon straight up," he requested.

"Are you sure you really want that?" Susan asked him softly.

John took the glass from the steward. "It's more a matter of need than want. I hate to admit it, but I need a crutch to get me through this ordeal."

"Would it help if I held your hand when the plane lands?" she suggested.

He attempted a smile. "Are you flirting with *me* now, young lady?"

"You bet I am. I've always had a secret weakness for botanists."

"Is that right? Even old ones?"

"The older the better. Especially when they wear polka-dot bow ties."

John's smile became less strained as he touched his own polka-dot bow tie. The banter seemed to relax him a little. "Maybe I don't need this drink, after all."

The pilot's voice came over the intercom again, informing the passengers that there would be a bit of turbulence ahead and requesting that they fasten their seat belts.

"Turbulence," John repeated in a bleak tone. He placed his drink on the armrest between his seat and Susan's to snap his belt closed. As Susan was fastening her own belt the plane dipped. And John's drink toppled into her lap.

"Oh, no! I'm so sorry," he said.

Susan pulled tissues from her handbag and tried to sop up the strong-smelling liquid. But a big brown blotch remained on her skirt. John looked at her with repentant eyes.

"It doesn't matter," she told him.

"Yes, it does. I've managed to ruin your dress."

Well, he had. But he looked so miserable about it that Susan attempted a joke to make him feel better. "No sense crying over spilt bourbon," she said. "Luckily, I have some other clothes in my carryon."

As soon as they'd passed the rough area and passengers were allowed to move freely again, she took her small suitcase with her to the washroom and changed into a pair of cutoff jeans and a faded sweatshirt that she always took with her when she traveled—her version of a security blanket. Alone in a strange hotel room, she would slip into these old, comfortable clothes to relax and feel more at home. The short jeans looked ridiculous, she was sure, with her stockings and black, high-heeled pumps, but she couldn't very well wear the fuzzy slippers sporting bunny ears that she'd also brought along for security and comfort. They would look even more ridiculous. She rolled up her beautiful new dress, stuffed it into the bag, and returned to her seat.

John still looked crestfallen.

"No harm done," Susan assured him, although she felt far less presentable than she had before the unfortunate mishap. She didn't hold it against John, however, and when the plane began its descent she reached for his hand. It was clammy, but she kept a firm grip on it until they safely touched ground.

Max Kaiser waited at the terminal gate for Susan Barnes. He wasn't good at waiting—for anything or anybody. He knew that was one of his faults and had done his best to overcome it. But impatience seemed embedded in his nature. He checked his watch. Her flight had arrived thirty-nine minutes ago. He wondered if she was having a problem getting through Customs.

A woman dressed in a sensible suit came through the doors to the waiting area.

"Perhaps that's Miss Barnes at last, Daniel," Max told the chauffeur standing beside him. He hoped it was. She looked very capable and businesslike.

The chauffeur waved the Kaiser Grand placard he was holding to get the woman's attention. She glanced at it blankly and continued past them.

Daniel shrugged and lowered the sign. "Could it be that Miss Barnes missed her flight?"

That possibility did not please Max. "If she changed her plans she should have notified me." His secretary had called Miss Barnes to inform her that he would be meeting her plane.

Max resisted the impulse to check his watch again. Instead, he went to the information desk to find out if Susan Barnes had indeed boarded the plane in New York. He was told that she had. So where was she?

As he walked back to the waiting area he observed Daniel in conversation with a young woman dressed in snug denim shorts and high heels. Max let his eyes skim over her figure appreciatively. He didn't appreciate the chauffeur socializing while on duty, however. But then again, Daniel was only twenty, and Max didn't have to go back too many years to recall how easily a curvy-legged fräulein could distract *him* at that age. He purposely slowed his pace to give Daniel a few extra minutes of privacy.

When the young woman handed over her small suitcase to him, Max frowned. Had Daniel offered to drive her somewhere? He quickened his pace again. The Kaiser Grand limousine wasn't the boy's personal taxi service, after all. Let him pick up pretty girls on his own time.

But it turned out that Daniel was only doing his job. "This is Miss Barnes," he told his boss when Max joined them. "I'll bring her bag out to the car." And with that he hurried off, a model of efficiency.

Max tried to keep his expression polite as he scrutinized Susan Barnes. She was . . . what was the American expression? . . . a knockout. Creamy complexion and wavy dark hair. Wide-set eyes and softly rounded cheeks. Without those high heels, not very tall. The clinging red sweatshirt she wore had the name of a popular American beer emblazoned on it. The gold letters curved over her full breasts. Her short jeans were unraveling at the edges. He wondered if the frayed material tickled her slender thighs when she walked.

Max made himself stop wondering. He didn't approve of her outfit. Not at all. You would think someone who called herself a hotel consultant would know the importance of first impressions. And his first impression of Susan Barnes was that she would never be able to understand, let alone appreciate, the Kaiser Grand's high standards.

"How do you do, Miss Barnes? I'm Max Kaiser," he said flatly.

Strike one for me, Susan thought. Max Kaiser's icy stare of disapproval was enough to make her shiver. Yet instead, she felt a rush of heat as he looked her over. She'd never felt such an immediate, powerful attraction to a man before. He exuded a magnetism that drew her to him despite his coldness.

Still, she resented his quick, critical judgment of her and held back an apology for the way she was dressed. She took the hand he offered and shook it briefly, feeling little charges of electricity tingle her palm. "It's very nice to finally meet you, Mr. Kaiser."

He didn't reply in kind. "Where's the rest of your baggage?" he asked in a clipped tone.

"Good question. I've been trying to find out what happened to it. That's what held me up. The airline assures me they'll track it down. But right now all I have is the clothes on my back." She paused. "Which you obviously don't approve of, Mr. Kaiser."

Was it that obvious? Max hadn't meant it to be. He gave Susan Barnes credit for at least being perceptive. And direct. Good. He never beat around the bush himself. "Frankly, I was going to ask you to change into something more appropriate before going to the hotel. I've arranged a meeting with the major shareholders."

"Well, since I can't change, they'll have to accept me dressed as I am," she said, keeping her voice light. And so will *you,* she added silently.

"I have a suggestion," he said. "We can stop at a clothing shop before we go to the hotel. Come along." He headed toward the exit.

That hadn't been a suggestion, it had been an order, Susan realized, lengthening her stride to keep up with him.

Sitting beside her new boss in the back seat of the roomy limousine, Susan tried to relax. But she found it hard to do in Max Kaiser's presence. Although he had an outwardly cool, calm demeanor, his inner intensity was almost palpable. It attracted her and frightened her a little bit, too.

She hadn't expected him to be so young. In his early thirties, she guessed. And she hadn't expected him to be so good-looking, either. Tall and angular, with sharply defined features and electric blue eyes, he had a forceful physical presence that was hard to ignore. Despite his somber attire—a beautifully tailored charcoal suit and black cashmere turtleneck—there seemed to be a golden aura about him. His lean face had a golden tan. And his thick, longish hair, combed back from his high forehead, was gold, too. Not blond, but a dark, rich, lustrous gold.

Mr. Perfect, Susan silently dubbed him, more as a put-down than a compliment. With a sidelong glance she studied his profile and decided that his nose was too sharp and prominent. It reminded her a bit of an eagle's beak. Finding something about him to criticize made her feel a little more at ease.

"Did you have a good flight?" he asked her. He spoke English without an accent, but so precisely that it was almost like having one.

"Yes, except for a little turbulence toward the end. Because of it, the man sitting next to me spilled his drink on my dress. So I had to change into the only other clothes I'd packed in my carryon." Susan brushed a piece of lint off her sweatshirt, congratulating herself on explaining her appearance without actually apologizing for it. "There's an expression in America you may not be familiar with, Mr. Kaiser. Never judge a book by its cover."

"Oh, I'm familiar with that expression, Miss Barnes. I've spent a great deal of time in the States. And I didn't mean to be judgmental. If I came across that way, forgive me. To coin another American phrase, it seems we started off on the left foot."

"The wrong foot."

"Right. That is, I mean wrong." He smiled.

It was the first smile he'd allowed himself since they'd met, and Susan was surprised by its shy sweetness. It transformed him, softening all his hard edges. The image of a glacier melting sprang into her mind.

Then his smile evaporated. "You're not going to have an easy time of it at Kaiser Grand," he told her. "The family isn't too receptive to outsiders and can be very critical. That was my chief concern when I saw the way you were dressed."

"It was my understanding that I'd be working for you alone."

"Yes, of course. I'm the hotel's general manager now. It's a family-owned business, however."

"I'm aware of that," Susan said. "But I didn't think that all the Kaiser shareholders were involved in the day-to-day running of the operation."

"Some of them would like to be involved in the minute-to-minute running of it. You know how families are."

She didn't really. From the time she was eleven until she was eighteen she had lived in various orphanages and foster homes. For the last ten years she had been on her own. "Maybe you need a family counselor instead of a hotel consultant, Mr. Kaiser," she remarked.

He laughed sharply. "What I need is to get the Grand back on course."

"How did it get off course?"

"If I knew, I wouldn't have hired you, Miss Barnes. I expect you to give me the answer by the end of your stay here."

His bright blue eyes bored into hers. She didn't look away. "You may not like the answer I come up with, Mr. Kaiser."

"Just so it's the right one." That settled, he released her from his piercing gaze.

The limousine sped down the highway, weaving in and out of the morning traffic. Susan thought that the chauffeur was driving far too fast, then she noticed that every driver on the road seemed to be a speed demon. The rolling green fields near the airport gave way to office and industrial complexes, modern and neat, and sooner than Susan expected, they reached the city itself.

Max leaned forward and spoke to the driver in Swiss German. "I asked Daniel to take us to a shop in town before we go to the hotel," he explained to Susan, switching back to English. "I don't know much about women's clothes, but my sister and mother patronize this shop, so I'm sure you'll be able to find something more presentable to wear there."

The last thing Susan felt like doing at the moment was shopping. Although it was ten in the morning in Zürich, her body hadn't adjusted to the time difference. Back in New York it was 4:00 a.m.

"Is that really necessary, Mr. Kaiser?" she asked. "Surely I'm presentable enough as I am until my luggage is found."

"No, you're not," he told her point-blank.

Susan wondered if he acted so imperiously with everyone, or only with women, or worse yet, just with *her*.

The chauffeur took a few turns that brought them into the heart of the city. Susan had expected high-rise buildings and bustling traffic, but Zürich looked more like a cozy village than an international financial center. Ancient church towers rose above the clay rooftops of pastel buildings with long shutters and window boxes. The cobblestoned streets were narrow. In the blink of an eye, it seemed, they had traveled a century or two into the past.

"How lovely Zürich is," she said. "Like some magical place out of a fairy tale."

"We Swiss are far too practical to believe in magic, Miss Barnes," Max told her. His expression remained serious, but Susan thought she discerned a twinkle in his eye.

The car pulled to a stop in front of a small shop with a dark green awning. Max pushed up the sleeve of his jacket to check his watch.

Susan recognized it as the most expensive timepiece a man could own. Swiss, of course. Perfectly crafted and guaranteed to last a lifetime, it was a watch that would never let one down. Susan found herself wondering if the man who wore it could claim the same fine attributes.

"We have a good hour before the meeting I scheduled," he stated. "Will that give you enough time to select something?"

"Plenty. I usually make up my mind very quickly."

"Good. Some women take forever." As Daniel opened the car door for her, Max settled back and unfolded a newspaper that had been lying on the seat.

"You're not coming in with me?" Susan asked him, trying not to sound too relieved about it.

"I trust you'll be able to find something suitable on your own, Miss Barnes."

Sure that she heard a note of condescension in his voice, Susan had an inclination to needle him. "Yeah, with lots of sequins and a feather boa," she said.

Max lowered the paper and looked at her. "You're joking, of course."

The man obviously lacked a sense of humor, Susan thought; she hopped out of the car without answering.

She entered the elegant shop and hoped she could find something "suitable" without spending too much. She hadn't had the chance to exchange dollars for Swiss francs at the airport but noted a sign on the glass counter that displayed her credit card, among others.

"Excuse me, do you speak English?" she asked the saleswoman behind the counter.

"Yes, of course," she replied haughtily, giving Susan a swift once-over. She turned up her nose, ever so slightly. "How can I help you?"

"I need a dress to wear to a business meeting," she told the woman. "Something understated and classic."

"What size are you, please?"

"An American size six. I don't know what that's comparable to here."

The woman sized her up again, this time with friendlier eyes. "Thirty-four," she replied. "But more a thirty-eight on top."

"Yes, that's always been a problem," Susan said.

"Most women wouldn't consider it one, madame."

Susan always had. Her full breasts, which looked all the fuller because of her petite frame, had caused her problems since puberty. Whenever she entered a new school, boys would snicker and point at her. That was bad enough. Much worse was the way grown men, sometimes in the households where she'd been temporarily placed, would make her a target for unwanted attentions. She'd come close to being raped once. By the time she was fourteen she'd concluded that no man could be trusted.

"Here's something that should fit you well," the saleswoman said, taking a navy dress from a small rack and holding it out at arm's length. "The cut is exquisite, and the light wool fabric is perfect for autumn."

If dresses could be called well-bred, this one certainly was, Susan thought. It had a high collar and short sleeves and looked both stylish and demure. "I'll try it on," she said.

The woman ushered her into a dressing room. "Call me if you need any help, madame."

Left alone, Susan searched the garment for a price tag. There was none. She tried it on, anyway, and examined herself in the full-length mirror from every possible angle, imagining all the family and staff members of the Kaiser Grand critically examining her from every angle, too. But she could find no fault with the way she looked in the dress and doubted that they would, either. It fitted perfectly. It went well with the black pumps she wore. And best of all, she felt great in it. Susan had never placed too much importance on clothes, but this particular dress seemed made for her alone. It was even better than the ruined silk she had bought on sale. And she wanted it. Very much. She was even willing to pay full price for it, something she rarely did. She stepped outside the dressing room to ask the saleswoman how much it cost.

At that moment Max Kaiser stepped into the shop. He paused in the doorway, silently taking her in. Susan held her breath and waited for his reaction. He said nothing.

"Well? What do you think?" she asked him.

"Perfectly acceptable, Miss Barnes."

His mild response disappointed her. "Did you come in to check up on me? I was joking about the feather boa, you know."

"I realized that. No, I came in because I neglected to tell you that I will of course pay for your dress, since I'm the one who insisted that a change of clothes was necessary."

"Oh, don't be ridiculous," Susan said huffily. "I pay for my own clothes." She reminded herself that he couldn't possibly know how sensitive she was to anything that smacked of charity. "But thanks, anyway, Mr. Kaiser," she added more graciously.

The saleswoman, who had been visibly pretending not to listen to their conversation, dropped the pretense. "Herr Kaiser?" she asked Max. "You are not by any chance related to Karin Kaiser?"

"My sister," he replied.

"One of our most treasured customers! And your dear mother, too. Both ladies have such excellent taste."

"Yes, I know. I see the bills," Max said dryly. He turned his attention back to Susan. "Are you sure you won't let me pay for your dress?"

Adamant, Susan shook her head.

He accepted her refusal with a slight shrug. "Very well. I'll go back to the car and wait for you." With that he left the shop.

Susan went to the counter, opened her purse and took out her charge card. "How much is it, anyway?" she asked the saleswoman, sure she wouldn't like what she heard but resigned to pay the price.

"Two thousand francs, madame."

Not only didn't Susan like what she heard, she was stunned by it. "Two *thousand* francs?" Although the sum made her head swim, she still managed a quick calculation. "That works out to almost fifteen hundred American dollars! For a plain little dress!"

"Yes, but of the finest quality." The woman smiled sympathetically. "Americans are often amazed at the price of clothes here in Zürich."

"Do you have anything less expensive that you could show me?" Max Kaiser would just have to wait a little longer, Susan decided.

But the saleswoman shook her head. "I'm afraid not. And nothing that would suit you so well, either. That dress is an excellent investment because it's so basic."

Susan could think of far better things to invest her money in than an overpriced piece of clothing. She earned a good income but had never forgotten what it was like to be poor. She had promised herself she never would. "I'm sorry to have wasted your time," she told the woman, and went back to the dressing room to change.

Max returned to the car, satisfied with Miss Barnes's selection. But the little joke she'd made earlier stuck in his mind. He smiled to himself, imagining her in a sprinkle of sequins, a feather boa, and nothing more, parading down a spotlit ramp. She had a figure as good as any he'd seen gracing the boards of the Folies-Bergère in Paris.

He blinked away the image of Susan Barnes as a skimpily clad show girl, feeling a twinge of guilt. She was his employee now, and he intended to view her in a professional capacity only. That was why he'd held back complimenting her on how stunning she'd looked in that little dark dress. He was determined to always hold back with her.

That wasn't going to be easy, Max knew. She was both petite and voluptuous, a combination he would find hard to resist. And her big, luminous eyes were the most fascinating color, gray tinged with violet. Luckily, he was a man of supreme self-control.

As Max was telling himself this, he saw her come out of the shop dressed in the same cutoff jeans and scruffy sweatshirt she'd worn in. He groaned. He had enough problems, and now it appeared that the woman he'd hired to help him solve them would be an additional one.

Chapter Two

"I didn't buy the dress," Susan announced, getting back into the car.

"Obviously." Max waited for an explanation.

"It went against my principles to pay that much."

"But I already offered to pay for it myself," he reminded her.

"And I already refused your offer."

"Then I'll renew it."

"It's not that simple, Mr. Kaiser."

"It seems so to me," he said, making an effort to remain patient. "You refuse to purchase a dress because you think it costs too much. Fine. I accept that. But since you are not being required to spend your own money, why be concerned about it?"

"Because it also goes against my principles to have someone buy my clothes for me."

Max noted the stubbornness in her softly contoured face and felt himself growing equally stubborn. "We seem to be at an impasse," he said evenly.

"Not really. Surely Zürich has stores with more reasonably priced merchandise."

"We don't have time to go bargain searching, Miss Barnes."

She refused to let herself feel intimidated by him. "Fine, then," she said. "We can go straight to the hotel. I'll explain why I'm dressed as I am and be done with it. I thought this was an unnecessary stop to begin with."

That was because she didn't realize what she would be up against, Max thought grimly. He'd already warned her that his family could be difficult. And now she was being difficult, too. He wasn't going to waste time arguing with her. As far as he was concerned, they'd wasted enough.

"Very well, Miss Barnes. On to Kaiser Grand." He gave the order to the driver and said no more.

Susan looked out the window as they crossed over a bridge spanning the river. The historic buildings along its banks glowed in the sun. A large lake stretched on the other side of the bridge. Pleasure steamers and sailboats dotted the calm blue water. Susan wished for a moment that she could be in one of those boats, sailing far away from the aloof Max Kaiser. Instead, she attempted to draw him out with a little conversation.

"What's the name of the lake we're passing, Mr. Kaiser?" she asked.

"The Zürichsee."

"And the river on the other side. What's that called?"

"The Limmat."

"The water looks clean enough to swim in."

"It is."

Oh, the heck with him, Susan thought. She folded her arms and clamped shut her lips, giving up the effort. What a remote man Max Kaiser was! It took away from his physical attractiveness. And that was just as well. She didn't want to feel attracted to him. She wanted no emotional entanglements in her life.

And right now she could easily do without Mr. Kaiser's taciturn company altogether. He'd disapproved of her at first sight, and nothing she'd done since had made him change his opinion. She considered asking him to take her back to the airport, so she could catch the next flight back to the States. He'd probably be relieved if she did.

Susan rebuked herself for such a defeatist thought. She'd never been a quitter, and she'd managed to work with difficult people before. Winning Max Kaiser's approval would be no easy accomplishment, but she needed a good recommendation from him if she wanted to make it on her own—which she did, more than anything. She had left a secure position to become a free-lance consultant, and having the general manager of the prestigious Kaiser Grand as her first satisfied client would be the best start she could make.

Besides, she'd only signed a three-month contract. She could last it out with him for that long. But as Susan was giving herself this pep talk, a part of her despaired. Even this ride with her new employer seemed an eternity, although no more than ten minutes had passed.

They were now in a more residential area of shady streets and sunny parks. Susan glimpsed an old lady pushing a child on a swing and thought of her grandmother. This section of Zürich reminded her a little of Boston when she'd lived there with her grandmother twenty years ago. How safe she'd felt, how loved and wanted. But then Grandma had become too ill to take care of her, and Susan had never felt that way again.

Max heard Susan sigh, and he regretted his own irritation with her simply because she'd refused to go along with his wishes. Perhaps he'd grown too used to giving orders and having them followed without question. He considered this possibility for a moment, then spoke.

"I think you were right, Miss Barnes."

Susan looked at him, amazed. "Right about what, Mr. Kaiser?"

"About not buying that dress. I believe in holding fast to one's principles."

Susan continued to stare at him. His face, in sharp profile, remained stern. "I appreciate your understanding."

"I didn't say I understood you. Your reasoning still remains cloudy to me. But since I never explain myself to people, I don't expect them to explain themselves to me. That's all I have to say about the matter."

Since that was more than Susan had expected from him, it was enough. She appreciated his attempt to put their relationship on a more cordial basis. At least they were on speaking terms again. The tenseness in her chest eased.

The car was now climbing a twisting, hilly road that ran through a forest of pines. "How much farther is it to the hotel?" she asked Max.

"It's right up ahead," he told her.

She saw it a moment later on the crest of the hill—the Kaiser Grand in all its glory, four stories high and built of white stone that shimmered in the sunlight. Its rooftop turrets, sporting bright, flapping banners, poked their pointed roofs into the cloudless heavens. Carved wooden balconies hung beneath long French windows, and a wide porch, decorated with latticework that looked like lace, swept around the front and sides of the building. The porch overlooked an expanse of emerald lawn.

Susan couldn't decide if the Kaiser Grand reminded her more of a medieval castle, a Victorian mansion or an elaborate Swiss chalet. It reminded her of something else, too...a place she'd been to in her deepest dreams. She had the odd sensation of coming home, but discounted this feeling of déjà vu. Of course the hotel looked familiar to her. She had seen pictures of it in brochures.

"Quite an architectural hodgepodge, isn't it?" Max said. "So many changes and additions have been made to the original structure through the years."

"I think it's perfectly wonderful," Susan said from the heart.

"Do you really like it?"

His question surprised Susan. He had sounded almost...diffident. "Of course I do, Mr. Kaiser. It looks exactly the way a luxury hotel should look. Very impressive."

"Perhaps a bit too fanciful, though."

"That's part of its charm."

"The turrets and balconies were my grandfather's idea. I doubt my great-grandfather, who founded the Grand, would have approved. Josef Kaiser liked to keep things simple. So do I."

Susan had guessed that about Max from his appearance. Yet she also sensed that a very complicated man lay beneath the perfect facade.

"A great-uncle was responsible for that gingerbread porch," Max went on. "Actually, his wife Gerda was. She was quite a beauty, I'm told, and he indulged all her little whims. Almost bankrupted the hotel in the process. But then she ran off with an Italian count, and the hotel survived for yet another generation."

Max's sudden willingness to talk delighted Susan. She didn't interrupt him.

"My father added a modern wing in back, which you can't see from here. He did a lot to update the hotel without taking away from its character. Kaiser Grand flourished during the years my father managed it. He had a real talent for running a hotel. I don't think that's something that can be inherited."

Neither did Susan. Her own skills in the business, which she took pride in, came from diligence and hard work, plain and simple. Unlike Max Kaiser, nothing had been handed to her on a silver platter. The only thing she'd ever inherited was a cameo brooch from her grandmother.

When the limousine stopped in front of the hotel's main entrance, a doorman wearing a top hat and burgundy uniform trimmed with gold braid opened the door for them.

"This is Miss Barnes, Rolf," Max told the doorman when they got out. "The consultant from America I told the staff to expect today."

"Welcome to Kaiser Grand, madame," Rolf said. But he offered no welcoming smile to go along with his words and turned abruptly away from her to open the limousine trunk.

Max took out the carry-on bag himself and slung the strap over one broad shoulder. "No need of a porter, Rolf. I'll take Miss Barnes to her room."

Max swiftly guided her up the marble steps carpeted in red, through the glass doors, and into the hotel lobby. Large areas of the glossy parquet floor were covered with Oriental rugs in glowing colors. Massive chandeliers from the *belle époque* around the turn of the century added to the warm aura. And huge lacquered columns, supporting the domed and carved ceiling, added to the grandeur. Susan stopped in her tracks.

Max walked on. Noticing that she wasn't keeping up, he turned back. "Something wrong, Miss Barnes?"

"Not at all. I just want to take a look around."

"Of course. I didn't mean to rush you. I only thought you were eager to freshen up before the shareholders' meeting. We don't have much time."

Susan longed for a hot shower and nap and wished he had scheduled the meeting for later in the day. As it was, she barely had enough time to wash her face and comb her hair.

Beyond the registration area she saw an airy salon paneled in oak, and a large hall with a curving staircase. A youth wearing a jacket with gleaming gold buttons and a little pillbox hat trotted up the stairs, balancing a silver tray on the palm of one white-gloved hand.

Susan had never seen a real live page boy before. She didn't think hotels employed them anymore. But obviously the Kaiser Grand still did. She wondered how much of the staff was unnecessary show. It would be part of her job to find out.

"Would you like to go into the salon?" Max asked her. "Or see the office space I arranged for you?"

"Not now. I *am* a little rushed at the moment." She couldn't keep the peevishness out of her voice.

"We would have had more time if your luggage hadn't been lost. Not to mention that useless stop at the dress shop."

"Well, since you did mention it, Mr. Kaiser, I feel the need to point out that it was your idea, not mine."

"Let's not quarrel about it."

He took hold of her elbow and led her toward the elevators. A woman carrying a toy spaniel stepped out of one of the cars.

"Good morning, Lady Stilton," Max said.

She nodded to him and threw Susan a disapproving look. "I thought the Grand had a dress code," she murmured in passing.

Susan felt the heat of a blush as she and Max entered the empty elevator.

"That wasn't very kind of her," Max said softly. "Sometimes the nobility can be a noble pain in the butt."

Susan gave him a grateful smile. "Maybe I should have curtsied." Delicately holding the ragged edges of her shorts between her fingertips, she did just that.

Max chuckled and pressed the top button. "You'd better be prepared to get the same reaction from my mother. We *do* have a dress code here, you know, and she's the main enforcer of it. She once asked a sheikh to leave the dining room because he was dressed in a tennis outfit. He became enraged and threatened to leave—and take his entire entourage with him. The hotel would have lost thousands, but my mother didn't waver."

"What happened?" asked Susan.

"He went up to his suite and changed."

Susan's heart sank as the elevator rose. "Maybe my luggage will arrive before I meet your mother," she said hopefully.

Max checked his watch. "Only if it's delivered within the next seventeen minutes."

"Then she'll be at the staff meeting?"

"Wild horses couldn't keep her away."

"You mean wild horses couldn't drag her away, Mr. Kaiser."

"That, too. My mother rarely leaves the Grand. She resides here. So does my sister. And my aunt and her husband. This is more than a business to them. It's their home."

"But you don't live here," Susan guessed.

"No, I need to get away at the end of a day and be by myself."

The elevator stopped, and Max motioned her out. He led the way down a carpeted hall and up a flight of stairs. A solitary door stood at the top. Max took out his master key and opened it. Susan followed him inside.

"Good heavens!" she cried.

Striding across the large sitting room on his way to the bedroom with her bag, Max glanced over his shoulder. "Something wrong, Miss Barnes?" he asked once again.

"This is a suite, Mr. Kaiser. Much too..." Too good for the likes of me, she'd almost said. "Much too big for only one person. I'd be just as comfortable in a smaller room."

"Nonsense," he said. "You'll be here for three months. And this will make up for the small office I've had to give you downstairs."

"But my apartment in New York was smaller than this!" Susan protested. She gazed around the sitting room, decorated in tones of rose with accents of pale green. The wall-to-wall carpeting was plush, a design of interwoven flowers, and the sofas and chairs were upholstered in gold brocade. Swags of green- and rose-striped silk decorated the long windows along the curved wall. "And it's nowhere near as fancy," she added.

"But you feel comfortable here, don't you?" Max asked. "It's not too fussy for you? Too overdone?"

"It's lovely," she told him. "It's just that I'm not used to being treated like a princess."

"Really? I should think you would be, because you certainly look like one."

Susan laughed at that, sure he was being ironic.

"A princess in disguise," he amended. He turned away, heading for the bedroom again. "Come see the other half of the tower."

A wall with an arched doorway divided the circular room in half. The bedroom, decorated in soft blues and mauves, had a lace-canopied bed and an embroidered rug. When Susan was a little girl, she'd fantasized about having a beautiful bedroom like this, all to herself. She almost told Max that, but decided to keep it to herself. What did he care about her childish daydreams?

He placed her bag on a stand and pushed back a gauze window curtain. "Come take a look at the view."

Susan came forward and stood beside him. From this hilltop vantage point she could see the rooftops of Zürich, the glittering lake, and even the white-capped Alps beyond. But it was Max's proximity that excited her more than the distant panorama. How easily they could touch, if only one of them leaned toward the other a little! She could feel her body swaying in his direction. Although he stood as still as a statue, he seemed to pull at her like a magnet. But she stepped away from the window without so much as brushing her arm against his.

"Really, Mr. Kaiser, I'd be as happy with simpler accommodations," she said. "Since I'm not a paying guest here, I don't think it's right for me to occupy such an expensive suite."

Max waved away her protest. "Don't concern yourself about it. Actually, the tower suites aren't in great demand. Many of the guests who stay at the Grand are elderly and don't appreciate having to climb a flight of stairs to reach their rooms."

"How much do you charge for a suite like this?" Susan asked him. When he told her she gave a low whistle. "That's pretty steep. What's the occupancy rate?"

"I don't know offhand," he replied with an edge to his voice, as if her question had been out of line.

"That's the kind of information I need to have to assess the hotel's operating efficiency," Susan reminded him.

"Yes, of course," he said, sounding a shade more co-operative. "I'll check those figures for you. And supply any others you need."

He showed her how to work the temperature regulator and how to raise and lower the coral awnings that shaded the balconies. Then he headed for the door, wishing her a comfortable stay.

Susan laughed. "I have the urge to give you a tip, Mr. Kaiser. You would have made an excellent porter."

She wondered if he would take offense at that. He didn't. Instead his wide lips tilted up at the edges.

"It so happens that I was a fairly good porter in my day," he told her. "And before that a fairly bad page boy. I disliked wearing the silly uniform. I didn't mind being a waiter, though. Or even a dishwasher."

"So you learned this business from the bottom up," Susan said.

"That's right. All the Kaiser men do."

"What about the Kaiser women?"

Max shrugged off that question. "They don't get involved in management."

"By choice or restriction?"

"Tradition," Max said.

Susan didn't press him. What the Kaiser women did was none of her concern. "So you washed dishes and waited on tables," she said in a challenging tone. "I started out in the hotel business as a chambermaid. But I didn't make beds and scrub bathrooms for the learning experience. I did it because I needed the money to eat."

"Apparently you did learn from it, though," Max pointed out. "Or you wouldn't be where you are now."

"Yes, here I am," she said, waving her arm around the beautiful suite. "At the very height of luxury." She wasn't being sardonic. She truly appreciated how far she had come.

But Max seemed to have lost interest in such a personal conversation. He looked at his watch. "You have ten minutes, Miss Barnes," he told her. "The meeting will take place in a conference room called the Gallery. The desk clerk can direct you to it."

"I am a little nervous about meeting the shareholders," Susan admitted. "Especially dressed as I am."

"That was your choice," he reminded her, without the slightest trace of sympathy. But Susan hadn't expected any from him.

"I'll send up the room maid to collect that dress you wore on the plane," he added, his tone a little more solicitous. "The valet might be able to clean it for you in time for dinner." He left her alone, shutting the door softly behind him.

As Susan was washing her face a few minutes later, she heard a knock. Dabbing her face with a towel, she hurried to the door, hoping her lost luggage had turned up in the nick of time. But when she opened it all she saw was an empty-handed young woman in a black skirt, frilly white blouse and apron.

"Herr Kaiser sent me up to collect something that needs to be cleaned," the girl said.

"I don't think it can be, but come see for yourself." Susan beckoned the maid into the bedroom and took her silk dress out of her carryon.

The girl raised her hands to her face, as if horrified by the sight of the stain on the skirt.

"It's whiskey," Susan informed her. "I have doubts it'll come out."

"Yes, silk is such a delicate fabric. Strong cleaning fluids could damage it even more."

"I agree. It's a lost cause."

"A pity," the maid said. "Such a pretty dress. But the top part isn't soiled. It would make a nice blouse."

"What a good suggestion." Susan sized up the girl. About her size, she estimated. "Do you happen to have a spare skirt on the premises?" she asked.

"But of course, madame. All the staff members have backup uniforms in order to look neat at all times."

"Would you let me borrow it?"

The girl hesitated.

"Please," Susan said. "I have nothing else to wear at the moment, and I don't want to meet Mrs. Kaiser dressed the way I am."

"Ah, you will be meeting Frau Kaiser." The maid nodded, as if suddenly understanding Susan's dilemma. "I will be right back with a skirt for you," she said, hurrying out of the suite.

The moment she left Susan took a pair of manicure scissors from her bag and began cutting her ruined dress in half. She smiled to herself as she snipped. She would be walking into the conference room looking much more respectable than Max Kaiser expected.

"I must have a word with you, Maximilian!"

Max was gazing out his office window, musing over the way the color of Susan Barnes's eyes reminded him of the autumn crocuses that were blooming high in the Alps right now. Hearing his mother's sharp voice address him in his native Swiss German, he swiveled around in his desk chair to face her. Frau Kaiser stood in the doorway. As always, she looked neat as a pin, every hair in her silvery bun in place, her tailored gray suit buttoned up to the neck, her slender figure erect.

Max leaned back in his chair and smiled. "Please come in and sit down, Mother. Surely you can spare more than one word with me."

He usually took a polite but ironic tone with her. Although Max loved and respected his mother, he did not have an especially close relationship with her. He'd never been her favorite son.

"Oh, I have plenty to say," she assured him, remaining rigid in the doorway. "But there isn't time before our meeting. I only wanted you to know that tongues are already wagging."

"About what?" Max asked; he knew, of course.

"About *her*. That American you imported. I considered it a bad idea from the very beginning, and now I've been proven correct."

"Nothing has been proven, Mother. We must all give Miss Barnes a chance."

"To do what? Make more of a spectacle of herself? I heard about that skimpy costume she arrived in!"

"Not all that skimpy," Max said. "It's just that her figure...calls attention to itself." He smiled. "And there is a good reason why Miss Barnes arrived here dressed as she is." He didn't go on to supply it, however.

Frau Kaiser didn't need him to. She had her own version. "Yes, Daniel told Rolf that she spilled liquor all over her dress on the plane. She must have been drinking rather heavily."

"Another passenger spilled *his* drink on her, Mother."

Frau Kaiser sniffed. "Or so she claims."

Max shook his head. Susan Barnes had been at the Kaiser Grand for less than half an hour and already had a bad reputation to live down. Hotel gossip, he knew, spread like wildfire and kept growing with each passing moment. He also knew that trying to douse it only made it flare all the more. It would die out on its own if no extra fuel was added.

"I accept Miss Barnes's explanation," he said. "Now let's please forget about it."

"I would like to forget about her entirely. The last thing we need at this hotel is a... What is that word she calls herself?"

"A consultant," Max supplied.

Frau Kaiser sniffed again. "I can think of better words to describe her."

"You haven't even met her yet, Mother!" Patience, he reminded himself. He offered her a conciliatory smile. "If I see that I made a mistake in hiring Miss Barnes, I'll be the first to admit it."

"Yes, I know you will," Frau Kaiser conceded. "Even

as a child you were always your own worst critic, Maximilian. At times I thought you were much too hard on yourself.''

Then why, Max wondered, hadn't she ever made it easier for him? He couldn't remember a time when he and his mother hadn't been at odds with each other. If he had been his own worst critic, she had certainly run a close second in that role.

"Gerhard had a far more easygoing personality," she added wistfully.

His mother had always compared him unfavorably to his elder brother, and Max was tempted to tell her that Gerhard's "easygoing personality" had contributed to the Grand's present financial straits. But he'd never spoken a word against his brother while he was alive and wasn't about to tarnish his mother's shining memory of him now. What good would that do?

He checked his watch, his automatic defense mechanism. "It's almost eleven o'clock, Mother. You'll get to see Susan Barnes for yourself in a few minutes."

"That should prove extremely interesting. But there is one other little matter I'd like to clear up with you first."

"Oh?" Max waited attentively.

"I learned at the reception desk that you gave the Barnes woman one of the tower suites."

"That's correct. You haven't wasted any time collecting information this morning, have you?"

"I never waste time," Frau Kaiser replied. "And I would like to know why you gave her the very best accommodations the Grand has to offer? I thought you'd arranged to have her stay in one of the efficiency apartments on the fourth floor."

Max had impulsively decided to give Susan a tower suite as they'd gone up in the elevator together. He rarely acted on impulse—and he didn't know why he'd given in to this one. But he had no intention of admitting this to his mother. Once he made a decision, even a spontaneous one, he never backed down.

"Since all the tower suites were free, I saw no reason not to let Miss Barnes have the use of one of them," he said.

"But what if we get reservation requests for all of them while she's here?"

"That's highly unlikely at this time of year. They weren't even fully booked during the busy tourist season."

"Unlikely but possible," Frau Kaiser persisted. "And what if that happens, Max?"

"Then I would ask Miss Barnes to change rooms, of course. She understands the hotel business. Don't forget, that's why she's here in the first place."

"Oh, *I* haven't forgotten! How could I possibly forget that you've asked an outsider to come here to tell us how to run our business? That isn't the Kaiser way of doing things."

Max knew that well enough. Kaisers weren't inclined to ask help from anyone. The whole family had been against the idea of bringing in a stranger for advice. But now that he had become general manager, he couldn't sit back and let the Grand steadily lose money. He had as much stubborn pride as the rest of the Kaisers, but he wasn't as insular or as conservative as they tended to be. He believed in taking action when it was needed.

"Perhaps it's time we changed the Kaiser way of doing things," he told his mother. His tone was gentle, however, and when he stood up he offered her his arm. "Let's go to the Gallery now. All I'm asking is that you keep an open mind concerning Susan Barnes."

He could tell by her pinched expression that she wasn't mollified. But she took his arm and said no more. He was the boss now. That much was understood between them. His mother, along with the rest of the shareholders, had pressured him into taking on the position of general manager, and she would now respect his authority.

As Max and his mother walked across the lobby, a smartly dressed young woman with red hair caught up with them. She took Max's free arm and fell into step with them.

"I've heard all about her, Brother dear," she told Max in a hushed tone.

Max didn't have to ask his sister Karin whom she was referring to. "Whatever you've heard has been greatly exaggerated," he said.

"You mean she isn't shaped like a rabbit?" Karin asked him. "That's how our chauffeur describes her."

"A rabbit?" Max didn't understand.

"You know," Karin said, switching from Swiss German to English. "Like in that American magazine with the nude centerfold."

Max laughed. "Ah, you mean a bunny. Yes, I would agree with Daniel's description of her physical attributes." He saw no reason to deny that Miss Barnes had a sensational figure. She would be displaying it to all the shareholders momentarily.

Frau Kaiser frowned. "What's this about rabbits and bunnies? Are you talking about that Barnes woman, Karin?"

"Who else, Mother? Apparently she travels light. She arrived here without any luggage to speak of. I suppose she intends to wear a sweatshirt and shorts every day."

Frau Kaiser's frown deepened. "She cannot expect to be seated in the dining room dressed that way."

"Her luggage was lost at the airport," Max said wearily.

"Poor Miss Barnes hasn't had a very good start here in Switzerland, has she?" Karin's voice dripped with insincere sympathy.

"Perhaps that's because she doesn't belong here," Frau Kaiser said.

Max looked from one woman to the other and saw that their faces were set. It didn't look to him as if they planned to give Susan Barnes a very warm reception.

He was curious to know how she would handle herself during the meeting. Recalling her stubbornness when they'd argued over the dress, he felt a sudden spurt of impatient anger. Miss Barnes had been foolish to disregard his advice. The Swiss weren't used to dealing with women in business, to begin with. So how did she expect to be taken seriously in a pair of cutoff jeans and high heels, dammit?

Entering the Gallery, he checked his watch again. Two minutes past eleven. The four other key shareholders had already assembled around the conference table, and he nodded his greetings to everyone. Karin and Frau Kaiser took their seats.

Max remained standing at the head of the table. Everyone turned to him expectantly. And then all heads turned in the opposite direction as Susan Barnes entered the room.

Max did his best to hide his surprise at the change in her appearance. She looked the picture of propriety in a beige silk blouse and simple black skirt that landed at knee level. She had twisted her hair into a neat chignon at the base of her neck. And she exuded a confidence that he couldn't help but admire.

Maybe, just maybe, she will work out, he thought.

Chapter Three

Susan disliked being the center of attention, and meeting new people always made her nervous. But she knew that outwardly she remained poised. She'd mastered the art of doing that long ago. Even as a child she'd hidden her fear and insecurity with a brave, bold smile. So she smiled now at the people seated around the table, the tremor in her lips so slight she was sure it wasn't noticeable. None of them smiled back, but simply stared at her. They looked as stern to Susan as the portraits hanging on the walls behind them.

Her eyes darted to Max Kaiser across the room. He was watching her intently. Catching the glimmer of approval in his gaze gave Susan the confidence to utter a phrase that she'd practiced over and over again with the room maid.

"Gruezi mitenand," she said in a clear, distinct voice. It meant "Greetings, everyone," and Susan felt relieved that she hadn't stumbled over the tongue-twisting words.

She saw eyebrows rise at her Swiss German salutation, and heard an echoed muttering of *"Gruezi"* in return. Then a hush fell over the room. What do they expect me to do now? Susan wondered. Hop onto the table and tap-dance?

"This is Susan Barnes," Max announced.

That seemed to be the formal cue everyone had been waiting for. Chairs scraped against the polished floor and they all stood up.

Max took Susan's arm and steered her toward a tall, silver-haired woman whom he introduced as his mother.

"Welcome to the Kaiser Grand," she said, but Susan heard no welcome in her tone. Her touch was cold and limp when they shook hands.

"And this is my sister Karin Kaiser," Max said.

Susan estimated Karin to be a few years younger than herself. Perhaps they might become friends, she thought. But Karin's tone was as flat as her mother's when she welcomed Susan, her handshake as noncommittal.

Next Susan met a plump, middle-aged woman named Berta Maier. "I'm Max's aunt," she said. She actually smiled at Susan. "And this is my husband Fritz." Berta indicated a short, stocky man with a goatee, who was standing beside her.

When he took Susan's hand she felt him tickle her palm with his thumb. Did she imagine it? Then he winked at her with such quick slyness that Susan once again doubted her own perception.

"Fritz is the Grand's financial comptroller," Max told her. "I'm sure he will be happy to help you with any questions you have concerning the hotel's day-to-day expenditures."

"Of course," Fritz said. He bowed to Susan, clicking his heels together. "I am at your service, Fräulein Barnes."

Susan wasn't sure if he was making fun of her or not. His slyness put her off. She formed an instant distrust of the man, then cautioned herself to keep an open mind.

She next met a shy young man whom Max introduced as his cousin Ernst Kaiser. Ernst mumbled a few awkward words of welcome, apparently more intent on studying Susan's shoes than her face.

Only one person remained to be introduced. Max brought Susan over to a glaring old fellow with hoary whiskers and an old-fashioned suit that had seen better days.

"This is my Great-uncle Anton, Miss Barnes. He came down from the mountains to meet you today."

Anton grabbed Susan's hand and shook it energetically. His grip was hard and callused. His eyes were hard, too, but with a twinkle in them. He grumbled something to Susan in a harsh, guttural voice.

"I'm sorry," she told him. "But I don't understand German."

"Even if you did, you probably couldn't understand Uncle Anton," Max said, his tone fondly humorous. "He insists on speaking his village dialect even though he knows at least four languages, including English."

Anton rattled off something else, practically shouting into Susan's ear as he continued to pump her hand.

Max laughed. "He says you were worth the trip down the mountain, Miss Barnes."

Although the old man's strong grip was a little painful, Susan's smile never wavered. "Well, thank you," she told him. He released her hand and she flexed her numb fingers behind her back.

Everyone sat down around the table again. Only one seat remained free, at the opposite end, across from Max. Susan took it. Her eyes felt scratchy from lack of sleep. It was now 5:00 a.m., New York time. She regretted not taking a nap during the long plane ride, but she'd been too excited.

Max cleared his throat. "Thank you all for coming today," he began, giving a special nod to Great-uncle Anton. "I thought it fitting to hold this shareholders' meeting in the Gallery, surrounded by portraits of the men who have made the Kaiser Grand what it is today."

Susan looked at the gilt-framed oil paintings hanging around the room. She saw Max's aquiline nose in one of the portraits, his blazing blue eyes in another, the dark gold of his hair in the beard of a third.

"As all of you know," he continued, "I had little preparation before taking on the position of general manager last April."

Maybe everybody else in the room knew that, but it was news to Susan. She'd assumed Max Kaiser had been in charge for years. He certainly acted like a man who was used to being in control.

"Of course, I was fortunate to have had some guidance from Fritz Maier in the beginning," he said. "Fritz, having been with our hotel since my father's day, knows operational details better than most family members here."

Susan glanced at Fritz. He kept his eyes down and pulled at his goatee.

"Of course, Fritz has recently become a family member and major shareholder, too," Max added, looking in Berta's direction. "By marrying my favorite aunt."

"And you are my favorite nephew, Maxie darling," Berta said, beaming at him. Then she seemed to remember that this was a formal meeting and put on a serious face.

"But even with the help and support of our respected financial comptroller," Max went on, "I decided that outside advice would be beneficial. The world is rapidly changing, and the Kaiser Grand must change with it."

No one said a word, but there was a general shifting in chairs that seemed to demonstrate discomfort over Max's last remark.

"Change is not necessarily *bad,*" he stressed. "We should remember that Josef Kaiser changed the established concept of what a hotel should be when he founded Kaiser Grand in 1890."

Susan noticed how everyone but Max looked in the same direction then, at the portrait hanging above his head. She, too, regarded the picture of the man with the golden beard. He had been painted in keeping with turn-of-the-century fashion, stiffly posed in formal attire, his silk cravat perfectly tied, his high collar primly starched. But his intense expression was that of a man who had better things to do than sit for a portrait. His strong, clearly drawn features appealed to Susan.

She lowered her eyes a few inches and regarded Max Kaiser with the same objectivity. His features were as angular as those of his great-grandfather. And like the man in the portrait, he too seemed to be hiding a restless nature behind a facade of propriety and reserve. Was Max also enduring some kind of pose that wasn't to his liking? As this thought occurred to Susan, Max looked directly at her. All her objectivity dissolved. Her heart turned over.

While everyone else in the room continued to stare at the portrait, Susan and Max regarded each other across the length of the glossy table. Only a few seconds passed. It seemed like an eternity to Susan. She had trouble breathing. Max pulled his eyes away from her and cleared his throat again.

"And to change, we need fresh insights," he continued without missing a beat.

His words sounded muffled as Susan tried to regain her equilibrium. For a moment there she had felt quite disoriented, as if she were still in the plane and falling, falling. She told herself that she was experiencing jet lag, that was all.

"And so I contacted a search firm to help me find someone who could advise us," Max said. "One name kept coming up. Susan Barnes."

Hearing her own name pronounced so distinctly cut through Susan's momentary confusion. She paid closer attention to what Max was saying.

"Miss Barnes has made quite a reputation for herself in the industry," he informed the rest of his listeners. "She was instrumental in making the Golden Key chain of hotels in America a prestigious operation."

Susan had to delve deep to find her own voice but managed to speak up. "You give me too much credit, Mr. Kaiser. The guiding force behind Golden Key has always been Tony Armanto, not me."

"Miss Barnes is being too modest," Max said. "As Mr. Armanto's chief executive for the last three years, she changed his company's direction. Golden Key moved away from its image as a cheap motel chain by acquiring a string of luxury hotels in major American cities." He turned his penetrating gaze on Susan full blast. "Am I correct, Miss Barnes?"

Susan had never regarded the motels Tony had built his empire upon as *cheap*. They provided clean, efficient lodging for travelers. She had seen the possibility, however, of making outmoded city hotels into efficient money-makers, too. And she'd managed to do just that in Boston, Saint Louis, New Orleans, Baltimore, San Francisco. Even New York.

"Yes, I did have the responsibility of turning a number of hotels around and making them more profitable," she said a little reluctantly, because it sounded too much like bragging. But this was the time to toot her own horn, she realized. Max Kaiser apparently expected her to. And those stern, unsmiling faces now looking at her around the table seemed to be expecting something from her, too.

Max gave her a nod. She took that to mean she had said the right thing.

"The search firm I employed contacted Miss Barnes and made her an offer to come here as a consultant," Max went on. "And we are fortunate that she accepted."

Susan nervously touched the chignon at the base of her neck. She had accepted the offer because her position at Golden Key had become too uncomfortable. Tony Armanto had suddenly taken it into his head that he'd fallen in love with her, and because Susan had no reciprocal feelings, they had both been miserable for a while. When the offer from Kaiser Grand came to her by way of a headhunter in the business, Susan told Tony about it straight out. And they had both agreed it would be best that she leave Golden Key and go off on her own. But nobody in this room, especially Max Kaiser, had to know about her personal reasons for leaving.

Apparently Max's mother thought differently. "I would like to know why Miss Barnes gave up her important position in America to come here," she said, looking at her son rather than at Susan. "Compared to the Golden Key organization, we are a small, rather insignificant establishment."

Susan spoke up. "Hardly insignificant, Mrs. Kaiser. This hotel is regarded as one of the finest in the world. I'm sure I can learn a great deal here."

"Oh, I'm sure you can, too, Miss Barnes," Frau Kaiser said. "But what have you to offer *us?*"

Rather than be offended by her blunt question, Susan appreciated her directness. "I believe what I have to offer you is a new perspective. And years of experience in the business."

"Years?" Frau Kaiser narrowed her eyes. "You don't appear to be old enough to be able to claim that many. And what about your formal training?"

"Miss Barnes isn't here to be interviewed, Mother," Max said. "I've already hired her."

"Oh, I don't mind answering questions about my qualifications," Susan said. "I have a degree in hotel management from Cornell University. And I paid my way through college by working in various hotels, which gave me plenty of hands-on experience in the business. I became part of the Golden Key organization after graduation and was eventually promoted to executive vice president. In that position I implemented financial and operating studies to ascertain the earning potential of hotels Golden Key was interested in acquiring."

"I would like Miss Barnes to do such studies here," Max put in. "In order to discover our hotel's strengths."

"And weaknesses," Susan felt obliged to add. "After analyzing the results, I'll suggest ways to fine-tune operations. Or to do a major overhaul, if necessary."

No one said a word. But they all stared at Susan as if she had uttered a blasphemy. Even Max, whom Susan was counting on for support, seemed uncomfortable with her last statement. "I don't think Miss Barnes's approach will be as cold-blooded as it sounds," he said.

Cold-blooded? Had she come across that way? That hadn't been Susan's intention. She turned to Max, feeling as if he'd somehow betrayed her. "I thought you valued my objectivity, Mr. Kaiser," she said. "And that's the way I'd describe my approach. Objective."

"Of course," he agreed. "A much better choice of words, Miss Barnes."

At least she'd gotten him to concede that little point. But Susan sensed that even though it had been his idea to bring her here, Max's allegiance remained with the others seated around the table. They were his family, after all. And she was the outsider. Oh, well, she was used to that. For as long as Susan could remember, she had been an outsider. She hadn't seen this as much of an advantage while growing up, but now she believed that a certain detachment was one of her strengths. In the business world, anyway.

"I'll be happy to answer any more questions," she told the Kaiser clan.

No one seemed to have any. They all sat as silent as stones. This disappointed Susan. Weren't they curious as to how she would implement her analysis of their hotel? Or had they already decided to discount her findings before she had even presented them? In their silence she could hear doors slamming shut.

At last Great-uncle Anton muttered something. Everybody nodded in agreement and stood up. Susan looked to Max for a translation.

"Uncle Anton suggests we all go to lunch now," Max told her. While the rest of the Kaiser family filed out of the conference room without giving Susan a backward glance, Max waited for her by the door.

"I went over like a lead balloon," she muttered to him.

"Not at all. The meeting went as well as could be expected." Max patted her shoulder perfunctorily, then dropped his hand. "Certainly much better than if you had shown up in those ripped-off jeans of yours. Tell me, Miss Barnes, how did you manage to make yourself look so...?"

"Presentable?"

"Well, yes. Did the airline deliver your lost luggage at the last moment?"

Susan shook her head.

"Then how did your sudden transformation take place? Surely your fairy godmother didn't appear and wave her magic wand."

Susan laughed at that. "I don't have one, Mr. Kaiser. I learned a long time ago that if you wait around for fairy godmothers to come to your rescue, you don't get very far in life. And that goes for knights in shining armor, too. I pity the poor woman who thinks *they* still exist."

Max regarded her a moment. "You talk a lot tougher than you look, Miss Barnes."

She became defensive. "You mean I'm sounding cold-blooded again?"

"I didn't intend for you to take that remark as a criticism."

"Well, that's the way I took it."

"I was only trying to assuage the family's fear of great changes taking place at the Grand. Whether you realize it or not, you came across rather strongly with your comment about a major overhaul."

"Oh, I realized it wasn't appreciated when everyone stared at me as if I were some sort of alien from outer space."

Max smiled. "I'm sure they don't consider you a Martian. But if you're going to talk tough, you should have a thick skin to go along with it."

"Mine's thick enough," she assured him.

No, it wasn't, Max thought, contemplating her. She had skin as delicate as the petals of the Alpine flowers she seemed to constantly call to his mind. Then Max remembered that mountain wildflowers, despite their fragile appearance, had a resilience that enabled them to survive harsh winters. Perhaps Susan Barnes was that sort of survivor, too. What had she managed to survive? Max caught himself wondering about her personal life, which was certainly none of his business, and looked away from her.

"Shall we join the others in the dining room now?" he asked her. "Knowing my family, they'll be more relaxed with you while we all share a pleasant meal together."

Maybe Max Kaiser didn't know his family as well as he thought, Susan reflected; they were still ignoring her at lunch. The meal, served with flawless precision, consisted of many courses, one more delicious than the next, but Susan didn't have much of an appetite.

Not that she was nervous anymore. She'd learned which fork to use long ago, during her waitressing days, and even knew enough to keep both hands on the table at all times, because she'd read that the Swiss considered this proper dining etiquette. Although she made no attempt to try to eat in the European manner, she had to admit it was highly efficient, as she watched Great-uncle Anton stacked food onto his fork with his knife, then somehow manage to balance it there until it reached his mouth.

The old man could really pack it away, Susan marveled with a certain admiration. Everyone at the table ate quickly and heartily. They finished everything on their plates before the waiter whisked them away to serve yet another course. Susan had ample time to observe their eating habits since no one bothered to talk to her. Instead, they chattered away in Swiss German, not seeming to care that she didn't understand the language.

Max, who was seated too far away from Susan to hold a personal conversation with her, made a few attempts to include her by raising his voice and asking her polite questions in English. But nobody else seemed particularly interested in her responses. Off they would go again, talking in their German dialect. Finally Max put down his knife and fork and made a gesture to Susan—palms up with a shrug. She took it to mean he'd given up trying to include her. Would that always be his response?

She appreciated the fact that Max didn't join the others in their exclusionary conversation. Like her he remained silent throughout the remainder of the meal. She noticed that he kept checking his watch. He reminded her of a man who had a train to catch, and missing it was a matter of life or death.

Susan realized she already placed far too much importance on Max Kaiser's every gesture and word. He fascinated her. She couldn't stop looking at him during the luncheon although her glances in his direction were quick and—she hoped—discreet. Mostly she concentrated on her immediate surroundings.

The Kaiser Grand dining room was impressive without being ostentatious. While the service was formal, with many waiters in tuxedos milling around, and the decor was elegant, with tapestries hanging on the high walls and a wealth of fine linen, china and crystal on the table, the atmosphere was relaxed. Easy. Unpretentious. Susan knew how difficult it was to attain the perfect ambience that made diners feel wrapped in luxury, yet comfortably at home, too. Not only did the Grand dining room have the right atmosphere, it had another great advantage. The view. One wall of the room was solid windows, showcasing the Alps in the distance.

At last the dessert course was served, a chocolate soufflé in its unassuming little baking dish. Susan broke the thin crust with her big silver spoon and took a bite. Perfection. Like eating a chocolate cloud. Chocolate was her favorite indulgence, and she closed her eyes to better concentrate on tasting. When she opened them again she caught Max watching her. He looked away quickly. So did she.

The chef came to visit their table, wearing his high, puffy hat and immaculate white jacket with covered buttons. He bowed to Max. It wasn't a servile bow by any means, Susan noted. She knew a proud man when she saw one, and this chef, with his florid face and luxuriant gray moustache, was as proud as they came. His chest was as puffy as his hat, almost making the buttons on his jacket pop. He asked Max in French if he'd enjoyed the meal. Susan knew just enough of *that* language to understand his simple inquiry.

"It was delicious, Alain," Max responded in English. "And I appreciate your taking the time to come talk to us."

Susan approved of Max's show of regard. She knew the importance of keeping a good *chef de cuisine* happy. Without an excellent restaurant, a luxury hotel could lose its five-star rating.

"Let me take this opportunity to introduce you to Miss Susan Barnes." Max gestured in her direction. "Miss Barnes, this is our esteemed chef, Alain Duprés."

They nodded across the table to each other. Like everyone else Susan had met at the Grand, M. Duprés gave her a wary look. Then he turned his attention to a lady he obviously felt much more worthy of it.

"Was everything to madame's liking?" he asked Frau Kaiser.

"The lobster was not as sweet as I would have liked it, Alain," she responded. The chef's face fell. "But the sauce accompanying it was excellent." He looked relieved.

Susan barely made out the exchange, again in French, but she could plainly see how Alain Duprés valued Frau Kaiser's opinions. She surmised that although Max was general manager of the hotel, his mother still played an important role. That meant trouble for her, Susan knew. Frau Kaiser had made it clear that she had no use for an outside consultant. And Susan had already sized her up as a difficult opponent. Not that she didn't feel up to the challenge of taking her on if the necessity arose. She only hoped it wouldn't.

After Chef Alain returned to his kitchen, and everyone finished dessert with a resounding clang of spoons against porcelain, Max stood up.

"Thank you all for coming today to meet Miss Barnes," he said in that formal way of his.

He shook hands with them all, even his mother, and then they all shook hands again with Susan. She couldn't remember a time when she'd pressed more palms and still felt so excluded. The Kaiser clan departed, and Max and she were left alone at the table.

"Well," Max said with a sigh of relief. "Wasn't that fun?"

"Surely more fun than if they'd burned me at the stake," Susan replied, matching his sardonic tone.

"They're saving that treat for dinner, Miss Barnes. You're the main course."

She didn't laugh. "How can I function here at the Grand if I'm viewed as the enemy, Mr. Kaiser?"

"But you're not," he protested lightly. "We Swiss have no enemies. We're a neutral country, don't forget."

"Families are never neutral," she shot back. She knew that much about them.

He didn't disagree this time. "Would you care to take a stroll around the grounds with me?" he asked instead.

Susan readily accepted his unexpected invitation. They left the dining room through French doors that opened onto a large, crescent-shaped terrace overlooking sloping lawns and gardens.

Among the people eating lunch out here, at glass-topped tables with coral umbrellas, Susan noticed Lady Stilton. Her little spaniel was on her lap, licking ice cream from a silver bowl. Susan shook her head at the sight. Her work often brought her close to wealthy people, but she still found it hard to accept the indulgences they took for granted.

Max led her down the terrace steps, and they followed a flagstone path through a formal garden. It was as perfectly maintained as the hotel's interior, with clusters of purple, gold, and white chrysanthemums artfully arranged around clipped bushes and pruned trees. The path, lined on both sides with late-blooming nasturtiums, was just wide enough for Max and Susan to walk abreast. Each time they brushed arms, they would quickly move apart; it was as if they'd given each other an electrical shock by merely touching. Susan tried to keep her mind on business.

"Does the hotel employ an outside landscaping service?" she asked Max.

"No, we have a grounds keeper and three full-time gardeners on the staff," he said. "Seasonal workers, too."

"Pretty high operating expenses for no return in revenue," Susan remarked.

"Most women would appreciate the beauty of the gardens rather than be concerned about expenses and revenue, Miss Barnes."

"But I'm not most women. I'm an efficiency consultant. I presume all these outdoor plantings change with each season."

"Of course. Our guests expect beautiful surroundings as well as comfortable accommodations."

"Well, you sure give them *that*," Susan said, pausing by a low garden wall to look at the snow-capped mountains beyond. "At least this great view doesn't have to be maintained."

"You're not suggesting that the Grand do away with its gardens, are you?" Max laughed, as if such a suggestion would be absurd.

"No," Susan answered seriously. "I can appreciate the part they play in the Grand's overall image. But using an outside service instead of employing your own gardeners could cut maintenance costs by at least a third. Once I have some exact figures to look over, I can show you how much you can save by—"

"Forget it," Max interrupted.

Surprised by his abruptness, Susan took a step back, bumping into the stone wall. She sat down. "Forget what, Mr. Kaiser?"

He stared at her, a frown on his face. "It will be a waste of your time to analyze costs concerning these gardens," he told her.

"I don't think so." Chin up, Susan stared at him. The sun was behind him, making his dark gold hair gleam. But his black sweater and dark suit seemed to absorb the light, giving his tall, looming figure an almost ominous look. Still, she persisted in making her point. "Surely it's not a waste of time to ascertain how much money you could save if you—"

"I don't give a hang how much money we could save by doing things differently," he interrupted again. "We've employed the same family of gardeners for the last two generations. Sometimes tradition is more important than efficiency, Miss Barnes. But perhaps you can't appreciate that."

Susan looked away to hide her hurt feelings. "I'll do my best to appreciate Kaiser traditions while I'm here," she said softly. "But I *can't* appreciate being snapped at when I'm only trying to do the job you hired me to do."

Max immediately regretted his impatience with her. He sat down on the wall beside her, so close that their thighs touched.

"My mother loves these gardens," he told her in a gentler tone. "She spends a great deal of time working in them alongside the gardeners. It's one of her chief pleasures in life now, and I could never take that away from her. That's why I sounded so adamant about it."

His explanation mollified Susan somewhat. But not completely. "I had no way of knowing that," she pointed out.

"No, of course you didn't, Miss Barnes. You're a stranger here. I have to keep that in mind." He shifted away from her slightly so that they no longer touched.

Susan missed the solid, muscular feel of his leg against hers. Then she also shifted her own body so that they sat even farther apart. "I don't want to step on any toes while I'm here, Mr. Kaiser," she said.

Max smiled tightly. "Then I hope you packed ballet slippers, Miss Barnes. Because you'll be required to do a lot of tiptoeing around here."

"That wasn't part of the job description," she commented dryly. "I came here with the understanding that you need my practical skills in hotel management. I don't dance around anything. I prefer the direct approach."

"So do I," he said. "That's why I like you, Miss Barnes."

He liked her? That was news to Susan. As she was digesting this piece of information, a breeze plucked a strand of hair from her neat chignon. It fluttered against her cheek. Before she could push it back into place Max reached out and did it for her, grazing his fingertips against her skin as he tucked it behind her earlobe.

Susan's heart leaped. But outwardly she gave no sign of acknowledging his gesture. It had happened in an instant and was easy enough to ignore... or was it? Her skin burned where he had touched it. She turned away, pretending a great interest in the mountain scenery over her left shoulder.

"Well, now I can claim I've seen the Alps," she said. "It's odd, but I feel a pull toward them, an immediate attraction. I want to get closer." She could have been talking about Max Kaiser, she realized.

"That's not so odd," he said. "Mountains arouse something deep in human nature."

Susan sighed. So did he. "At the same time they seem so cold and intimidating."

"Maybe from far away. But not when you get closer," Max assured her.

She shrugged. "This is as close as I'll probably get while I'm here."

"That would be a shame. I'll take you on a hike through the Alps before you leave." Max's offer came with the same spontaneity as his hair-tucking gesture had. And it surprised him just as much. Hadn't he decided to keep his distance?

"I'd enjoy that," she told him. She looked away from the mountains and directly at him then.

And Max knew he couldn't keep his distance while he gazed into her lovely violet-flecked eyes. He wanted to touch her again, feel the softness of her skin beneath his fingertips. He stood up abruptly.

"Shall we go back to the hotel, Miss Barnes? I have an appointment to keep."

Susan felt more disappointed than she knew she should. She'd just started to relax a little with Max in this peaceful setting. "Do you have any more meetings scheduled for me today?"

"No, I thought you would appreciate some free time to yourself after your long trip. I'll introduce you to the staff tomorrow. Stop by my office at eight."

"So I won't see you again until then."

Max hesitated. "Unless you'd care to have dinner with me this evening."

Susan wondered if his invitation came from a sense of obligation. "I was thinking of having dinner sent up to my room," she said, testing.

"Of course," he agreed. Much too readily, she thought.

They parted in front of the elevators, and Susan went up to her suite. When she entered it she found the room maid in the bedroom, unpacking her two suitcases.

"Oh, they found my luggage at last!"

"Yes, Miss Barnes. The airline delivered it about half an hour ago." The young maid smiled at her. "I'm sure you must be pleased."

Susan was as pleased to see a friendly face as her lost luggage. "What's your name?" she asked the maid. She'd been too nervous about the shareholders' meeting to inquire earlier.

"Heidi."

"Really?" Susan smiled. "You're not making that up, are you?"

"Why would I make up my own name?" She sounded a bit offended.

"I'm sorry," Susan said quickly. "It's just that *Heidi* was a book I read as a child, and I always wanted to go to Switzerland and meet her."

"Well, I'm not *that* Heidi, of course," this one said, neatly folding Susan's underwear and putting it in the drawer of a big wood-inlaid armoire.

"Close enough," Susan said. The maid had curly brown hair and rosy cheeks. "You acted like a heroine by lending me your spare skirt."

"Did Frau Kaiser notice it was part of a hotel uniform?"

"Probably. I doubt anything slips by her sharp eyes."

"Oh, nothing does," Heidi replied in an awed tone. "But since the great tragedy she has taken less interest in the hotel. She stays in her suite a good deal of the time now."

Susan didn't let her curiosity get the better of her and ask the maid what this great tragedy was. It wouldn't be right, she felt, to gossip about the Kaiser family's private life. She offered to do the rest of the unpacking herself, but Heidi wouldn't hear of it.

"This is part of my job, Miss Barnes."

The guests at Kaiser Grand certainly got personal service, Susan thought, glad that her underwear was of good quality. Besides chocolate, she had a weakness for pretty lingerie. She considered those her only two vices, and they seemed harmless enough.

Happy to have Heidi's company for a while, Susan sat on a chaise lounge by the window and watched her. "Do you enjoy working here?" she asked.

"Oh, yes! My sister also works here, and I used to be so jealous of her. I couldn't wait to be old enough to get a job here, too. Now all the other girls in my village are jealous of *me*."

"You mean they all want to work for a hotel in the city?"

"Not just any hotel, Miss Barnes. Only the Kaiser Grand. And the Kaisers are very particular about who they hire. You have to speak good English, for one thing. And it helps if you're a relative, of course."

"You're related to the Kaisers?"

"Almost everyone in our village is in one way or another," Heidi said. "I'm a third cousin twice removed."

While Susan was trying to figure that out, she yawned. "Excuse me," she said. "But I lost a night's sleep traveling here."

"A nap would do you good." Heidi began turning down the chintz bed quilt.

"Oh, I never take naps," Susan said. "Besides, I'm too wound up. I may even have trouble sleeping tonight."

"Perhaps you should take a sauna, then. It will surely relax you."

"The hotel has a sauna room?"

"But of course! And we also have an excellent masseur. We have the best of everything here."

Susan smiled. "And you're the best ambassador the Grand could have, too." She made a mental note to tell Max Kaiser that. If the rest of the staff had Heidi's enthusiasm, then management must be doing something right.

After Heidi left Susan paced her luxurious rooms, unable to decide what to do with herself. She considered going down to the lobby and observing how the staff functioned, but until Max officially introduced her to them, that could seem too much like spying. She should just relax for the rest of the day, she knew, but she wasn't very good at doing that. Perhaps she should follow Heidi's suggestion about indulging in a sauna. She'd never taken one before, and now seemed as good a time as any. She'd come to Europe for new experiences, hadn't she?

When Susan entered the sauna room, her towel tightly wrapped around her naked body, she found another woman already occupying it.

"Oops, pardon me," she said, quickly glancing away; the woman was sitting on her own towel instead of covering herself with it. "I didn't realize anyone was here. The attendant told me to go right in."

"Why shouldn't she have?" the woman asked. "There's plenty of room."

Obviously, taking a sauna wasn't the solitary occupation Susan had expected it to be. The hot, wood-paneled room smelled of eucalyptus. Stones were being heated in a little stove. Almost stubbing her toe on a water bucket, Susan climbed to a wooden platform opposite the one where the other woman so boldly perched. Giving her another quick glance, Susan recognized her as Lady Stilton. She looked different without her tweeds and accessory spaniel. Following Lady Stilton's example, she took off her towel, spread it over the platform and sat on it.

"I always enjoy a little company while I sweat, don't you, my dear?" Lady Stilton asked in a cordial tone that suggested the pouring of tea and offering of crumpets.

Actually, Susan preferred to do her sweating in private. But she didn't have to answer the question because Lady Stilton chattered on.

"One often meets the most interesting people in a sauna," she said. "Why, just the other day I struck up a conversation with a gentleman in here, and we soon discovered that we had a mutual avocation. He also raises rare orchids."

"Not right here in the sauna?" Susan asked in amazement.

"Of course not, dear girl. At his country estate."

"No, I mean, you and he were in here *together?*"

Lady Stilton trilled a laugh. "Of course. It isn't in the Continental spa tradition to segregate the sexes. They're much more relaxed about such things here." She must have noticed that Susan wasn't. "But don't worry. This sauna is rarely used in the afternoon. You're sure to have it all to yourself when I leave, which I must do right now or I shall melt into a puddle."

With that Lady Stilton moved her great bulk off the bench, bade Susan a jaunty "Cheerio," and departed.

Susan contemplated leaving, too. But the dry heat and scent of eucalyptus were extremely soothing, and she decided to chance staying a few minutes more. She leaned her head against the timbered wall and closed her eyes. They flew open a moment later when she heard the door creak.

Max Kaiser entered the small room, filling it with his presence.

"Oh, hello, Miss Barnes," he said as casually as if they had been fully clothed.

Chapter Four

"Mr. Kaiser, fancy meeting you here," Susan said in a weak attempt to sound nonchalant as she hugged her legs to her chest, covering up as much of herself as she could.

Max tried not to smile. It always amused him, though, that Americans were so puritanical when it came to simple nakedness. In deference to Miss Barnes, he kept his towel wrapped around his waist. After giving her a quick appraisal that didn't miss one delightfully exposed inch, he maintained sauna protocol and kept his eyes on her face, which was as red as a poppy. He guessed embarrassment more than heat had caused the flush.

"So you're a sauna devotee, too, Miss Barnes."

Susan's eyes darted from his smooth, golden chest to his earlobe. She couldn't quite look him straight in the eye. "Actually, this is my first time in one."

She looked so ill at ease that Max almost offered to leave. But he just couldn't make himself do it. Damp tendrils from her upswept hair curled at the base of her neck. Her white shoulders gleamed with a film of perspiration. No, he wasn't going anywhere because he was exactly where he wanted to be at that moment.

Susan's immediate inclination was to flee. But in order to do that she would have to stand up, and she couldn't get up the nerve. She squeezed her legs closer to her body.

"Would you like me to steam things up for you?" Max asked her.

"Steam things up?" Susan repeated. Her eyes, as if they had a will of their own, skittered over his upper torso again. His shoulders were wide, his arm and chest muscles well-defined. He had the powerful, graceful lines of an athlete. She swallowed hard. "I'm not sure what you're talking about, Mr. Kaiser."

The absurdity of addressing each other by their last names while she was stark naked and he practically so did not escape Susan. Would he keep that small, low-riding towel wrapped around him? It was so loosely tied that it looked as if it might slip off if he made the slightest movement. She made a quick check to see if it was still in place. Lord, his stomach was flat. His legs were long and strong. Even his feet were well formed and attractive. She evaluated his male assets in less than a second before forcing her eyes back to his face.

"I'll show you what I'm talking about," he said. "But first I'll make sure we're not disturbed." He twisted the lock on the door.

The loud click made Susan's heart jump. "I'd just as soon the door remained unlocked, Mr. Kaiser."

"No, we don't want anyone coming in for a while. That would ruin everything." He moved toward her, loose-jointed. "You'll enjoy this," he assured her.

"Enjoy *what?*" she asked with a fluttering of apprehension. Surely he wasn't planning to take advantage of the situation? But why the locked door?

In fact, Max intended to take as much advantage of the situation as he could. He saw no harm in teasing Susan Barnes a little. The temptation was too hard to resist. He'd just had a vigorous workout in the hotel gym and felt relaxed and at peace with himself, as he always did after hard exercise. He'd worked out to drive disturbing thoughts about Susan from his head, but now that he'd discovered her here in the flesh, all that effort had been wasted. At the moment, however, Max didn't mind one bit.

"You'll enjoy the benefits of a master at work," he told her, making each word slide slowly off his tongue.

Susan caught the smile tugging at the corners of his wide mouth. It occurred to her that he was putting her on, and her fear lessened. "That depends on what you're a master of, Mr. Kaiser," she drawled back, going along with him.

"The art of steam," he declared, picking up the wooden ladle that rested against the water bucket. "Which is a very precise and exacting art. That's why the door must remain closed while I'm performing this little ritual."

"Well, you've got my interest now," Susan said. As if he hadn't from the moment he'd stepped into the small hot room, half-naked.

"Good," he said. "Watch closely."

He dipped the ladle into the bucket beside the stove, then slowly poured the water over the hot stones neatly piled on top of it. They sizzled and steam rose in a cloud.

"See that?" he said.

"Wow, magic." She kept her tone flat. "If that's your great trick, I'm not terribly impressed."

"Not yet you aren't. But once I remove my towel, I assure you that you will be, Miss Barnes."

She'd played along with him for long enough, she decided. "That won't be necessary, Mr. Kaiser."

"But it is. Producing the steam is the easy part, of course. Directing it takes a certain skill. The artistry comes in with the towel-swinging." He began untying the knot in his. "In fact, I've had occasion to receive applause after my performance." With that, he whisked off the towel. But before Susan could blink, much less avert her eyes, he turned his back to her.

He'd given her enough of a glimpse to satisfy her curiosity, however. Her eyebrows shot up. She was glad he'd turned away before he could see the good impression he'd made. Now she couldn't help but admire his strong, wide back and tight buttocks. Hard and smooth as marble.

He began twirling the towel through the air, sending the heavy cloud of steam in her direction. His motions were energetic and theatrical. And he sang as he swung, supplying his own musical accompaniment to his actions.

Since Max's singing was so badly off-key, Susan didn't recognize the tune. She did recognize a man who took a delight in the absurd and didn't mind making a fool of himself for the sake of entertaining a woman. She'd never expected the proper, reserved Max Kaiser to be that sort of man. And as she laughed at his antics, she felt her heart expanding in the heat. Expanding to make room for him.

Her body soaked up the steam drifting toward her in damp, warm gusts as the sound of Max's lusty singing vibrated through her. He lowered his voice a few decibels and began humming a waltz. Since he kept his back turned, Susan loosened her taut leg muscles and allowed herself to lean back until she touched the wall behind her. She relaxed for the first time since she'd arrived at the Grand. Her bones seemed to be melting. She inhaled deeply and could feel the coolness of eucalyptus in her throat. She had a sensation of floating.

She imagined herself a cloud—a fluffy, aimlessly drifting cloud. She sailed along without a care in the world, allowing the wind to lift her higher and higher. How thrilling it was to be taken by the wind! How easy it was to give up control and let it take her anywhere it pleased! She had no fears, no reservations. The nice thing about being a cloud was that nothing could hurt you. She felt safe now. Happy.

"Miss Barnes, wake up."

Hearing Max softly call her name, Susan sighed and stretched her arms above her head. She had never felt so at ease with herself and her body. Her lids fluttered open, and she turned her eyes in his direction. He was still standing by the stove, but he faced her now. The intensity of his expression roused her to full wakefulness and she quickly folded herself up again.

"I must have dozed off," she murmured.

"Yes, despite my horrible singing." He made an effort to smile but his facial muscles remained tense.

How long had he been watching her? She noticed that he'd tied his towel back around his waist.

"It's not wise to fall asleep in a sauna," he said. "That's why I called to you. You shouldn't stay in here much longer." He stepped forward and offered her his hand to help her down from the platform.

Susan hesitated before taking it. But at this point modesty seemed pointless; he must have had a good enough look at her as she'd stretched. Even so, the moment she stood she let go of his hand, snatched up her towel and covered herself.

Max sighed. "What a shame to hide such perfection." His low voice took on a husky intimacy. "You're very beautiful, Susan."

How strange her name sounded from his lips. *Zooh-zahn.* Strange and wonderful. How easy it would be to let go of her towel now, let it slip to the floor. What would he do then? She clutched the terry cloth in her fist, keeping a firm grip on it—and on her own wayward inclination. She pretended he had never uttered his soft compliment although his words hung in the air, mingling with the steam.

"I'd better go take a shower now," she managed to say, but couldn't manage to move.

"Yes, the colder the better. In the mountains we run into the snow after a sauna."

"That sounds like torture."

"No," Max said. "It's bliss. Strong sensations can be one or the other."

Something in his voice told Susan that he was a man who craved strong sensations. She met his eyes and the glint in them told her the same thing.

"I prefer more moderate ones." She had trouble forming those sensible words. She wished he would stop looking at her like that. But she didn't look away.

"Do you, Susan? Then perhaps you don't know what you're missing." He touched her shoulder with one finger, gliding it slowly across the silky slope.

Hot as she was, his touch made her shiver. His finger trailed down her collarbone and paused at the base of her neck. Could he feel her pulse throbbing there? She could hear it herself.

He slowly lifted his finger to his mouth. The sensuality of his gesture reverberated through her system. She knew then, with every female instinct passed down to her from Eve, that Max Kaiser's sexuality had a depth that could make a woman drown in the unexpected pleasures of it. And she, who had struggled all her life to keep her head above water, didn't want to be that woman. The door leading out of the sauna was less than two feet away. She could throw the bolt and be gone in a minute.

But she remained motionless, finding it difficult to breathe in the hot, heavy atmosphere of steam and eucalyptus. If he lowered his face to kiss her now, she would do nothing to prevent it. She felt weak, powerless. Her fingers grew limp as they clutched the towel. She had to press it with her palm to keep it in place. She could feel her chest rise and fall with each rasp of breath she took. She could feel her own heart pound beneath her hand. She felt as if she were suffocating.

At the same time, she felt invigorated and pulsing with life. He could take her now, she realized vaguely through the haze of shimmering heat. He could take her with one kiss and the sliding off of two towels. Sex had always seemed so difficult and awkward. But now it appeared natural, inevitable. He had told her she was beautiful, and she had never seen a more beautiful man. His eyes glinted with desire. And she desired him. It really was so simple. She swayed toward him, lips parted and waiting. She had never given less thought to what she was doing or why.

As her eyes closed she felt the grip of his hands around her upper arms, his strong fingers indenting the soft flesh. He shook her gently.

"Susan? Are you feeling dizzy?" The sensual timbre in his voice had disappeared, replaced by concern.

It was as if he'd awakened her from another dream, this one not as innocent as her cloud fancy. "I'm fine," she said, feeling foolish now. She averted her eyes.

Max took hold of her chin and tilted up her face. "You're not used to so much heat." He dropped his hand and stepped back. "I suggest you get out of here. For your own good."

He unlocked the door and threw it open. All the steam rushed out. And so did Susan, because she knew he was right. It was for her own good.

"Would you care for some coffee while we talk, Miss Barnes?" Max asked, ushering Susan into his office the next morning. They had spent the last hour meeting with the Kaiser Grand's managerial staff, and Susan had received no warmer a reception than she had during the shareholders' meeting the day before.

"No, thanks. I try to limit myself to only one cup a day." She sat down across the desk from him.

"I admire your restraint," Max said.

Susan heard the archness in his voice. Was he remembering how little restraint she'd shown as she'd swayed toward him in the sauna? This was the first time they'd been alone since they'd parted the day before. Not only had Max Kaiser gone back to addressing her formally, he was acting cooler toward her than ever.

Which was fine with Susan. She perfectly understood his determination to keep their relationship on a strictly business level. She had an equal determination to do that. Maybe she couldn't quite forget about her weak moment in the steamy sauna, but she wasn't going to dwell on it, either.

One thing she knew for sure. It was a lot easier to keep an emotional distance from Max Kaiser when they both had their clothes on. He was dressed in a dark blue suit today, which made his eyes look even bluer.

"The coffee here is much stronger than I'm accustomed to," she said.

"I'm sure. Americans don't know how to make real coffee. They serve up a watered-down version of it at restaurants, anyway. I notice that whenever I'm in the States."

"Do you visit often, Mr. Kaiser?"

"Not as often as I'd like to."

"But you told me that you'd spent a great deal of time in America."

"Oh, you remember my mentioning that."

Susan remembered everything he'd ever said to her about himself. Which wasn't very much.

"Yes, I spent a good part of my reckless youth in America," he said now. "I raced in a lot of competitions there."

"You were a race-car driver?"

"No, I used to race on skis for a living."

Susan could easily picture him as a fierce competitor, pushing himself to the limit at breakneck speed. It must have been the ideal outlet for all his self-contained energy.

"What made you give it up?" she asked him.

"Old age."

She laughed. "You don't look that old to me."

"Anyone over thirty is racing against time in that profession."

"So you decided to manage the family business instead."

"No. I decided on something else."

"What?"

"Something else," he said again and quickly changed the subject. "Well, now that you've met the Grand managers, I'd like to know what most impressed you about them."

Susan found that an easy question to answer. "They're all men."

Max frowned. "That's not entirely correct. What about Ursula Schmidt?"

"Of course. The only woman with any responsibility here is Frau Schmidt, in charge of housekeeping."

"A highly responsible position."

"Still, a traditional woman's role. Do you have a training program to encourage women who work here to become managers?"

"No, but we don't have a training program for men, either, so don't make an equal-rights issue of it, Miss Barnes."

"It was just a simple question, Mr. Kaiser," she said evenly. There had been an undercurrent of tension between them all morning.

He nodded and continued with more patience in his voice. "The Grand's management staff has simply evolved through the years. The people in positions of responsibility here have been with the hotel since my father's day. And since most Swiss women weren't interested in having careers outside the home until recently, the Grand's lack of female executives stems from tradition, not prejudice."

"It seems we always come back to tradition," Susan remarked.

"It's one of the Grand's strengths," Max reminded her.

One of its weaknesses, too? It was too early for Susan to ascertain that. "Do you have an organizational chart I could study?" she asked Max.

"We've never had any need for one. Everyone knows his function here."

"Or *thinks* he does, anyway. But the complexity of this business can lead to confusion and false perceptions about functions. For instance, your financial comptroller seems to be under the impression that he's in charge of all the other departments."

"Yes, Fritz Maier considers himself indispensable."

"Is he?"

Max considered her question a moment. "If he is, he shouldn't be."

"You don't trust him?"

"I don't distrust him," Max replied quickly. "Fritz has been with the Grand for many years, and he was an enormous help to me when I took over as general manager. The only reason I said that he shouldn't be indispensable is because it's my responsibility to be in charge, not his. I can't...what's that American expression?...pass the bucket."

"The buck," Susan said with a little smile. Max Kaiser spoke such precise English that she found these occasional slips endearing.

"Ah, yes, the buck," he repeated. "Anyway, Fritz cares a great deal about the Grand, especially now that he's become a major shareholder through marriage. Perhaps at times he oversteps his authority, or interferes with other departments, but it's best to take him with a grain of pepper."

"Salt," Susan automatically corrected. And then she caught that little smile of his, barely there but tugging at the edges of his lips. "You do that on purpose, don't you?"

"Do what, Miss Barnes?" Max's expression was one of surprised innocence.

"Those little twists on clichés. They're intentional."

He shrugged, admitting nothing.

But Susan was on to his little trick now. Max Kaiser was a teaser. He'd teased her in the sauna, too, and made her laugh with his antics. So unexpected. So unlike him. But she had no idea what he was really like, did she? He was such a contrast of coolness and warmth, humor and reserve. The coldness in him put her off. The heat she felt from him whenever they got too close pulled her right in. She didn't want to be pulled in.

"I think the first thing I should do is formulate an organizational chart for the Grand," she told him, getting back to business. "Not only would it make managerial functions clear, it would help me get acclimated, too."

"Of course, Miss Barnes. If you think it's necessary."

He had decided to give her free rein because his confidence in her had increased considerably since their first meeting at the airport. Although he thought she'd come on a little too strong with the family shareholders yesterday, he'd still admired her forthrightness.

And her professionalism had impressed him all morning. Her questions to his staff had been intelligent and right to the point, proving to Max that she knew the hotel business well. In fact, a lot better than he did. He didn't mind admitting that—to himself. His limited experience was one of the reasons he'd hired a consultant.

The trouble was that he was having more and more difficulty viewing Miss Barnes in a strictly professional capacity. It would have been a lot easier if he hadn't hired a consultant with a nose that turned up so charmingly, he thought as he regarded her across his desk. And he hadn't expected big violet eyes, either.

Nor had he expected to see all her other assets uncovered, and the power of that particular image hit him right in the belly every time it sprang into his mind. Which was about every five minutes or so. Maybe less. The intervals when he wasn't picturing Susan Barnes naked seemed to be getting shorter and shorter.

At thirty-three, Max had enjoyed his share of amorous adventures. But his Swiss nature made him discriminating, and he believed in limitations. He considered Susan Barnes off-limits. When he thought back to their time in the sauna, he congratulated himself on his restraint. He'd wanted her then, more than he'd ever wanted a woman before. But when she'd swayed toward him and parted her lips, he had realized that she didn't know what she was doing. He'd never taken advantage of a woman before. And he could never take advantage of one stupefied by heat.

He did his best to pay attention to what she was saying. Something about an organizational framework?

"A distinction should be drawn between operating departments and support service departments, don't you think, Mr. Kaiser?"

He nodded. He had no idea what she was talking about now, but it sounded as if she did.

"So the chart I have in mind will block out the various service groups and how they connect," she continued. "I think the breakdown should be administration, operation and maintenance. These areas tend to overlap, of course, but designating functions on a chart makes everything so much clearer."

Max nodded again, paying more attention to the way Miss Barnes's full lips moved when she formed her words than to what she was saying. He caught himself recalling her naked again. He looked at his watch and promised himself he wouldn't let the image invade his mind for a full three minutes. He pictured a bright red helicopter hovering over an icy cliff instead. He added two people on the cliff. Then he put himself in the pilot's seat. It was the one place he always felt most in control. This would be a tricky maneuver. How could he get close enough to pick up those people without smashing into the side of the cliff? Certain risks were involved. But they were calculated risks. He turned the helicopter around in his mind and made it come in even lower and closer.

"All heads of departments report directly to the general manager, I assume," Susan said. She waited for a response. None came. She realized he wasn't listening. "Mr. Kaiser? Are you still with me?"

"Yes, of course, Miss Barnes." He managed to catch the drift of her question despite his inattention. "Everyone reports directly to me."

He didn't sound too happy about it, Susan noted. He'd seemed distracted all morning, and she'd noticed him checking his watch. His lack of interest irked her. He had a position she would have given her eyeteeth to have. And one of these days, she'd promised herself, she would be running a hotel as fine as this one. That was why her experience here was so valuable.

Meanwhile, she would do her best to fulfill her assignment and discover why the Grand's profit had been steadily shrinking over the years. Was Max Kaiser himself the key to the problem? Then she recalled that he'd only taken over as general manager last April. Who had been in charge before him?

Susan was about to ask Max this, but he spoke first. "How long do you think it will take you to do this chart of yours?"

"A week or so. Then I can go on and do productivity studies."

Max almost smiled at the eagerness in her voice. "You really enjoy your work, don't you, Miss Barnes?"

"Hotel management fascinates me."

"You're lucky then," he said with a note of wistfulness. "You're doing exactly what you want to do."

"And you're not," Susan guessed aloud.

Max picked up a silver pen and threaded it through his long fingers. "I'm fulfilling my destiny," he finally said.

Because his reply brought her no closer to understanding him, it disappointed Susan. "I don't believe in destiny," she said. "Life is what you make it."

Max laughed sharply. "What a very American attitude, Miss Barnes. We Europeans accept our lot in life more easily than you do."

She wondered if he realized how condescending he could sound at times. "Listen, Mr. Kaiser," she said, leaning toward him. "If I'd accepted my lot in life, I would be nowhere right now. Instead I went ahead and made something of myself."

Max could smell her perfume as she leaned toward him, a mixed bouquet of sweet and sharp. How proud she was, he thought. He liked that about her even more than her physical attributes, which were compelling enough.

So she'd made something of herself. Good for her. Without knowing anything about her background, Max envied Susan Barnes.

"Perhaps you had more freedom of choice than I had," he said. The words tasted bitter in his mouth.

"Well, I sure didn't have the advantages!" she shot back.

They stared at each other, and a distance as vast as the Atlantic Ocean seemed to separate them. Neither understood the other. Both doubted they ever could.

A knock on the door broke their locked gaze.

"Come in," Max said, relieved by the interruption. He'd been tempted to take the plunge and swim across the vastness for a moment there. To simply reach across the desk and touch Susan's cheek. He'd been longing to touch her all morning.

His sister Karin walked in. She looked from Susan to Max. *"Entschuldigung,"* she said, and continued to talk in Swiss German to her brother. "I thought you were alone, Max. I came to ask you to have lunch with me. We need to talk."

"Don't be rude like the others, Karin. Please speak English in front of our consultant," Max replied sharply in their mother tongue. Then he switched to English, turning to Susan. "My sister just invited us to join her in the dining room, Miss Barnes."

Hearing the exasperation in the breath Karin Kaiser let escape from her lips, Susan knew his translation was less than accurate.

"Oh, I think I'll skip lunch," she said.

"I won't hear of it," Max insisted. "We Swiss never skip the midday meal. And neither should you while you're here. We would be very disappointed if you didn't join us."

Susan had no doubt about his sincerity. But a quick look in Karin's direction told her that it wasn't a mutual invitation. At the same time, she wanted to get to know Max's sister better. Despite Karin's barely concealed antagonism toward her, Susan sensed they could eventually become friends. Or maybe that was just wishful thinking on her part. She badly needed a friend at Kaiser Grand.

"Yes, please join us, Miss Barnes," Karin said, her effort to sound gracious not lost on Susan.

Always the outsider, Susan had grown up knowing that any chance to be included shouldn't be refused. "Thank you. I will," she said.

As they were about to leave the office Max's telephone rang. "I'd better get that. It's my private line," he said. After listening for a few minutes he told whoever was on the other end that he would be right there and hung up. "Please excuse me, ladies. I must leave immediately."

"That was Sabine, wasn't it?" Karin said. "You always drop everything when she calls, day or night. Mother thinks it interferes with your duties at the hotel."

"Let Mother think what she wants. I have other obligations, too. Sabine needs me today. I can't refuse."

"Just be careful, Max."

"You needn't worry about me."

He quickly kissed his sister's cheek, then said goodbye to Susan and hurried off without further explanation.

Susan burned to know who Sabine was. Max's lover, she guessed. Who else could have such a power over him? Her call had electrified him with energy. She'd seen it crackle in his eyes.

"That leaves just the two of us, Miss Barnes," Karin said flatly.

"You're under no obligation to have lunch with me now," Susan told her. "I realize you only included me because your brother insisted."

Karin didn't deny it. "Well, now that I have, we might as well go through with it."

On that resigned note, she led the way to the dining room. They sat down at a table by the windows. Karin checked over the place settings with a proprietary air. She plucked a wilted rose from the small vase of fresh flowers on the table, moved the vase a fraction of an inch to center it better, then lifted a crystal glass to scrutinize it by the light from the window. Apparently satisfied that it was spotless, she set it down again and gave her attention to Susan.

"The house Riesling is very nice," she said. "I could order us a small carafe if you'd like."

Susan agreed, and when the wine was served Karin lifted her glass. "It's customary to say *'Zum Wohl'* before drinking, Miss Barnes."

Susan raised her own glass and repeated the words. "I assume it's also customary to address people formally. I'm beginning to forget what my first name sounds like." Perhaps that was why, whenever she recalled Max's soft murmuring of it in the sauna, she melted a little.

"I can understand why you would find the formality strange, being American," Karin said. "But to call someone by their Christian name here is an invitation to be friends for life. Not a step to be taken lightly."

"Then I guess I made a mistake calling my room maid by her first name."

"It would be more proper to address her as Fräulein," Karin told her. "Who is your room maid, by the way?"

"Heidi. She has curly brown hair and—"

"Yes, yes," Karin said. "I know Heidi. She comes from our village. She's very bright."

"And enthusiastic," Susan added. "If given a chance, she could go far at the Grand."

"My opinion exactly. That's why I offered to pay for her further schooling. The way I see it, the Grand must encourage young women who work here to get managerial training. I don't know if you've noticed, but we have only one female executive on our staff. And of course she's in charge of—"

"Housekeeping!" Susan said, in unison with Karin.

They both laughed.

"This must change," Karin continued, becoming serious again. "Men have always advanced from the bottom ranks of the Grand, and it's high time women did, too. So I take it upon myself to sponsor any young woman who shows interest and potential. Like Heidi."

Susan sat back, impressed. "You and I seem to be on the same wavelength, Miss Kaiser. Yet I get the feeling you resent my presence here."

"Oh, I do," Karin admitted, softening the bluntness of her reply with a smile. "But don't take it personally, Miss Barnes. I would resent any outsider coming here to give advice, because my own suggestions have always been ignored by the family."

"Why is that?"

Karin shrugged. "Kaiser females stay in the background while the men run the hotel. All that's expected of me is that I marry well."

"What an outdated attitude!" Susan couldn't help but remark.

"Things are different here than in America. Women didn't even have the right to vote in Switzerland until 1971. And some cantons held out giving them the right until very recently. So we have a lot of catching up to do."

"But surely your brother will let you get involved in the business. He can't be prejudiced against women. He hired *me*."

"Yes, Max would support me. But that would mean going against Mother, who has very old-fashioned ideas. And I don't want to ask him to do that right now because he has enough problems."

Susan wondered if a woman named Sabine was one of them. Hadn't Karin warned Max to be careful after he'd received that phone call? She wished she could think of a way to ask more about this mystery woman without sounding too obvious about it. Her burning curiosity was giving her indigestion. Or maybe it was just the wine on an empty stomach.

"Poor Max," Karin went on in a sad voice. "The last thing he expected was to get saddled with running the family hotel. But he was forced to take over when we lost Gerhard."

Yet another mystery. The Kaiser family seemed to be filled with them, Susan thought. She felt she had a right to get this one cleared up, however, since it involved hotel business. "Who's Gerhard?" she asked.

Karin looked surprised that she didn't know. "Our elder brother. He was killed in a car crash last March."

"Oh, I'm so sorry. No one told me."

"No doubt Max would have, eventually. But we don't like to talk about the tragedy. We have not yet recovered from the shock of it. And Mother may never recover. Gerhard was her favorite. As the eldest male, he took over running the hotel when Papa died six years ago. Now it's up to Max."

So that was what he'd meant when he said it was his destiny. He'd made it sound like a life sentence.

Chapter Five

"So how is that Barnes woman working out?" Frau Kaiser asked her son as they strolled through the hotel gardens together.

"Very well, thank you," Max replied. Knowing how much his mother resented Susan's presence at the hotel, he figured the less he said about her, the better. The path they took began to ascend more steeply, and he took his mother's arm, just in case she needed his support. She'd had a mild heart attack soon after Gerhard died, and although she'd fully recovered, Max still worried about her.

"I hear she's interfering in everybody's business."

"Who told you that, Mother?"

"Fritz."

Max laughed. "It's Fritz who constantly interferes. Miss Barnes has to familiarize herself with all areas of the Grand, and I expect the staff to cooperate and answer all her questions."

"Has she complained to you that they aren't cooperating?"

"No, but I doubt anyone's making her job any easier for her."

"Except for you, of course, Maximilian."

"Actually, I haven't seen much of her all week. We've had a few meetings, that's all." It wasn't as if he'd been avoiding her, Max told himself. But she seemed to be working well on her own, and he saw no reason to interfere. It was best to keep a certain distance. Miss Barnes's value, after all, was her objectivity.

"Then you haven't taken her on any more little shopping trips?" his mother asked.

"What?" Max didn't understand. Then he remembered. "Oh, you heard that I brought Miss Barnes to a dress shop the day she arrived here."

"Yes, the saleswoman mentioned it to your Aunt Berta, who passed the information along to me."

This didn't surprise Max. People were always passing information along to his mother. She had an intricate network of friends and family who kept in close touch, and although she rarely left the hotel grounds, she knew what went on all over Zürich, or at least anything that had to do with her two children or the Grand.

"Since when do you offer to buy employees expensive clothes, Maximilian?"

His mother already knew about Susan's lost luggage, so Max didn't bother to explain himself. He rarely explained his actions to anyone. "Miss Barnes didn't accept my offer," he replied.

Frau Kaiser sniffed. "Perhaps it wasn't big enough."

"Now what do you mean by that, Mother?"

"Never mind." She disengaged her arm from his and bent to pluck a weed she'd apparently spotted in the chrysanthemum bed. She yanked hard, pulling it up by the roots. "If there's one thing I can't abide, it's weeds," she said vehemently.

Or outsiders, Max thought. "Miss Barnes will be gone in a few months," he said.

"Unless you ask her to stay longer."

"I can't foresee the possibility of that. She's a consultant, not a permanent employee."

"You couldn't take your eyes off her during the shareholders' meeting. And I wasn't the only one who noticed. Fritz thinks you hired her more on her looks than her ability."

"That's ridiculous!" Max took a calming breath. He had promised himself always to be patient with his mother. "I hired Miss Barnes without even meeting her because she had excellent qualifications. And of course I looked at her during the meeting. It would have been rather rude not to."

He didn't mention how rudely the family had behaved toward Susan during the luncheon. Better to let such things pass rather than make an issue of them. All Max wanted was to have the ship he now guided to sail smoothly and avoid troubled waters.

"But you find her attractive?" Frau Kaiser's voice was sharp.

The answer to that was so obvious that Max didn't bother replying. His mother spotted another weed and went on the attack. As she extracted it, Max took the opportunity to lead the conversation away from his interest in Susan.

"How would you like to go to the opera with me tonight, Mother?" He loathed opera, but knew how much she enjoyed it. Or used to, anyway. She took little joy in life now.

"No, thank you, Max," she said. "I really don't feel up to it. Besides, you would probably get bored and restless by the second act. I remember how badly you behaved when I took you to the opera as a child."

Patience, Max reminded himself. "But I'm an adult now," he reminded his mother.

"Yes, I'm sure you wouldn't crawl under the seats and tickle people's legs anymore."

"Well, thank you for your confidence!"

"But it wouldn't be the same without Gerhard sitting in the box beside me. *He* appreciated opera."

Max tried again. "You haven't been to any lectures at the university lately, have you, Mother?" She didn't go anywhere anymore, and Max worried about this as much as her heart condition. He took a brochure out of his pocket. He'd stopped by the university to get it for her. "Just look at all the interesting talks listed this month," he urged.

She gave the brochure a cursory glance. Something caught her eye. "John Morgan is going to be speaking this evening. He's a well-known American botanist."

"Really?" Max pretended a great deal more enthusiasm than he felt. "Then we must go hear him talk."

"Oh, Max, you've never cared that much about plants."

He knew she did, though. And he cared about her. "I'm always ready to expand my horizons," he said, which was true enough. "There's nothing I'd like better than to take you to that lecture, Mother."

She thought about it a moment. "All right. We'll go. Perhaps Herr Morgan will take questions from the audience. If I get up the nerve, I'll ask him about propagating rhododendron. Oh, how I would like him to see the Grand gardens!"

"Why not invite him to visit you here?"

Frau Kaiser looked shocked by his suggestion. "I couldn't do that without a formal introduction, Max. It would be far too presumptuous. No, it will be enough just to hear the man talk." She patted Max's arm. "Thank you for offering to take me. You can be very kind and thoughtful when you want to be, my son."

She rarely gave him compliments, and when she did she always tempered them. Still, this one warmed Max's heart, even though he knew he could never replace Gerhard in hers.

"Now I must go have a word with the gardeners," she said. "This weed situation is getting out of hand."

"Two weeds don't exactly constitute an uprising, Mother."

"Two too many," she replied and strode away, still clutching the evidence. Max felt a moment's pity for the gardeners.

He continued along the path, knowing he should get back to the office but reluctant to do so. Administrative work bored him. Sitting behind a desk giving orders had never been his goal. He'd always preferred more physical work as an outlet for his energy. Gerhard had been the one groomed to take over managing the hotel, and he'd seemed ideally suited for the position, with his outgoing personality and friendly manner.

But now that Max had replaced his brother, he realized that Gerhard hadn't kept on top of things as he should have. His easygoing nature had made him popular with the staff, and the guests had appreciated his warmth and hospitality. But when it came to basic business skills, Gerhard had been lacking. He'd allowed Fritz Maier too much authority, for one thing. He'd approved costly but unnecessary expenditures, for another. And perhaps Miss Barnes would uncover more.

But much as Max wanted her to find solutions to the Grand's current financial problems, he didn't look forward to implementing them. He knew he would have to tread carefully. Both the staff and the family would balk at change. Max understood, even sympathized with their reluctance to depart from established procedures. The Grand was more than a business to them. It represented a way of life that had been passed down for generations.

And now that Max had been entrusted with ensuring the financial security of generations to come, he felt the full weight of this responsibility. He could no longer lead a life independent of family demands. Still, whenever Sabine called, he had to go. He had other commitments, too, which he'd made long before he became general manager of the Grand. He always felt pulled in opposite directions now.

He thought back to the time in his life when he'd been responsible only to himself. All that had mattered then was winning; he'd been as free as the wind and as fast. How indestructible he'd felt in those days! It had made him too reckless.

Max had reined in the reckless side of his nature since then. He believed restraint to be a sign of maturity. But if he had met Susan Barnes a few years ago he wouldn't have held back with her the way he was doing now. He would have pursued her with passion, not caring about anything but the pleasure they could give each other. Instead, he was doing his best to cool the heat he always felt in her presence by constantly reminding himself that it was her brains he needed now, not her body. Ah, maturity! Max almost laughed.

As he followed the path leading back to the hotel, he spotted Susan sitting on a bench just ahead, engrossed in the book on her lap. Her hair was loose today, the way he liked it best. It fell over her cheeks, dark against pale. And the willow she sat under dappled light and shade over her, an ever-moving pattern in the breeze. She munched on a big red apple as she read, and seemed so content that Max was about to turn around and leave her in peace. Before he could, she glanced up.

"Guten Tag. Wie geht es Ihnen?" she said, greeting him and asking how he was in German.

"Danke, gut," he responded, surprised. He sat down beside her. "I assumed you didn't know a word of the language, Miss Barnes."

"Only a few so far. But I thought it would help me fit in better here if I could speak a few simple phrases." She showed him her book.

He read the title aloud. *"German the Easy and Fun Way."* That made him smile. "I'm afraid you won't find us Swiss German that easy or so much fun, Miss Barnes. We tend to be complicated and serious."

"Oh, you're not always so serious." She took a bite of apple.

He watched her chew. He liked watching her do anything. "Don't ruin your appetite for lunch." He considered inviting her to join him. They could discuss business, of course. The scent of the apple mingled with her delicate perfume.

"This is my lunch today," she said.

"What? You prefer an apple to Chef Duprés's fine cuisine?"

"No, but if I indulged in a big midday meal every day, I'd get fat."

Max tried to imagine her fat. He couldn't. The image of her naked perfection was still too vivid in his mind. It should have faded by now, dammit.

"And every time I go back to my suite I have another temptation to resist," she went on. "I found a big box of expensive Swiss chocolates on my dressing table my first night here."

"Do you always resist temptations, Miss Barnes?"

"I try, but sometimes I fail. I must admit I've made a dent in the chocolates. They're deliciously irresistible."

"I'm glad you're enjoying them."

"Oh, I am, but I think you overindulge your guests, Mr. Kaiser. In most hotels the maid leaves a few candies on the pillows when she turns down the bed. A nice touch. But an entire box of them! I intend to calculate how much that costs the Grand each year."

Max shifted uncomfortably. "Don't waste your time doing that."

Susan shot him a sidelong glance. "Another area I should tiptoe around? Don't tell me you have a relative who makes chocolates?"

"No." Max wished she would drop the subject.

But she didn't. "Well, then I have a suggestion to make. Fruit arranged in a basket wrapped in colored cellophane makes a lovely presentation and would cost less." She held up her hand to keep him from interrupting. "Oh, I know you're going to say pinching pennies has no place in a luxury hotel. And I agree. But I've observed that most wealthy people are very weight and health conscious, and would probably appreciate fruit more. Also, you'd be surprised how all those gratis extras can add up and eat into hotel profits. Just to prove to you that I know what I'm talking about, I'm going to get some estimates on fruit baskets, compare the cost with what you're spending on boxes of chocolates, and do a five-year projection of potential savings.''

Max sighed. This woman, who looked as delicate as an orchid, had the tenacity of a bulldog. Once she set her mind to something, she would not let go. The only thing left for him to do now was confess. He did so stiffly.

"There's no need to do any cost projections, Miss Barnes. It isn't our policy to give guests free boxes of chocolates. That was my personal gift to you. I had the maid bring them up to your suite.''

Her violet-gray eyes widened in amazement. "But why did you do that?''

Max almost wished he hadn't, now that he had to explain his actions. "Because I observed how much you liked chocolate at the shareholders' luncheon. And I wanted you to feel more comfortable here.''

Susan could tell that admitting this embarrassed him. He had wanted his kind gesture to pass without acknowledgment, and this made her appreciate it even more. But before she had a chance to thank him, he abruptly changed the subject.

"How is your organizational chart coming along, Miss Barnes?''

"I should have it completed by this evening. I could stop by your office after dinner and go over it with you.''

"No, I won't be staying as late as usual. I'm taking my mother to a lecture at the university. Some botanist from America is the guest speaker.''

"Not John Morgan?''

"Why, yes, that's his name. But how did you know? Do you share my mother's avid interest in botany?''

Noting how surprised he looked that she and his mother could have anything in common, Susan set him straight. "I don't know the first thing about the subject. But I met John on the plane coming over here, and he told me he'd be giving a talk.''

''So you're on a first-name basis with him.''

''That's not as big a deal between Americans as it is among the Swiss, Mr. Kaiser,'' she said dryly. ''We tend to be more relaxed and open with strangers. By the end of the flight, John and I considered each other friends.''

''Would you like to come to his lecture with us?''

His unexpected invitation pleased Susan enormously. Perhaps Max Kaiser was beginning to consider her a friend, too. But how would his mother feel about having her come along? Whenever they passed in the lobby, Frau Kaiser looked right through Susan as if she didn't exist.

''Are you sure your mother wouldn't mind?''

''She'll be delighted,'' Max assured her. ''There's nothing she'd like better than to ask John Morgan to come here and see the gardens, but she thinks a formal introduction is necessary. And you, Miss Barnes, will be able to make it.''

So that was it, Susan thought. He'd only invited her because she knew John. But it would nice to see him again, and perhaps an evening together would break the ice between Frau Kaiser and herself. Besides, she wanted to do Max this small favor. It would be her way of thanking him for the chocolates. She agreed, and they made arrangements to meet in the lobby that evening.

''Well, I'll let you get back to your lesson book,'' Max said.

''Can I practice a little with you?'' Susan didn't want him to go right away. It seemed he never had much time to spare for her.

''Of course,'' he agreed. He glanced at his watch.

Susan wished he would stop doing that whenever he was around her for more than five minutes. ''Am I keeping you from something?''

''No, please go ahead. Say something in German.''

She asked him where the train station was.

"Are you thinking of taking a trip?" he asked back in English.

"No, but my conversational skills are somewhat limited. I can also count to ten."

"Yes, that does limit conversation." Max again reminded himself that he had work waiting back at the office. Then Susan crossed her legs and her pleated skirt slid above her knee. The work could wait a few minutes more, he decided. "Let me hear you count to ten, Miss Barnes."

She began, but he interrupted her when she reached five.

"*Fünf,*" he corrected.

"That's what I said."

"Not quite. Listen." He said the word again.

She repeated it.

"You're not rounding your lips enough."

"You mean like this?" She pursed them.

"Yes, that's perfect," he said.

She had the most perfectly formed lips Max had ever encountered, the bottom one full and pouty, the upper one pert. On impulse he dipped his face and kissed her, grazing his own mouth against the pliant softness of hers, tasting apple and her special sweetness. Nectar. But he only allowed his appetite to be whetted instead of appeasing his hunger for her. Realizing he'd overstepped his bounds as a language instructor, he drew back immediately.

"Excuse me, Miss Barnes."

She laughed and felt color spring to her cheeks. "You make it sound as if you just stepped on my toe."

"Well, I hope that's not what it felt like," he said gruffly.

She didn't reply. She wasn't going to tell him that all the nerve endings in her body were singing now.

"Let's skip over *fünf* and go on," he suggested after a moment of awkward silence.

"I can't seem to remember what comes next."

"*Sechs,*" Max prompted.

It sounded like Sex to her. "I think we should talk about what just happened," she said.

Max groaned. "Why do women always want to talk about such things? I realize I shouldn't have kissed you, Miss Barnes. I respect you as a professional and intend to keep our relationship on that level. Emotional entanglements would be imprudent for both of us. What else is there to say?"

"Nothing. You've summed it up quite nicely." And coldly, Susan silently added.

"Perhaps I should add that I find you ... deliciously irresistible, to borrow a phrase from you."

"I was talking about chocolates."

"Yes, but we all have our weaknesses. Mine is beautiful women."

She gave him a swift look. "And you like to sample as many as you can?"

"I don't feel the need to do that anymore. I know exactly the shape and size and taste that please me, Susan Barnes." He picked up her hand, pressed the back of it against his warm cheek, then let it go. "And when you know what you like, it's sometimes hard to resist." He stood up abruptly. "Excuse me again for kissing you. I'll meet you in the lobby at eight this evening." He began walking away.

"Mr. Kaiser?" She couldn't help it. She had to call him back to say one thing.

"Yes, Miss Barnes?"

"It did feel a lot better than if you'd stepped on my toe, by the way."

He smiled with the shy hesitancy she found so attractive. "Well, that's good," he said. Then he left her alone in the garden.

Susan nibbled on her apple, without much appetite now. She leafed through the pages of her book without much interest. Less than ten minutes ago she had been relatively content by herself. Now she felt restless and confused. Max always had that disturbing effect on her. It seemed they were in a tug-of-war of emotions—drawn to each other, but always pulling away.

*   *   *

Susan came down to the lobby ten minutes early, sure that Frau Kaiser was a stickler for promptness. She wore a conservative brown tweed suit and white blouse that buttoned high at the neck, so high that when she lowered her chin the edging of lace tickled it. As she'd gotten dressed she'd thought how perfect her grandmother's cameo brooch would have looked on the blouse.

She doubted she would ever get over the loss of that brooch because it had symbolized too much to her. It had been her grandmother's only treasure, all she'd been able to pass down to Susan. And when it had been stolen, it had made Susan realize that she had nothing left to get her through life but her self-determination. She had been eleven at the time.

And she'd come pretty far on the strength of her own determination, she thought now, glancing around the richly appointed lobby. It didn't matter to her that her position at the Kaiser Grand was only a temporary one, or that she was here to work rather than enjoy herself. She'd grown up in temporary places. And her work *was* her enjoyment. Sure, she'd had a lot of bad luck in her life, but she'd also had the good luck to find a career that suited her perfectly.

From the big challenges down to the nitty-gritty details, hotel management fascinated Susan. That was why she couldn't understand Max's indifference to his job. He obviously cared about the Grand, but his heart didn't seem to be in his work. Perhaps he was just a spoiled playboy who resented having to take on the responsibilities of the family business. The only other occupation he'd mentioned having was skiing, and Susan didn't consider racing down mountains work.

Still, he didn't seem like a playboy to her. She'd known more than a few. They were easy enough to meet in the hotel business. And easy enough to reject, as far as Susan was concerned. She had no use for womanizers. She had no time for lightweights. Max Kaiser didn't strike her as being either.

But maybe she was wrong. She hardly knew the man, after all. And doubted she ever would. His cool reserve and her deep caution would surely keep them from ever getting close. And there was no sense in getting close to someone you would be leaving in three months' time. No sense at all.

She was glad he'd kissed her, not for the brief pleasure it had given her, but because they had gotten it out of the way. It shouldn't have happened, and it wouldn't again. They were in complete agreement about that. She knew she should feel relieved. So why didn't she?

Lost in thoughts about Max, she didn't notice Fritz Maier approach, and he apparently took advantage of this to slip his arm around her shoulders and give her a squeeze. "Susan, my pet, how are you this evening?"

She pulled away from him. She'd met with him a few times this week, and he'd taken more than one opportunity to touch her in sneaky little ways. He was the only one at the hotel who called her by her first name. Ironically, he was also the only one Susan felt unfriendly toward. But she tried her best not to show it. She needed to get along with the man.

"Just fine, Fritz. And you?" She forced a smile.

"How could I feel anything but good in your company, my lamb?"

He was always calling her cute little names like that, too. Susan didn't take it as flattery. She felt he meant it as a power play, a way to demean her. Yet she could hardly protest without seeming prim and making an issue of something he would no doubt shrug off.

"Are you waiting for someone?" he asked. He shifted his bulging briefcase from one hand to the other. "Or just snooping around?"

"Snooping around?" Her smile remained firmly in place.

Fritz laughed and squeezed her arm again. "That's your job, isn't it, Susan? I thought perhaps Max sent you on a spy mission to see how the reception staff was performing its duties this evening."

"Mr. Kaiser doesn't send me on spy missions, Fritz. Actually, I'm waiting for him and his mother. We're going to a lecture together."

"Oh, really?" Fritz stroked his goatee. Black, with a streak of white down the center, it reminded Susan of a skunk pelt. "Frau Kaiser actually agreed to spend an evening in your company?"

Susan felt the jab, which was none too subtle. "Are you assuming that she would find my company too offensive?"

Fritz looked pleased to have made a direct hit. "*I* certainly don't, my dove."

If he squeezes my arm one more time, Susan thought, I'm going to yank his goatee. Hard. But the idea of actually touching it repulsed her and she took a few steps back, instead, just out of his reach.

"That financial report you gave me was a little sketchy," she said, to regain lost ground. "I need a detailed breakdown of expenditures, not rough estimates."

"I know exactly what you need." His little black eyes looked menacing. "And I'll give it to you in due time. But I have other matters to deal with right now. I can't drop everything to accommodate you, now, can I?"

"I don't expect you to do that." She kept her voice friendly, polite. "But my time here is limited, and I can't make much progress without concrete figures. I'd like them no later than next week, please."

"I don't take orders from you, Susan. Or from anyone."

"Not even Max Kaiser?"

"I'm as big a shareholder in this hotel as he is now."

Susan filed away this new piece of information. "But you're not general manager, Fritz."

He toyed with his beard. "Unfortunately not."

"Why unfortunate? Don't you think Mr. Kaiser is doing a good job?"

His eyes shifted around the bustling lobby, as if he'd just remembered that their private discussion was taking place in a public place. When he looked back at Susan his expression was guarded. "Of course I do. Max is a highly intelligent and determined young man. I will do everything in my power to help him succeed, just as I helped his brother and his father before him."

"Then help me out a little bit, too," Susan said. "We're all working toward the same goal, to make the Grand as profitable as possible."

Fritz made no reply. Instead he looked over her shoulder, his eyes still hard, his lips forming a smile.

Susan turned to see Max striding toward them. He was dressed casually, or as casually as she ever expected to see him, anyway. The cut of his navy blazer and gray flannel slacks was European, the lines fluid and relaxed.

Fritz greeted him with hearty affability. "Max, my boy, I was just talking about my dedication to the Grand. Isn't that so, Susan?"

"Among other things," she replied. "We were also discussing my need to get cost breakdowns as soon as possible. Isn't that so, Fritz?"

He didn't deign to look at her. "This young lady of yours is quite a taskmaster, Max." His smile turned sly. "Or perhaps I should say taskmistress."

"Miss Barnes is my consultant, not my... young lady," Max corrected him coolly. "Is there a problem about giving her the figures she needs?" He gave his financial comptroller a flat, steady look.

"None whatsoever." Fritz shifted his briefcase again. "As a matter of fact, I plan to work on the report she needs tonight in my suite. Berta has been complaining that I spend too much time in the office away from her."

Max looked concerned. "Really, Fritz, I hope you're not ignoring Aunt Berta because you have too much work to do. Hire an assistant if you need one. And delegate some of your duties."

"I don't need to do either," Fritz said in an adamant tone. He softened it. "You know how women are, Max. They want constant attention."

"Well, I can understand Aunt Berta wanting to spend more time with you. You haven't been married that long. Only a month, isn't it?"

"Two, but it seems a lot longer." Fritz quickly changed his glum tone to a cheerier one. "I mean, it seems as if Berta and I were always married. That's how well we get along. She's such a treasure to me."

"Oh, I'm sure," Max said.

He hoped he hadn't sounded too sardonic. He'd noticed how Fritz ignored his aunt and couldn't help but think he'd married her more for her shares in the hotel than out of love. In that way she certainly was a treasure to him. Max didn't like thinking that way, though. All he wanted was happiness for every member of his family.

"And I'm sure Miss Barnes can wait for the figures she requested from you," he added. "So why not pay attention to Aunt Berta tonight, Fritz, instead of burying your nose in hotel accounts?"

Susan silently fumed. She had trouble enough getting any information out of Fritz, and now Max had let the little worm off the hook. She considered objecting, then decided against it. This wasn't the time or the place. And it wasn't her place to insist that Max's dear aunt be ignored because she, Susan Barnes, needed a detailed balance sheet. This mixing of family concerns and business ones didn't sit well with her. She held her tongue and tapped her foot. It made no sound as it hit the plush Oriental rug in the center of the lobby.

Max noticed the tapping foot. He noticed everything about Susan at all times, even when he seemed to be directing his attention elsewhere. She'd twisted her thick mane of wavy hair into a tame little bun, and her practical suit and demure blouse would have met with his mother's approval. He wondered if Susan had dressed with that in mind. If so, her effort to please had been wasted. His mother wouldn't be putting in an appearance this evening.

Before telling Susan that, Max thought it best to get rid of Fritz. "Well, good night, Fritz. I'm sure you don't want to keep Aunt Berta waiting." He considered adding a wink but thought that would be overdoing things.

Fritz didn't budge. "Oh, she can do without me for a few more minutes. I'll stay until your mother comes down, Max. Susan tells me you're all going to a lecture together. How nice."

Curse the man, Max thought. He was making an awkward situation much worse. "Mother has decided to stay in for the evening." He turned to Susan. "She isn't feeling well and sends you her regrets, Miss Barnes."

At that moment Susan learned something important about Max Kaiser. The man could not lie. Or rather, he couldn't do it well. Either he lacked the practice or the inclination, because his face gave his thoughts away. He looked as if he'd just swallowed something distasteful. And his eyes didn't connect with hers for once. He pretended to look directly at her, but Susan knew he was staring at her forehead instead. She could tell the difference. When their eyes really connected, she always felt a jolt in her stomach.

"I'm sorry to hear that," she said.

"Not feeling well?" Fritz interjected. "But when I saw your mother during my afternoon stroll, she seemed perfectly fine, Max. In fact, she was digging in some flower beds with the gardeners and stopped to tell me how much she was looking forward to going to a talk about plants with you this evening." Fritz paused to examine his manicured fingernails. "She didn't mention that Miss Barnes would be accompanying you, however."

Max did more than curse Fritz now. He wished him to hell. "Perhaps Mother overdid things," he said, his teeth on edge. "Because she feels too tired to go out this evening."

Susan felt a slow heat rising over her, a wave of humiliation brought on by Frau Kaiser's snub. "May I talk to you in private please, Mr. Kaiser?" she said softly, twisting the lace around her collar between her fingers.

"Oh, don't mind me," Fritz said, his expression gleeful. "I'm off to make my little bride happy." He shuffled off to the elevators, swinging his briefcase.

"I've never been able to warm up to that man," Max muttered as he watched him depart.

Susan had little interest in discussing Fritz now. Something else had to be settled right away. "I'm not going to be the cause of your mother missing this lecture, Max," she said, forgetting to address him by his last name.

"She has a headache," he said curtly.

"And I'm the cause of it!"

Max didn't deny it. He saw the hurt in Susan's eyes and looked away.

"Go call her on the reception phone and tell her to come right down," Susan urged him. "Assure her that I won't be here when she does."

"I'll do nothing of the kind."

"I really don't mind," Susan said, wishing she were a better actress.

"Well, I do."

"You shouldn't have included me in the first place, you know."

"That was my decision to make."

"No, it wasn't, Max. You should have discussed it with her first."

He released an exasperated breath. He'd just had exactly the same argument with his mother. He found it ironic that Susan was supporting her now, leaving him still caught in the middle. He'd never expected his mother to react so strongly about including Susan. He'd thought it would be a good chance for them to get to know each other. Instead, she had stubbornly refused to come along. He had left her suite, furious that she was denying herself the pleasure of attending the lecture because of a prejudice against a woman she hardly knew. And now Susan was digging in her heels, too! He didn't have the time or the patience for this sort of female nonsense. He checked his watch.

"We'd better go, Miss Barnes, or we'll be late for that damn lecture."

"I'm *not* going," she insisted. "I want Frau Kaiser to go instead."

"But she won't now, even if you don't come. And I'm not going to go by myself, dammit!"

"There's no need to swear. You're the one who created this situation, Mr. Kaiser. Good night."

Max watched Susan walk away, shoulders back, head high. He caught up to her before she reached the elevators and captured her arm in a firm grip. He noticed that the front-desk clerk was watching them, along with a few of the porters. He didn't want to make a scene in front of them, but didn't want to let her go, either.

"All I ever had was good intentions," he told her softly. "But somehow I've managed to offend both my mother and you and end up in the dog pound."

If his intention was to make her smile, it didn't work. "Doghouse," she corrected. "And I already told you I'm on to that trick."

"That's right, you did. You can read me like a newspaper."

"Oh, stop that!" But now she was smiling.

"Please come with me, Susan. Why pass up the opportunity to see your friend from America?"

Why indeed? Susan thought. She would like to see John Morgan again, and it seemed silly to boycott this lecture just because Frau Kaiser did. Besides, Max had said "please." And he had called her by her first name. Susan wondered if she would hear him do either ever again. She agreed to go with him.

"Why, it's my angel in the sky! What a delightful surprise this is!" John Morgan exclaimed, taking Susan's hand and pressing it between his big, freckled paws at the reception following his talk. "Are you here alone?"

"No, I came with someone. He's at the buffet table getting us some champagne."

"I knew it wouldn't take long for a pretty young woman like you to find a beau here."

Susan smiled at the old-fashioned term but shook her head. "Nothing like that, John. He's my boss, not my beau."

"One doesn't necessarily discount the other."

"For me it does."

John nodded. "That's probably wise."

Susan knew it was and dropped the subject. "I had no idea you were such a famous man, John."

"Oh, I'm not famous. I doubt more than a handful of people know who I am."

"Looks like more than a handful to me." Susan waved her hand around the crowded reception room.

"I never expected such a big turnout. The Swiss, it seems, have quite an interest in botany."

"I know of one lady in Zürich who admires you very much."

"Did she come this evening? I'd like to meet her. Any friend of yours is a friend of mine, Susan."

"No, Frau Kaiser couldn't make it. And I wouldn't exactly call her my friend," Susan said ruefully.

"Yes, I've noticed that the Swiss take their time making friends. Not that I haven't been treated with the utmost cordiality. I've been made to feel very welcome here."

Susan wished she could say the same. The staff continued to remain wary of her, Fritz was downright antagonistic, she hadn't seen Max's sister since their lunch together, and his mother refused to have anything to do with her. She had, however, survived more hostile situations. She could take this one in stride for the sake of her career.

Max came up to them then, carrying two glasses of champagne. Susan introduced the two men. Max gave one glass to Susan and shook hands, then offered John the second glass.

"Thanks, but no thanks," John said. "Alcohol goes straight to my head. Just ask Susan. I spilled a drink all over her on the plane."

"So you're the culprit," Max said.

"Turbulence was more to blame than John," Susan put in quickly.

"You were very understanding about it," he said. "I only wish I could have your hand to hold on the flight back to the States."

"You'll do fine on your own," Susan assured him. He'd been in such self-command during his talk that she found it hard to believe he was the same anxious man she'd sat with on the plane. But fear did strange things to people, Susan knew, making them act against their own nature at times. "When will you be going back, John?"

"Now that I'm here, I thought I'd stay awhile. There are some superb botanical gardens and greenhouses in Zürich that I want to explore."

"You must add the Kaiser Grand gardens to your list," Susan told him. "They're surely worth seeing while you're here."

"Oh, I don't know if they would hold much botanical interest for Mr. Morgan. The Grand gardens aren't all that special," Max said.

He was such an odd combination of modesty and pride, Susan thought, not for the first time. "They are," she insisted. "And the lady I told you was such a fan of yours, John, happens to be Mr. Kaiser's mother. I know for a fact that she'd like nothing better than to have you visit."

"I'd be happy to come," John said. "What about tomorrow?"

Susan smiled sweetly at Max. "Do you think your mother will be feeling better by then?"

"I'm sure of it." He kept a straight face but his eyes twinkled back at her. "And I'm sure she'd like Mr. Morgan to have tea after the tour."

"You're in for a treat, John," Susan said. "The Grand afternoon teas are famous. Does two o'clock tomorrow suit you?"

"Suits me fine," John said. "Count on my being there."

Other people came up to compliment him on his talk, and Susan and Max drifted away.

"That was extremely kind of you," Max said, resting his hand on her shoulder.

She could feel the heat of it through her jacket and blouse. "It was no big deal," she said.

"Yes, it was. You overlooked my mother's behavior and did her a good turn. I'll be sure to point that out to her."

"Please don't. It would be better to let her think that you invited John, not me. She'll be able to enjoy his visit more that way. And I'll make sure to stay out of the way."

"Don't be ridiculous. You must have tea with them. I'm sure Mr. Morgan is expecting you to."

"Oh, I'll use work as an excuse." She'd used work as an excuse plenty of times before to stay away from people. "I can see John on my own some other time."

"Why are you being so considerate of my mother's feelings? She certainly wasn't of yours this evening."

"I just don't like to butt in where I'm not wanted, that's all."

Max trailed his hand across her shoulders and lightly stroked the back of her neck. His fingertips sent currents vibrating through her body. "How could anybody not want you, Susan?" he asked, his voice as soft as his caress.

She slowly raised her eyes to his, and need met need. Neither of them looked away.

Chapter Six

Someone jostled Susan's elbow. Champagne splashed over the rim of her glass and trickled down her wrist.

"Entschuldigung!" the man who'd bumped into her exclaimed, as he offered Susan his cocktail napkin.

But Max had already taken out his handkerchief. He gave the other man such a glare that he moved on without further apology.

"This seems to be your week for getting drinks spilled on you," Max said, conscientiously blotting Susan's hand and jacket sleeve.

A week? Was that all it had been since she'd arrived in Zürich and first laid eyes on Max Kaiser? And now here she was, *making* eyes at him. She didn't need water thrown into her face to make her realize that she was getting carried away. A trickle of champagne was enough. Time to pull back and get her priorities straight. Needing a man wasn't one of them.

"It's too crowded here. Let's go," Max said.

"Back to the hotel?" She almost laughed. It sounded like a question a woman would ask her lover.

"No, I want to be alone with you for a while," Max said. "There's no privacy at the Grand. Too many eyes always watching. That's why I keep an apartment in town."

"You're not suggesting taking me there, are you?"

His smile came slowly. "If I wanted to *take* you, Susan, I wouldn't merely suggest. I would convince."

She'd had only the briefest taste of him, but enough to know he could be very convincing. She was thankful they were in a crowded room now. The smart thing to do would be to make sure they were never alone again.

"I'd just as soon go back to the Grand," she said.

For some reason she felt safe there. Not because of all the prying eyes minding everybody's business, but because it somehow felt like home to her. For all its grandness and despite the problems she had to deal with there, the Grand gave Susan a cozy, warm feeling she'd rarely experienced since she'd lived with her grandmother.

Not that there was the slightest similarity between Grandma's humble apartment and the luxurious suite she now occupied. But the quality of light streaming through the windows was the same. Or perhaps Susan's glowing memories of her grandmother's place made her remember it infused with golden light all day, the way her suite was now.

"Of course we'll go back to the Grand, if that's what you want," Max said. "But you seemed so enchanted with Zürich that first day we drove into town that I thought you might enjoy a little walking tour."

"You mean now?"

"Why not? The evening's still young." Max paused. "And so are we."

Susan had never felt young. She'd been forced to grow up too fast. But what could be the harm in taking a walk with this man? She felt fidgety; she always did in his company. It was as if the heat of his own inner energy managed to seep into her veins, too. And whenever they parted, she was left restless. Since they *would* part tonight, she decided a walk would help her sleep better. For the second time that evening, she agreed to go with him. They said goodbye to John and left.

Max took Susan's arm as they headed down the flight of steps leading from the imposing granite university building. He did this automatically. It was as if he took charge of a woman's destiny when she accompanied him, as if it was up to him to set the pace. Susan didn't mind. She took pleasure in having a strong male arm linked with hers because she knew that she didn't really need it. She had set her own pace and destination in life long ago.

It was one of those clear, crisp autumn nights that had an edge of excitement. The harvest moon shone brightly, and stars sparkled with the intensity of fireworks.

"I hope you don't mind taking a tram," Max said. "I sent the limousine back to the hotel."

"I don't mind at all. I don't usually travel by limo, anyway."

"Neither do I," Max said. "I arranged for Daniel to drive us to the lecture because I thought Mother was coming, too, but I prefer riding my motorcycle."

"You have a motorcycle?" That didn't fit Susan's image of him. A sleek, expensive sports car would have.

"It's the only practical way to get around," he said. "Are you cold? If you are, I'll give you my jacket."

"Then you would be cold," Susan pointed out.

"I'm never cold. Even in the dead of winter I always feel too hot."

"You must have a high metabolism rate," Susan said casually, at the same time thinking how good it would feel to snuggle up to such heat on a cold winter's night. "Thanks for the offer, but I don't need your jacket. I'm perfectly comfortable."

"With me?"

They had reached the bottom step and Susan turned to him. "No, not really," she admitted. His face was in shadow, but a globe-shaped streetlight cast a halo around his head. "You keep putting me off balance."

She could see the glimmer of white teeth as he smiled. "How is that possible? I've never met a woman with her feet so firmly planted on the ground."

"Firmly planted as they are, I still don't know where I stand with you," she told him. "One moment you're warm and friendly, the next you're distant and formal again. It's very disconcerting."

"Which? The warmth or the distance?"

"And you keep asking me arch questions like that!"

"I'm only teasing," he said.

"Oh, is that all?"

"No." In one swift, easy movement he pulled her against him.

Susan instinctively put her hands against his chest to push him away. But she didn't. She stared up at him, trying to discern his features in the darkness. All she could make out was that his eyes sparkled as brightly as the stars. And he wasn't smiling anymore. He clasped her waist tightly and his taut thighs pressed against hers. Her heart thudded in her chest and she heard a rumbling in her ears, growing louder and louder.

Max glanced up. "That's our car," he said, releasing her so quickly she almost lost her balance. "If we run, we can catch it at the next stop."

He didn't bother to ask her if she wanted to run. He grabbed her hand and pulled her along. Susan was thankful she'd worn flats. When they reached the stop half a block away she was breathless but laughing. They had just enough time to jump on board before the car pulled away and clattered down the track again.

They took two seats by the door, and she heard Max swear under his breath.

"What's the matter? We made it, didn't we?" she asked. She placed a hand to her flushed cheek. As far as she was concerned, the streetcar had come in the nick of time. Her heart was beating no faster now than when she'd been held in Max's embrace.

"I didn't buy us tickets," Max replied.

He made it sound like the crime of the century. Susan glanced around the clean, brightly lit car but couldn't spot a ticket collector. The driver was in a little front cabin, isolated from the passengers. "Will someone come around to check?" she asked, picturing some fierce law enforcer popping up from his hiding place under one of the seats.

"No, but it's the principle of the thing," Max said.

They got off a few stops later at Paradeplatz, and the first thing Max did was put change into the outdoor ticket vending machine. When two tickets dropped out, he threw them into the trash container, having no use for them now that their ride was over.

"How honest of you," Susan commented. She was used to seeing people sneaking through New York subway gates.

"This system wouldn't work without honesty," he said.

She nodded. "I don't believe in taking free rides, either. In fact, I should pay for my own ticket." She opened her purse and felt around for change to repay him.

But he wouldn't hear of it. He grumbled something about being able to afford a two-franc ticket and hooked arms with her. They strolled down the wide, tree-lined boulevard. Many of the stone buildings had beaux arts facades with intricate carvings around the arched portals. None were more than five stories high, giving the street a turn-of-the-century feeling. The sidewalks were immaculate. Susan couldn't spot so much as a candy wrapper.

"No traffic," she noted with surprise. It couldn't have been later than ten.

"No motor vehicles allowed on Bahnhofstrasse. Only trams and pedestrians."

"So this is the famous Bahnhofstrasse. I read about this street in a guidebook. It's supposed to be the most expensive one in the world."

"Maybe because gold and silver worth billions are stored in bank vaults beneath our feet."

She looked down, as if she could see all that treasure through the concrete. Then she glanced into one of the well-lit store windows they were passing. The elongated mannequins were wearing luxurious fur coats of every style and hue. "Or maybe because of the merchandise for sale," she said.

They paused to look at the furs. "You'd look good in that one," Max said, pointing to a black coat with a hood.

Susan guessed it was sable, but certainly wasn't an authority on the subject. Whatever it was, she considered it too rich for her blood.

"I'd like to see you in it," Max mused, a little smile playing on his lips. "There's nothing more sensual than a beautiful woman draped in fur, and sable would look magnificent against your pale cheeks."

Ah, so it *was* sable. Of course Max Kaiser would know about such expensive things. Sensual things, too. And beautiful women. That he considered her one made Susan feel more delighted than she knew she should be. Irritated with herself, she knew she sounded irritated with him when she spoke again.

"I don't wear animal skins. Wool keeps me warm enough, thank you."

Max laughed. "Don't worry, Susan. I wasn't offering to buy it for you."

"I realize that!" She moved on to the next window and concentrated on a display of crystal decanters and vases. "These prices are absurd," she muttered, hoping he realized that she found his remark equally so.

Max ambled on up the street, hands in his trouser pockets, whistling to himself. Susan had never seen him so relaxed. He paused a few stores up.

Wondering what had captured his interest, Susan caught up with him. Of course. Watches. A window filled with them. "You have a fascination with time, don't you?" she remarked.

"What makes you say that?"

"The way you're always checking your own watch."

"Yes, I know I do it too often," he admitted. "It's become a nervous habit with me. But I've come to realize that time is the most precious commodity a person can have because there's never enough of it."

"The trick is to set priorities," Susan told him.

He laughed. "Spoken like a true efficiency expert. But you can't *set* priorities until you *have* priorities, Miss Barnes."

So he was back to calling her that again. He hadn't all evening. Now, for some reason, he was putting the formal barrier up again. She wanted to know why. "What are your priorities, Max?" She deliberately called him by his first name, hoping to draw him out again.

To her surprise, he didn't dodge the question with one of his light quips. "I have only two. The Grand, and my other work. That leaves me little time for anything else." He kept his eyes on the window display. "The last thing I need is to get involved with someone right now."

Well, who was asking him to? Susan skipped over that piece of information, but stored it away in her heart. "What other work?" she asked him.

Max shrugged. "Something that has nothing to do with the hotel." He said no more.

What was he, anyway? Susan wondered. A secret agent? She could easily believe it as she studied his sharp, strong profile. It looked carved out of stone at the moment. And since she didn't have a pair of pliers handy to pull out his fingernails, she gave up trying to get any more information out of him. Besides, torture wouldn't work. When Max Kaiser didn't want to divulge something, he became impenetrable. Yes, she decided. He would make an excellent secret agent. That was probably his true calling.

She moved on to the next store. This time he followed. "Diamonds, I think, would suit you better than rubies," he said.

Susan hadn't been paying much attention to what she'd been staring at through the thick plate glass window. She'd been mulling over the few kernels of information Max had given her instead. "Do you really?" she asked, turning her attention to the display of exquisite jewelry. Her tone was ironic. "I had my heart set on emeralds."

Max rubbed his chin, as if considering her stated preference, then shook his head. "None of those gems is quite right for you. Only that piece is." He pointed to a necklace on a black velvet pillow.

Susan recognized the stones set in platinum gold from a college course in geology. She pretended disappointment and sniffed, even though the price beneath the necklace had five figures. "But that's merely quartz," she said in her best attempt to sound haughty. She couldn't quite pull it off.

"Not merely quartz. Amethyst," Max stressed. "The glint in those stones is like the glint in your eyes."

What was he talking about? "My eyes are gray, not purple."

"With the hint of violet," he said.

The mirror had never reflected any such hints to Susan. But she thought it would be ungracious to argue over a compliment. She was used to men waxing eloquent about her figure. Big breasts seemed to inspire them to poetic similes, and her own had been compared to a cornucopia of fruits by intent suitors who ended up seeing little else of her anatomy than her cold shoulder. Amethyst eyes? That was a new one. She liked it. She didn't want to let on how much, though.

"Actually, I have little interest in jewelry," she said, moving away from the window.

"Yes, I noticed you never wear any." Max linked arms with her again. "Does owning jewelry go against another of your principles?"

"It goes against my practical nature. Why own something that can be so easily lost? Or stolen. I once had a cameo brooch that..." Susan stopped herself from sharing her sad little tale of loss with Max Kaiser, a man who had everything.

"What?" he asked. "What were you going to say, Susan?"

Back to being on a first-name basis, she noted. He didn't seem to mind getting personal when she was the one they were talking about. Well, she wasn't going to give away any more of herself than he'd given her of the private Max. She duplicated his shrug and echoed his words. "Nothing that has to do with the hotel."

"Touché," he said. He asked her no more about it. They continued up the street in silence. After a few moments Max broke it with a suggestion. "Let's go see a special lady not too far from here."

His proposal didn't thrill Susan. "I thought the Swiss didn't like unexpected visitors."

"They don't. But she won't mind."

Susan wasn't reassured. He'd also said that his mother wouldn't mind when he'd invited her to the lecture. "Listen, you go ahead and visit her, Max. I'll go back to the hotel." She knew she had no right to, but she felt deeply disappointed that he wanted to see another woman while he was in her company.

"Come on," Max urged, tugging her arm. "This lady reminds me very much of you, Susan."

Well, now he'd aroused her curiosity. "Is she a relative of yours?"

"In a manner of speaking."

"I really don't want to impose. It's a little late to pay a social call."

"Don't worry about it." A smile edged his mouth. "People drop by to see her at all hours."

Susan allowed him to lead her off the bright boulevard and down a few narrow streets, feeling the irregular bumps of cobblestones beneath the soles of her shoes.

"We're in Old Town now," Max said. "These streets go back to medieval times. Watch your step here."

"Which one?" Susan asked, looking up at a flight of stone steps, shallow and worn with age, reaching to the top of the steep hill before them. As Susan mounted the steps with Max, she imagined hearing the echoes of all the footsteps that had gone before. "I hope there aren't any ghosts from the past lurking about," she whispered, only half joking.

"I've never come across any," Max assured her. "Or vampires, either."

She hadn't even thought of vampires. But if they existed, this ancient section of the city, with its maze of twisting streets, seemed a likely hangout for them. Or for muggers, too, for that matter. Still, she wasn't the least bit frightened. Dark and deserted though the area was, its ambience was one of tranquillity rather than danger.

Besides, she felt safe with Max next to her, even though she knew he could be a danger if she let herself care about him too much. Nonetheless, she found comfort in his presence; it was as if he could lead her into treacherous emotional territory and still protect her from harm.

Did that mean she was beginning to trust him? Susan didn't dare consider the possibility and reminded herself that Max was taking her to meet another woman now, someone he clearly thought special. Who? The mysterious Sabine? She recalled how energized he'd become because of that phone call, how he'd hurried off to respond to whatever request she'd made.

"This is Lindenhof," Max announced when they'd climbed the steps to the top of the hill and entered a small, deserted park encircled by a stone wall. The only sound was the wind rustling through the linden trees.

Susan looked at him, puzzled. "But why did you bring me here?"

"Because the lady I wanted you to see is over there."

He pointed to a fountain, which Susan could barely discern in the moonlight. Gravel crunched beneath their feet as they walked toward it. As they got closer to the fountain she saw the bronze statue of a woman standing guard. She wore a helmet and chain mail armor. A sword dangled at her side, and she held a lance.

So Max had been teasing her again, Susan realized. She laughed, looking up at the statue. "She reminds you of me?"

"In spirit, yes," Max said. "This statue commemorates the day back in the thirteenth century when Zürich's women saved the city from an attack. All the men were fighting battles elsewhere, so the women donned armor, marched up this hill, and lined up along the wall. The encroaching enemy thought just what they wanted them to, that they were a trained army ready to defend Zürich. Rather than take them on, the invaders turned back."

Susan liked the story but still didn't understand what it had to do with her. She studied the statue for a moment. The expression of determination on the woman's bronze face gave the impression that she wouldn't hesitate to use her lance or sword. "Do I seem so tough to you?" she asked Max.

"I think you want to seem that way to keep away intruders. Just like this lady."

His observation rang true. Susan had no city to protect, only her own heart. And any man who broke down the defenses she'd built around it would have to be considered an intruder. Wouldn't he?

"What do you think she would have done if the bluff hadn't worked?" she asked Max, more comfortable discussing the statue than herself.

"We'll never know, will we? No man dared come close enough to see through it."

"She would have fought long and hard if he had," Susan stated, answering her own question.

"Or fled. That would have been the smartest thing to do."

Susan considered this a moment, her eyes on the statue. "No, she would never have run away. She really *is* tough."

"Maybe that's why I like her so much." Max put his arm around Susan's waist and pressed her to his side. He could feel her slender body tense and laughed softly. "Ready to do battle, Susan? Don't worry. You're not under attack." To prove it, he let her go.

Would he always be able to let her go so easily? Max wondered. She fascinated him. The more he got to know her, the more he wanted to know. How could he do that and still keep his emotional distance? He had no room for strong emotions in his life now. Tempted though he was to break down Susan's defenses, he had decided to forego the challenge. She had too large an arsenal of weapons. She could spear him with a flashing violet look, pierce him with a laugh, or wreck him with a light kiss. Better to retreat while he still had a chance. Some battles were best left unfought.

Taking this little detour had been a strategic mistake. If he wanted to keep his attraction for Susan at bay, then he should never have brought her to this dark, quiet spot where moonlight made her look all the more enticing.

"It's getting late. We'd better go," she said.

As she turned away he reached for her once again, surprising himself as much as her. He dug his fingers into her shoulders and dragged her against him, and all the wise counsel he'd given himself only a moment before dissolved into a blur of desire. He'd just told her not to worry, but he forgot about that, too, as his mouth captured hers. Let her fight him if she wanted to. He would still take his fill.

But Susan didn't fight. She'd been caught unawares. She felt he'd somehow tricked her, and at the same time was thrilled that he had. The heat of his unexpected passion melted her armor and radiated through her. Such a thick, sweet melting! She succumbed to the domination of his hard, hot mouth. No gentleness here. No tentative exploration. He kissed her as if he had a right to, as if she had no choice but to respond. And she did. She couldn't help herself. Infused with his heat, she tilted back her head to meet his lips completely. She craved more. With a sigh of surrender, she opened her mouth to him.

He moaned, plunging deeper as she melded to him. His heart sang with triumph. He could taste sweet victory. He released his tight grip on her, sure now that she had been conquered and would not pull away. He lifted his face to see her expression in the moonlight. She looked stunned. Her lips remained parted and moonbeams glowed in her wide eyes. She stared back at him. He stroked her hair, then began plucking out the pins that held it so neatly in place. She didn't protest.

"Toss your head," he commanded when the last lock fell free. He wanted to see the dark waves lap over her pale cheeks before he claimed her mouth again.

Susan did shake her head, slowly back and forth. "No," she said. It took great effort to form that word with lips that still burned from his kiss. It came out a whisper.

Max barely heard her. He pretended he hadn't. Her ardent response had given him the only answer he needed right now. He combed his fingers through her hair, spreading it around her shoulders, just the way he liked it. He took his time doing this, imagining how he would take his time with her all night. He lived only a short distance away. He could easily carry her there if he had to. But he believed that she would go with him willingly. Sure that one more kiss would confirm this, he dipped his face.

She averted hers. "No," she said, more clearly this time. "I didn't want this to happen between us."

He could have said the same thing. Five minutes ago he would have. Now desire had driven out all good sense. Nothing mattered to him but having her. He wanted to take her right there, in the shadow of the linden trees, on the rough gravel. Something about her brought out the savagery in him. At the same time her moonlit eyes brought out his tenderness, softening his lust, civilizing it.

He cradled her face in his hands, cupping his palms against the smooth, perfect roundness of her cheeks. "But it has happened, Susan." He brushed his thumb across her lips, tracing their lush softness. Desire made him impatient. "You must spend the night with me. That's all there is to it."

She almost laughed. He was always so direct, so dogmatic. No sweet sentiments from him. No options. No consideration of how they would deal with tomorrow if they let passion rule them tonight. Well, she would not be passion's fool. Or any man's, either. Perhaps his kiss had scorched her heart, but it hadn't seared her brain.

"No, that's not all there is to it!" Her voice came out strangled; her throat was constricted with exasperation, frustration and anger, too. "You assume too much."

He'd thought he'd won a battle, but realized now that it had only just begun. His fingers pressed into her cheeks, just hard enough to feel the unyielding bone beneath the pliant flesh. "Is my assumption wrong, then? Don't you want me as badly as I want you, Susan?"

To say no again would have been to lie. To say yes would have been total capitulation. So she said nothing and stared back at him. His lean face was tense, and his eyes looked silvery in the moonlight. The eyes of a hungry wolf.

To satisfy his hunger would have brought her pleasure. She knew that. And she grew afraid, not of him, but of her own wayward desire for him. The night seemed to be closing in on her, a dark confusion of old fears and new needs. She twisted her neck sharply to escape his hold on her face. She couldn't let him trap her like this.

Max dropped his hands immediately, afraid of hurting her.

"Don't you, Susan?" he asked again.

Now it wasn't so much a question as a demand for her acquiescence. He had no patience to stand in this park wasting precious time when they both knew the answer. The pleasures of fulfillment awaited them with just a simple nod from her.

Susan heard the demand in his voice. She heard the impatience. A man like Max Kaiser expected to get what he wanted as soon as he wanted it. And if she let him kiss her again, he most likely would. She backed away from him. At the same time she went on the offensive.

"Let's get something straight right now. You hired me as a consultant, not a temporary lover, Mr. Kaiser."

Max stepped back, too. She might as well have kicked him in the gut. She'd warned him that she could be tough.

She'd forgotten to add "brutal." "I don't need to *hire* a lover, Miss Barnes."

A nearby clock tower began tolling the eleventh hour. Susan pressed a hand to her throbbing temple as each chime vibrated through her. The hurt she had glimpsed in Max's face shot through her, too. She had spoken without thinking, flinging words like weapons to protect herself from his power. And there was no way to call them back; it was just as impossible as calling back time past.

"I'm sorry," she said when quiet returned and only the fading echo of the chimes could be heard. She meant the words as an apology for injuring his male pride.

He interpreted it differently. "I'm as sorry about it as you are now," he said coolly.

Susan could think of nothing else to say to him. They walked back to the Bahnhofstrasse. He had nothing to say to her during the cab ride to the Grand. He cleared his throat when the taxi stopped in front of the entrance.

"I'll see you to the elevators, Miss Barnes."

"Please don't bother."

"No bother at all. I'm going to drop by my office and see if there are any messages, anyway."

Rolf the doorman greeted them. Susan self-consciously ran a hand through her hair, sure that Rolf had noticed it was up when she left and would see that now it was down. Rolf noticed everything. He also shared his observations with the rest of the Grand's employees. She could well imagine the sly smiles she would have gotten from him and the staff if she'd stayed out all night with Max. Even now she discerned one on the doorman's face.

"Did you have a pleasant evening?" he asked politely.

"Yes, Miss Barnes and I attended a lecture at the university," Max replied. "Any interesting developments here tonight?"

"No, sir." Rolf looked from Max to Susan. "Not here."

"Good." Max took Susan's elbow and guided her through the lobby.

The desk clerk turned to look at the wall clock when they passed by. Two porters stopped their conversation to watch them. The cloakroom attendant leaned on her elbows as she watched them turn the corner.

"You see how impossible it would have been," Susan said softly when they reached the elevators.

Max gave her a blank look. "What would have been?"

Was he going to make her spell it out for him? "If I had spent the night with you," she whispered. "We would have been tomorrow's gossip here."

"I don't give a damn about gossip," he muttered.

"Perhaps you don't have to," she shot back, then remembered to keep her voice low. "But my reputation in this business is important to me."

"Obviously." He kept his face blank, his tone cool. He shook her hand, as if they'd just concluded a business meeting. "I leave you with an untarnished one, Miss Barnes."

He pushed the elevator button for her and walked away when the doors opened, one hand casually stuck in his jacket pocket.

Nothing in Max Kaiser's bearing would give away his disappointment. Nothing in his long stride would give away his longing to turn back and hold Susan in his arms again. And his face remained a mask as he dug his thumb into the sharp tip of one of her hairpins that he'd slipped into his pocket. No one watching him would discern the slightest pain.

Susan had only a glimpse of Max's wide, straight back before the elevator doors shut. She recalled the way his face had closed during the chiming of the clock in the park. Max and she could never be friends now, she thought with regret. The kiss they'd shared had ruined any chance of that. Perhaps, if she hadn't responded so strongly, if there hadn't been such an explosive chemistry between them, she could have dealt with it better. Instead, she'd made a terrible botch of refusing him.

But he *had* assumed too much. It seemed to her that men always did. That was why she'd always been so careful in the past never to behave in any way that could be misinterpreted. She'd had to watch her step around men since she was thirteen and should have known how to handle herself by now. What a fool she'd been to kiss Max Kaiser back like that!

And what if he hadn't been so direct about asking her to spend the night with him? Susan wondered as she let herself into her suite. What if he had just kept kissing her instead of giving her a moment to come to her senses while he unpinned her hair? Would this evening have ended differently? Would she still be with him?

If so, she would have been more of a fool than she considered herself already. She turned on the lamps in her sitting room and kicked off her shoes. The fact that Max had shown disdain over her concern about her reputation rankled. Didn't he appreciate how important it was for her to maintain a good one, if she wanted to have credibility as a consultant?

If he didn't, then he should, by God. He should know how quickly gossip spread throughout the hotel industry. Personnel moved around a lot, from one hotel to another, all over the world, and carried rumors with them like a virus. Susan had been aware of them circulating about her and her mentor, Tony Armanto. And there had been nothing to them, nothing, until Tony had tried to change their relationship. Susan had felt obliged to leave Golden Key after that, but at least Tony had waited five years before asking her to become his lover.

Max Kaiser had waited a week! Maybe her crack about him hiring her as a consultant, not a lover, had been a bit harsh, but surely he had an ego too large to be permanently injured by a little kick from her? Telling herself this made Susan feel less guilty about hurting his feelings. She'd never met a man who had everything before. She'd never met a man like Max Kaiser before. So cold. So hot. A man like that could drive a woman crazy.

"But not *this* woman," she said aloud.

The sound of her own voice in the empty room pulled Susan up short. She realized that she had been pacing from one end of it to the other for quite a while, her feet soundlessly sinking into the thick carpet. She suddenly felt exhausted, as if she'd been walking miles instead of yards, and flopped onto the brocade sofa. The memory of their kiss remained vivid. The heat. The melting. Oh, that sweet melting. She longed to feel it again. She longed for him.

No, she didn't. Absolutely not. Susan slapped her thigh, as if to reprimand herself for such wayward thoughts. She got up and went to the bedroom, dragged the dressing-table stool to the tall wardrobe, and stood on it. She'd put the box of chocolates on top of the wardrobe to keep temptation out of reach. Promising herself that she'd only have one, she took the box down.

She sat on the bed, opened it, and inhaled the aroma of rich chocolate. She took her time choosing and decided on a dark oblong rather than a light square. She popped it into her mouth whole, but didn't bite into it. She enjoyed the pleasure of letting it rest on the back of her tongue, slowly melting. She sighed and swallowed, feeling the sweetness coat her throat.

Just one more, she promised herself once again. This time she didn't take so much time choosing. This time she sank her teeth into it. And when it was gone, she took another. And another. She ate ten chocolates in a row. Then she fell onto the bed and went to sleep, still clutching the box.

Max had the Grand gym all to himself at this time of night. The equipment was of the highest quality, all state-of-the-art. The exercise room had been Gerhard's idea when he'd gotten on a health kick a few years ago. But the guests of the Grand, who tended to be elderly, rarely used it. Even the younger guests didn't. When people were on vacation, it seemed they forgot about resolutions to keep fit. Or maybe they just wanted to relax. The tennis court, golf course and swimming pool were enough for them.

But Max needed strong exercise tonight. He pumped, he stretched, he gave every muscle in his body a workout on every machine. He pushed himself to the limit, but it didn't help. His groin remained tight. And no machine could relieve that pressure. Only Susan Barnes could.

Why had he given her the chance to change her mind, dammit? Why had he pulled back and fooled with her hair instead of taking what he wanted? And he was as angry with her as he was with himself. A woman shouldn't kiss a man like that and then refuse him. A tease, that was all she was. He had no time to play games with a little American tease.

Max headed for the sauna. He had a good sweat going already and didn't want to lose it. He poured cold water over the hot coals in the stove. But he didn't go into his towel performance. He sat down glum and naked on a bench, then grew restless. He decided to call Sabine.

He left the sauna, showered and dressed, and went to his office. He quickly punched in some numbers and drummed his fingers on his desk as he waited for an answer. He didn't have to wait for more than two rings.

"It's me," he said, when she answered.

Sabine recognized his voice immediately. "It's late, Max. Are you still available?"

"If you need me I am."

"I do," she said. "Actually, I was just about to call you. Can you be here in ten minutes?"

"Five," he said. Now that Sabine needed him, he could forget all about Susan Barnes. For tonight, anyway.

Chapter Seven

Susan's hand shook as she took the cup and saucer Max Kaiser's secretary handed her the next morning. Sugar overload, she thought. She felt disgusted with herself for eating all those chocolates. Where was her self-control, anyway?

She glanced at Max. He was scrutinizing the organizational chart she'd just given him. She took a quick sip of coffee while he wasn't looking at her. She didn't want him to see that her hand trembled. She didn't want him to assume that his proximity caused the trembling.

The secretary left the office. Max still didn't look up. Susan waited silently. She had no idea how to proceed with him after last night. She didn't even know if she should address him by his first name or last. She'd avoided calling him anything since she'd come to his office a few minutes ago. She'd asked if she was disturbing him; he'd politely replied, "Not at all." She'd remarked that it was a lovely morning. He'd agreed and offered to have his secretary bring her coffee. She'd accepted. So far, so good. No awkwardness. No tension. No reason, Susan told herself, to be nervous.

Then Max looked up at her. Her heart gave a little jump. He smiled. Not warmly, to be sure. An absent smile that didn't reach his eyes. Still, it was better than a glare.

"Well, what do you think?" she asked him, referring to the chart.

"You've put everybody who works at the Grand into a tidy little box. We Swiss admire tidiness."

Was he being sarcastic or sincere? Susan could read nothing in his eyes. She noticed deep shadows beneath them. "Actually, I was more interested in illustrating the Grand's management structure than in being tidy."

"Of course. And I'm impressed. We've never had the chain of command laid out so precisely before."

"Then I'm glad I supplied one. Every staff member should know his specific responsibilities, and I suggest that you give each one a copy."

Max shook his head. "That may cause trouble. You haven't taken into account seniority, for one thing. Or personal relationships. Or how politics and favoritism influence the way the staff functions."

"But that's the whole point," Susan said. "Those things shouldn't be taken into account if you want a smooth-running operation. As it stands now, you've got too many staff members with overlapping responsibilities." She stood up and leaned over his desk to point out what she meant on the chart. "For instance, you don't need both a house manager and a front-office manager. One person can do both those jobs. As you can see, cutting staff in many areas could make for a more efficient—"

"No," Max interrupted so loudly that Susan jumped. "There will be no cutting of staff as long as I run this hotel."

Susan stepped back from his desk. For once she didn't argue with him. Although she'd felt it her duty to show him where reductions could be made, she didn't like the idea any more than he did.

"Many of our older employees will be retiring soon
enough," he went on in a softer tone. "And I won't replace them if their functions aren't necessary ones. But
what you have to understand, Miss Barnes, is that we're not
just a business. We're a family."

It always came down to that, Susan thought. Family.
Relationships. Traditions. She knew nothing about these
things. She began rolling up the chart she'd worked so hard
on. Max obviously had no use for it. Or for her.

"I think you hired the wrong person, Mr. Kaiser. My
training and experience don't seem to match your needs,"
she said, making sure to keep her voice steady. Although
she'd resolved, more than once, to stick it out at the Grand,
she saw no sense in doing so if she couldn't be useful.

Max said nothing for a moment. He was tempted to agree
with her and end their prickly relationship. He'd gotten
over his anger with her for refusing him last night. Not only
did she have every right to refuse him, he'd concluded that
she'd been much wiser than he for doing so.

The trouble was, he hadn't gotten over his desire for her.
Nothing he'd done after parting with her had quelled that
desire. And when she'd walked into his office this morning, he'd wanted to grab and kiss her all over again. Instead, he'd ended up shouting so loudly that he'd made her
jump. Things couldn't go on this way.

Now she was giving him an out. If he agreed with her,
offered to pay up her contract, she would be gone by tomorrow. An easy solution to an uncomfortable situation.

No, not so easy. He really did think she was the person
he needed to help him solve the Grand's problems. So far
she'd come up with perfectly good, rational suggestions,
and if he had rejected them, it was only because the Grand
wasn't a rational enterprise. So he wasn't going to let her go
just because he found her presence so damn disturbing. He
hoped he had a little more backbone than that!

"I don't think I hired the wrong person, Miss Barnes."
He caught her hands to stop her from rolling up the chart.

"And please leave that with me. I want to study it more thoroughly. Why are your hands so cold?"

She snatched them away.

"You're upset with me, aren't you? Because of my behavior last night."

Susan saw no point in denying it. "We didn't part on the best of terms."

"I should have made more of an effort to see that we did." It was as close as Max could come to making an apology.

"And I shouldn't have said what I did to you."

"No, you shouldn't have," he agreed. "A simple no would have done."

Since they were having a conciliatory conversation, Susan didn't remind him that she'd said no twice. "I think the best thing to do is to forget all about it and go on."

"Absolutely." Max had been about to suggest the same thing. "Does that mean you intend to stay on here?"

Susan shrugged. "That's your decision to make, not mine. If you don't feel I'm working out, you can send me on my way."

"Then I'd be right back where I started, no closer to solving the Grand's problems."

"You could always bring in another consultant."

"You're the one I want."

His declaration hung in the air for a moment as they stared at each other. Susan averted her eyes first. "Very well, Mr. Kaiser. I'll continue my investigation. I need a lot more facts and figures before I can come up with any detailed proposals for you."

"This chart you made up is a good start," Max said, relieved. "I may change my mind and distribute copies to the staff. I'll definitely show it to Fritz Maier. He's now under the false assumption that he has authority over everyone else. It's time he recognized his proper place."

Susan had come to the same conclusion, but it wasn't her role to make judgment calls like that. She was tempted to tell Max how much she distrusted the man, but she had no concrete evidence to justify such a statement. Not yet.

"I'm having trouble getting balance sheets from Fritz," she said. "He doesn't seem to take me very seriously."

"That's because you're a woman, Miss Barnes," Max replied offhandedly.

"If that's the problem, it's not an easy one to solve. I can't change my sex when I'm dealing with him."

Max smiled at that. "No, you certainly can't. I'll speak to Fritz about being more cooperative."

"I'd appreciate that. There's prejudice against women in business in America, too, of course. But it's not so overt as I find it here."

"Maybe American men have had more reason to cover it up than Swiss men, considering the laws against discrimination in your country."

That comment made Susan raise her eyebrows. "Spoken like a true male chauvinist, Mr. Kaiser."

He shook his head. "You can't pin that label on me, Miss Barnes. The fact that I hired you is proof of my open-mindedness."

True enough, but not good enough. "What about your sister Karin?"

Max frowned. "What about her?"

"Why isn't she involved in the Grand's management? She seems very interested in the business."

"Karin is still too young to take on responsibilities."

"She's only a few years younger than I am."

"But you come from different cultures, Miss Barnes. Different backgrounds."

Susan didn't need to be reminded of that. "But I think your sister could be a big help to you here," she persisted. "In the area of personnel training, for example. Or perhaps sales and marketing. Those are two departments where the Grand could use more management rather than less."

Max rubbed his tired eyes. "I agree. I intend to do something about that eventually. But other areas demand my attention right now."

Susan appreciated how much he had to deal with. A hotel like the Grand needed constant attention. And even though she sensed Max didn't relish his top position, she'd also noticed that he put in longer hours than anybody and didn't shirk his duties.

"And even if Karin could be a help to me," he went on, "I don't want to pressure her into the business. I want her to have the choice of doing whatever she wants to in life."

"But what if she wants to be involved in the business? If you don't give her a chance, you're not giving her a choice."

"I never looked at it that way before. It's hard for me to see Karin as anything other than my little sister."

"Well, I didn't mean to interfere in family relationships."

"Speaking of family, I called my mother this morning," Max said. "She's delighted that John Morgan will be coming today."

Susan had forgotten all about that. "I hope you didn't tell her I arranged his visit."

"Of course I did. She expects you to join them for tea at three." Max laughed when Susan's eyebrows shot up again. "Mother isn't the ogre you assume she is."

As yet, Susan had seen no evidence to the contrary. But she wasn't one to hold grudges. "All right. If she wants to include me, I'll be there."

"Good. I won't be able to make it myself. I've got a tight schedule today." Max checked his watch.

Susan saw that as her cue to leave. "Then I won't take up any more of your time."

"I wish I had more of it to give you, but there never seem to be enough hours in the day."

He looked exhausted. Susan had enough of an ego to wonder if he'd spent a sleepless night thinking about her. She pushed back the thought.

His private phone rang. He looked at it.

"Go ahead and get that," she said. "I'm on my way out."

"I just want to know one thing before you leave, Miss Barnes. Are we back on the right train?"

"The right track, you mean." She smiled. "And yes, I hope we are, Mr. Kaiser."

"I'll make sure not to derail us again."

She believed him. And she felt a strange combination of relief and disappointment. She turned away, and he picked up the ringing phone. She overhead a snatch of conversation as she walked out of his office.

"You're welcome, Sabine. It was worth losing a night's sleep, believe me. I'm glad I called you last night."

Blood rushed through Susan's ears, and she heard no more. She hurried away. She didn't need to hear more. It was enough to know that Max had called Sabine after they had parted. He'd spent the night with her. So that explained the shadows under his eyes. Damn his eyes!

She crossed the lobby, propelled by a spurt of rage. How easily Max had turned to another woman after she'd refused him! That was how little she meant to him. Cold comfort replaced hot anger. At least she hadn't been stupid enough to be his sexual outlet for the evening. Let Sabine have that privilege. Let any woman other than herself! And damn his eyes again, she thought, as tears stung hers.

"Then the plane dipped and my drink toppled into poor Susan's lap!" John Morgan said.

Frau Kaiser threw back her head and laughed, as if he'd uttered the punch line to some marvelous joke. Karin laughed, too. Susan could only manage a weak smile. It had been *her* lap, after all.

A waiter came to the table with a silver tray laden with goodies. Susan selected a fudge brownie. Her third. Let the others nibble away on triangles of bread with thin slices of cucumbers and baby shrimp topping them. She craved chocolate.

"Oh, Herr Professor, how amusing you are," Frau Kaiser said, pouring him more tea.

"It wasn't so amusing at the time, I assure you, Mrs. Kaiser," he said. "Poor Susan didn't think so." He winked at her across the table.

She didn't wink back. She was a little weary of being referred to as "poor" Susan. And her liking for John hadn't changed her foul mood. It had grown more and more foul since she'd left Max's office. But everybody else was having a wonderful time. Especially Frau Kaiser. She spoke English very well, Susan noted. Since the shareholders' meeting, whenever Frau Kaiser and she were in each other's presence, the matriarch had spoken nothing but Swiss German.

Now Frau Kaiser turned her smile in Susan's direction. "Thank you for inviting Professor Morgan to see the Grand's gardens today, Miss Barnes." Her eyes remained cold.

Susan appreciated her formal acknowledgment. "My pleasure," she said.

"Susan didn't have to twist my arm to come," John added.

"I should hope she didn't!" Frau Kaiser looked aghast at the very idea.

"What I mean is that she didn't have to ask me twice, Mrs. Kaiser," John said. "I'm a lonely man in a strange country, and I jumped at the chance. I'm glad I did. Not only did I get to see some beautiful gardens, but I got to meet the most elegant lady in Zürich." He picked up his teacup and toasted Frau Kaiser.

Karin nudged Susan's arm. They glanced at each other, looked away, and both hid smiles by dabbing their mouths with their napkins.

"You are too kind, Herr Professor," Frau Kaiser murmured.

"You're the one who's been kind," he replied. "And I wish you would stop calling me Herr Professor. Makes me feel like an old man."

Karin leaned forward to whisper in Susan's ear. "He *is* an old man!"

But Susan knew differently. Some men remained young all their lives and took great delight in female companionship. John Morgan was such a man.

Now Frau Kaiser was blushing like a young woman. "What should I call you, then?" she asked him.

"John, of course. And what's your first name, lovely lady?"

Apparently that was too much of a secret to reveal. Frau Kaiser changed the subject. "I wish you could have seen my roses in bloom," she said. "They were magnificent this year. But I'd like to ask you about the problems I've had with my rhododendron, if it won't be too much of an imposition."

"Ask me anything you please!" John urged.

They became lost in a discussion about plants. Karin nudged Susan's arm again. "Are you as bored as I am?"

With a nod, Susan admitted she was.

"Then let's get out of here," Karin said. "If I have another cup of tea I'll burst my bladder. It's an English custom I've never taken to."

Although tea had never been Susan's favorite. beverage, either, she hesitated. "But won't that be rude?"

"They won't even notice." To prove her point, Karin stood up. "Miss Barnes and I are leaving now, Mother."

"Very well." She turned back to John Morgan. "But I refuse to use chemicals," she told him, not missing a beat in their private conversation. "I will not poison the soil for future generations."

"I admire you for that," he said in the same earnest tone. He turned his head to look at Susan. "Catch you later." He dismissed her with a wave and devoted his attention to Frau Kaiser again.

Susan smiled to herself. John had obviously lost interest in his "angel in the sky" now that he had met a woman closer to his age and with the same interests here on solid ground. And she'd never seen Frau Kaiser so animated and friendly. Toward one American, anyway. Susan realized her own presence at the Grand was no more appreciated by Max's mother now than it had been from the start.

Karin appeared more willing to make an effort to accept Susan, though. She even linked arms with her as they walked out of the dining room.

"How would you like to go to the zoo with me now?" she asked.

Susan laughed at the suggestion, assuming that Karin was joking.

"It's my favorite place in Zürich," she went on. "I'm sure you would enjoy it, Miss Barnes."

"But I have work to do!" Susan protested.

"Oh, come on. It's not far from here, and we won't stay long. It'll give us a chance to talk about things. Max, for one."

Susan told herself that she had no interest in learning more about Max. At the same time she found herself agreeing to go. Because she wanted to get to know Karin better, of course.

The valet brought Karin's car around to the front entrance. It was the type of sports car Susan had assumed Max would own—an expensive, high-powered German model.

"This was my brother Gerhard's car," Karin told her as they traveled down the hill.

"Not the one he died in?" Susan reached for her seat belt.

"No. That car was wrecked beyond repair. Gerhard collected fancy cars. And fine porcelain. And rare books. He had expensive hobbies." Karin shifted gears. "Max has more simple tastes. He lives like a monk."

That description didn't fit Susan's impression of him. She bit her lip and said nothing.

"They were as different as two brothers could be," Karin continued. "You'd never guess they were even related by looking at them. Gerhard had red hair like me. And he was short and chubby. He was a gourmet and a wine connoisseur. Max is just as happy with a wurst sandwich and a glass of beer when he remembers to eat. And Gerhard . . . well, he had no interest in the opposite sex, if you know what I mean. Max, on the other hand..." Karin laughed. "I would say Max's only weakness is women."

"I thought you just said he lived like a monk," Susan said dryly.

"Oh, I meant his disregard for luxurious trappings. You should see his flat in town. Nothing in it but the barest essentials." Karin shifted gears again. "Or maybe you *have* seen it, Miss Barnes."

Susan had to smile. Grimly. "No, Miss Kaiser. And I don't intend to. Men who are constantly on the make don't interest me."

"Oh, but I've given you the wrong idea about Max!" Karin pulled into the parking area by the zoo. "He's not one to chase after every woman he sees. He's very discriminating."

"Bully for him."

If Karin heard the sarcasm she ignored it. "Actually, I don't think Max has been involved with anyone for a long time."

Susan couldn't help it. She had to ask. "What about Sabine?"

Karin turned off the engine and gave Susan a puzzled look. "What about her?"

"Well, he's involved with her, isn't he?" Susan tried to keep her tone light, as if they were discussing the weather.

"Yes, of course he is. But not in a romantic way."

"Oh, it's strictly sexual?"

Laughing, Karin got out of the car. She was still laughing when Susan joined her on the pavement. She continued to laugh all the way to the zoo entrance as Susan walked beside her, wondering what the big joke was. Karin didn't tell her until they'd gone in and paused at the flamingo enclosure.

"Sabine Holten is at least seventy years old, Miss Barnes," she said.

"Is this the same Sabine who calls Max on his private phone?" It wasn't a common name, but Susan still had to ask.

"Yes, day and night. She's a dispatcher for the organization he's so involved with. Whenever she needs him to go on mission, she calls. And Max goes."

"You mean like spy missions?" Susan asked in a hushed tone, although there was no one around to hear them but the birds.

Her question started Karin laughing again, and Susan began to feel as silly as the flamingos looked, each one balancing first on one impossibly long leg, then on the other.

"Didn't Max tell you what he does during every spare moment he has?" Serious now, Karin shook her head at her own question. "He wouldn't, of course. It isn't like Max to brag about his volunteer work. But being his sister, I'll do it for him. He rescues people."

Now Susan was totally confused. "How does he do that?"

"He flies a helicopter and rescues people stranded in otherwise unreachable places. Or people who need emergency medical treatment. Last night he flew to a remote village and brought a sick child back to the hospital here. Even now that he's taken over running the Grand, he still flies whenever they need him. I think he survives on about four hours' sleep a night."

Yes, Susan thought, time would be precious to a man like that. She felt small for assuming the worst of him. "He never mentioned a word of it to me," she said softly.

"Oh, that's Max for you," Karin said. "He doesn't open up much to family, let alone strangers."

That comment made Susan realize that a stranger was all she really was to Max. The few intimate moments they'd shared had been potent enough to rock her off her bearings, but hadn't brought her any closer to understanding him. She imagined him opening up to her slowly, slowly— like a secret door creaking open, revealing a beautiful hidden garden. But he would probably slam it shut again before she got a good look.

"Does it usually take you that long to decide?" Karin asked her.

"What?" Susan cut off her musing. "Decide on what?"

Karin smiled at her. "I just asked you if you wanted an ice cream, Miss Barnes. Where were you, anyway?"

In a beautiful secret garden, Susan almost answered. "Sure, I could go for an ice cream," she replied instead. "If it's chocolate."

"Max mentioned that you have a thing for chocolate," Karin said as they walked on.

"I'm surprised that he talks about me."

"Your name tends to come up in his conversations lately," Karin said. "But only with me. He never mentions you at all to Mother."

"She's not very pleased with my being here, is she?"

"No. She thinks you're some American gold digger out to get a rich Swiss husband."

Susan let out a laugh. "Nothing like being blunt about it! I can't decide if that's a Kaiser trait I admire or find offensive."

"Oh, I didn't mean to offend you, Miss Barnes. I assure you that I don't share Mother's opinion."

As if to make amends, Karin treated her to an ice cream on a stick that she purchased at a stand near the bird sanctuary.

"Tell your mother not to worry," Susan said, unwrapping it. "I'm not out to get her son."

"I hope you don't think I brought you on this little expedition to get information about your relationship with my brother."

Susan deposited her wrapper in a handy receptacle. The zoo was immaculately maintained, as was every area of Zürich she'd seen so far. "Then why did you ask me to come here with you? So far we haven't given the animals a moment of our attention."

"Oh, they'll always be here, but you won't be, Miss Barnes. I was hoping that perhaps we could..." Karin hesitated. "Become friends."

Like her brother, she could be so shy at times, Susan thought. "There's nothing I'd like better," she said.

"I'm very grateful to you," Karin told her. "I had a talk with Max today. He asked me if I'd be interested in getting more involved in the Grand. Of course I said yes, and he suggested that I take over personnel training and look into ways to promote the hotel. I jumped at the chance, and then he told me it had been your idea."

So Max had finally accepted one of her suggestions and done something about it. This elated Susan. "If you need any help getting started, just ask me," she suggested.

"There's one thing I'd like to ask you right now, Miss Barnes. Could we start calling each other by our first names from now on?"

"It seems unnatural for me not to be on a first-name basis with you."

"Then I'd like to go through a little ritual and make it special."

"Are we going to have to prick our fingers and mingle blood or something?" Susan hoped not.

"No, not quite that extreme, Miss Barnes. We're going to kiss each other three times on the cheek. And then we're going to shake hands and say, *'Wollen wir uns nicht einfach duzen?' Du* is the familiar form of address in German."

That seemed easy enough to Susan. "Let's do it!"

Karin held back. "That means we'll be friends for life. I want you to understand that."

Susan let the words sink in. "I've never had a friend for life before," she said after a moment. "I've always moved around too much for that. And I'll be leaving Switzerland in January."

"Friendships have no borders," Karin replied. "And I promise you that I'll never take advantage of my friendship with you if you accept it."

Susan believed her. "That goes for me, too."

And then they did it. They kissed each other three times on the cheek, shook hands and said the phrase as animals chattered in the background.

"Well, I guess it's official now, Karin."

"Yes, it is, Susan."

They both laughed, awkward for a moment.

But in the next they felt comfortable with each other as they strolled through the zoo. They stopped to watch the lions in an enclosed natural area that gave them limited freedom to roam.

"Oh, look at that one," Karin said, pointing to a male restlessly pacing back and forth in front of them. "Isn't he magnificent?"

The lion shook his golden mane. "Magnificent," Susan repeated. "But he doesn't look happy."

"Well, he should be," Karin said. "He has everything he could need here. He's well fed and taken care of and has plenty of female companionship. What more could he want?"

"Freedom?" Susan ventured.

Karin shrugged and walked on to look at the tigers. But Susan stayed put, fascinated by the lion's every graceful, restless move. Energy contained in a confined setting. She thought of Max.

"I just don't see why it's necessary," Susan told Max a week later.

They were having a breakfast meeting in the hotel dining room. Since they were both early risers, they'd found this the most convenient time to get together. Susan always looked forward to it. These brief meetings with Max made her day even though they both kept to business, neither straying into personal terrain. On this particular morning, however, he'd requested something out of the ordinary from her.

"I appreciate that it's an imposition on you, but I must ask you to go along with it, Miss Barnes."

"I have plenty to do right here at the hotel. I don't see why I have to go to the mountains to visit your great-uncle. He can't even speak English."

"Yes, he can. He doesn't choose to, though. He'll understand everything you have to say to him."

"But I have nothing to say to him, since he isn't involved with the hotel. I can't understand why he wants to see me again."

"According to his letter, it's because you're so pretty. And he's feeling a little lonely."

Susan rolled her eyes to the high ceiling. "I have better things to do with my time than entertain a lonely old man on a mountaintop."

"And I have better things to do than bring a pretty woman to him," Max replied. "But I'm fond of Uncle Anton, and I respect him. Because of that, I would like to comply with his wishes. And I hope you will, too."

When Max put it that way, Susan had difficulty refusing him, especially under the persuasion of his bright blue eyes. It occurred to her that she was arguing against something that at heart she wanted—this trip to the mountains would give her some time alone with Max. "How long will we be there?"

"Only for the day," he said. "We'll be traveling by motorcycle. It's the best way to get to my uncle's place. It's a little remote."

"What about taking a helicopter?" Susan wasn't serious. She just wanted to get him to talk about his consuming interest. He hadn't yet. "I hear you know how to fly one, Mr. Kaiser."

"Yes, I learned in the army."

"And now you fly rescue missions?" she prodded.

"That's right. But I don't think visiting Uncle Anton qualifies as an emergency. He only needs rescuing from a mild case of boredom." And that was all Max had to say about the subject. "Do you mind going by motorcycle?"

"Only if there's a risk of driving off the edge of the mountain. Are the roads safe?"

"I've traveled them hundreds of times before. Can you be down in the lobby by eight, ready to go?"

Susan nodded. "How should I dress?"

"Warmly. And wear sturdy boots."

"I only packed sneakers."

Max laughed. "You're in Switzerland now, Miss Barnes. Go get yourself some hiking boots."

"You neglected to mention that this visit to Uncle Anton's involved hiking."

"Only a little."

"Heights make me dizzy."

"Not once you get used to them." He reached across the table and patted her hand. "Don't worry. I won't let you fall."

She already had, she thought, as she looked down at the strong, lean hand covering hers. His slightest touch made her nerve endings sing. But she didn't plan on letting Max Kaiser in on her little secret.

"I'm not the least bit worried," she lied.

Susan waited for Max in the lobby the next morning, dressed in corduroy slacks, a thick woolen sweater and brand-new boots that laced above the ankle. The salesman at Bally had assured her the boots would give her excellent support on steep mountain trails. She'd told him the price was steep enough for her to believe that. She'd paid it, though. She wasn't going to go against Max's advice about proper attire again.

When he strode through the revolving doors her heart took a leap and went into a somersault. He looked about as sexy as a man could in jeans and a black leather jacket.

They went out to his motorcycle parked in front of the entrance. It was a big, glossy black machine. It looked beautiful but dangerous. Sort of like Max. He laughed as she regarded it.

"What's the matter, Miss Barnes? Having second thoughts about taking this trip with me?"

She put on a brave smile. "Not at all. I only wish the weather were better." It was a gray, foggy morning. The chill in the air seemed to seep into her bones.

"It'll be sunny on the mountains," Max assured her. He took something out of the motorcycle panniers. "But I want you to wear this as a windshield."

He handed her a leather jacket similar to the one he had on. Assuming it was his, Susan slipped it on, expecting it to be way too big. It fitted her perfectly.

"I bought it for you yesterday," he explained. "I was afraid you wouldn't dress warmly enough."

His thoughtfulness touched her. But she frowned. "I can't accept an expensive gift like—"

"Well, you're going to have to bend your principles just a little, Miss Barnes," he interrupted gruffly. "I don't want you whining in my ear about being cold as we drive up to higher altitudes." He shoved a helmet toward her. "And put this on, too."

"I *never* whine," she said as she donned the helmet.

"I know," he said, rapping her helmet with his knuckles. "You're tough." He put on his own helmet and straddled the saddle. "Let's go for a little ride, Miss Barnes."

She climbed onto the seat behind him and he revved the motor, no doubt waking up half the Grand guests. "Hang on," he instructed.

"On to what?"

"Me, of course."

She put her arms around his waist. He felt solid and good. They took off, pebbles flying as they looped the circular driveway. And then they flew down the hill, leaving the Grand behind them.

Chapter Eight

Susan had never traveled on a motorcycle before. She'd never had any desire to, sure she would dislike the experience. She loved it. Max expertly cut through the clogged morning traffic in Zürich and headed for the open highway. He drove much faster when they reached it, and she held on much tighter. But she relished the speed, the wind, the feeling that she and Max were one with the machine.

"This is great!" she shouted.

"Late?" he yelled back.

"No, great! It's thrilling."

"I told you it would be chilly."

"Thrilling!" she shouted again. It was clearly impossible to communicate on a big, loud bike. Maybe that was why Max liked driving one so much, she mused. Communication wasn't one of his strong points. But he had so many others. She leaned into his strong, broad back.

The Swiss countryside enchanted her as much as Zürich had at first sight. The rich green meadows, grazing cows and snug farmhouses reminded her of storybook illustrations. Everything seemed so perfect, so peaceful. The Alps looked hazy beyond the rolling landscape, like some vague promise in the distance.

"How long will it take to get to Uncle Anton's?" she shouted to Max.

"What?"

"Oh, never mind!" It didn't really matter. Time didn't seem to be so important now that they'd left the Grand.

The smooth highway took them past lakes and picturesque villages as it cut through the lush valley. Even though they traveled at breakneck speed, Susan relaxed completely, sometimes resting her head against Max's shoulder. He drove fast but took no stupid chances, and she trusted him to take her safely to wherever they were going.

She didn't know what to expect when she got there. She'd never been in the mountains before. But in this last month life had become an adventure for her, and she'd done a lot of things she'd never expected to do. Accepting a consulting job in Switzerland had been only the first of them. Falling for the man who had hired her, sight unseen, was definitely the last.

Susan wasn't ready to admit to herself that she loved Max. He'd given her no grounds to love him. All he'd done was kiss her one moonlit night and ask her to go to bed with him. Typical male behavior, as far as Susan was concerned, and hardly a request to hang hopes and dreams upon. He'd done nothing since that night to demonstrate that he had any intention of making such an offer again. Whatever attraction he'd felt toward her, it seemed, had been put to rest that fateful night as the clock chimed eleven.

And yet... those eyes of his whenever he looked at her. What did she see in them? A need? Maybe their crystal blue only reflected her own need. People saw only what they wanted to see, Susan knew. And yet, wasn't it possible that a man like Max Kaiser could yearn for her, too?

Neither his good looks nor his wealth made him seem so special to her, though. It was his restless energy that she adored. And now that she knew about it, his altruistic spirit, too. Or did he just go on rescue missions to keep the boredom he felt in running the hotel at bay? For all she knew, his show of interest in her had been out of boredom, too. And her awkward refusal had bored him even more. She suddenly loosened her grip around his waist and leaned back in the seat. She didn't need him for support. She could keep her own balance.

When Susan dropped her arms, Max immediately missed the feel of them gripping him. He'd been about to pass a row of cars but slowed down instead. He didn't want to take a fast swerve into the left lane and lose Susan Barnes in the maneuver.

"Hold on to me!" he shouted.

"I'm okay," she called back.

"I said hold on to me, dammit!" he yelled back.

She wasn't going to argue with a man on a motorcycle going over sixty miles an hour, or whatever that was in kilometers. She wrapped her arms around him again.

"That's better," he said. Confident that all was as it should be, Max easily overtook the row of cars.

The mountain range became more and more vivid as they drew nearer. Susan got a sense of heading toward looming, ominous giants. Max turned off the highway and took a country road, then stopped in front of a little restaurant.

"Time for a *zweites Frühstück*," he announced, cutting the engine.

Susan jumped off the cycle. "If that means a pit stop, I'm ready for one."

"It means second breakfast." He smiled as he watched her take off her helmet, toss her head and fluff up her hair. The waves in it never failed to fascinate him. They went inside.

As they were sipping coffee, another couple came into the restaurant and sat down at the table behind them. They spoke English, rather loudly.

"It was the worst experience of my life," the woman said.

"Well, at least we made it up and back down, honey," the man replied. "And you've got to admit, the scenery was terrific."

"How would I know? I kept my eyes closed the entire time! I couldn't bear to look down."

"Neither could I. I kept my eyes closed, too."

"Harry, you didn't!"

"No, honey. But I clutched the steering wheel so hard, my hands are still numb."

"My entire body is numb. What about those motorcyclists who kept passing us? They must be insane to drive so fast around those bends, not knowing what's coming the other way. Never again, Harry. I've had it with driving through mountains."

"Honey, I'm in complete agreement. We'll take a train next time."

Susan gave Max a questioning look. He shrugged. "It's not that bad," he said. "Those two aren't familiar with the roads, that's all. I could take them blindfolded."

"I prefer you didn't," she said. "And I hope you're not one of those crazy cyclists I just heard about."

He grinned. "Have I done anything so far to make you think I am?"

"You don't exactly drive at a snail's pace, mister."

"I like speed," he said. "But I like to be in control even better. As a professional skier, I learned how important it is to keep that balance at all times. The one time I got reckless, I paid for it."

"What happened?"

"Nothing much. I ended up with two broken legs."

Susan's heart tightened. "You call that nothing much?"

"I call that being lucky." He motioned to the waitress for the check and they left the restaurant.

"How far up the mountain does your uncle live?" Susan asked, putting her helmet back on.

"We'll be there before you know it."

The paved road they took started off just fine, curving gently around the mountain as it ascended. The valley below glowed in the sun; the pastures emerald, the lake sapphire, and the larch and poplar stands topaz. The farmhouses, barns and village shops looked like miniature toys.

But the higher they traveled, the narrower the road became as it carved its way into the rock face. And the more it twisted. It rose and dipped with all the stomach-lurching loops of a roller coaster and kept going back on itself with hairpin bends. There was no need for Max to tell Susan to hang on again. She clung to him as if her very life depended on it. She felt as if they could topple off the edge of the earth at any moment. Nothing would have kept them from going over, no guardrails or barriers of any kind. And the sheer drop was awesome.

Max overtook a few slower-moving vehicles on the way, one of them a long, wide bus. Susan held her breath, as if that would help him get past the bus safely. Apparently it did, and she let out a sigh of relief.

"How are you doing?" Max shouted, his voice floating back to her on the wind.

"I'm fine. This is wonderful!" Susan called back. And she meant it. She adored every hair-raising, heart-stopping moment of the ride. She found it exhilarating and hugged Max all the tighter.

It amazed her that people actually lived so high up on a mountain. But they passed modest homes, even a tavern and a steeply spired white church tucked in a cranny.

After a while Max steered off the paved road and took a dirt track that cut through high pastureland. The Alpine meadows were still a rich green, and grazing cows looked up at the sound of the motorcycle as it flew by. The ride was much bumpier now and still steep, but at least they were traveling away from the mountain's face. Susan ventured to break her embrace around Max's waist to wave to the cows.

Eventually the dirt road dwindled to a footpath. Max stopped, and they dismounted. "We have to walk from here," he announced, removing his helmet and propping the cycle on its kickstand. "About a kilometer. That's less than a mile. Think you can make it that far on foot?"

"Of course I can," Susan said indignantly. "And a heck of a lot farther than that, too."

"Maybe I'll take you up on that boast."

"What sort of challenge do you have in mind?" she asked.

He slipped off her headgear and smoothed back her hair, his fingers making a lingering trail through the thickness. "Not a challenge, Susan. There's a special place I'd like to show you, that's all."

She looked up at him, interested. "What's so special about it?"

"To me it's the most beautiful spot in the universe," Max answered softly. And she had the most beautiful eyes he'd ever encountered, he thought. He imagined making love to her there. His fingers tightened around a section of her hair, crushing the waves. Hell, he wanted to make love to her now. But he dropped his hand and stepped back. "I doubt we'll have time to go visit it today," he said, his tone gruffer. "I shouldn't have mentioned it." He started up the footpath.

Susan wished he hadn't mentioned it, either, if it was only to tell her he shouldn't have. And she wished he hadn't looked at her that way, piercing her with desire. How could he do that and then turn away so easily, so abruptly?

"Are you just going to leave your motorcycle behind like this?" she asked him. "What if somebody steals it?"

Max didn't bother to look back. "Who? A renegade cow?"

Susan shrugged and caught up with him. They walked in silence, with only the sound of cowbells accompanying them. Beyond the rich grazing land they now traversed lay bare, rugged mountain peaks. "It's beautiful here," she said after a moment. "But so isolated. I can understand why your uncle gets lonely at times. It must be a hard life."

"Not so hard," Max replied. "Uncle Anton has all he needs here."

"Does he chop his own wood and make his own bread and cheese?"

Max glanced at her, not quite smiling. "That's right. And when he has a moment to relax he smokes a pipe and whittles by the fire."

Just like Heidi's grandfather, Susan thought. Uncle Anton resembled the illustrations she remembered in the book she'd read as a child. Susan could easily picture where he must live—a rustic cottage, humble and quaint.

"How does he get in touch with people?" she asked Max. "I mean, what if he should get sick or hurt himself? How would he call for help?"

"Oh, no problem," Max assured her. "He would just blow on his alpenhorn."

"Really? They still use alpenhorns to communicate around here?" Susan narrowed her eyes. "You're putting me on, aren't you, Max Kaiser?"

"I would never do that," he assured her earnestly, taking off his leather jacket and swinging it over his shoulder. He began humming to himself.

Something caught Susan's eye in the rock face above them; it was the glitter of sunlight ricocheting off glass. She saw a large modern construction, all domes and windows, with a deck running around it. The intricate arrangement of cantilevered supports gave the impression that the building was hanging in midair off the side of the mountain.

"What's that? An observation site?" she asked, pointing to it.

"No, that's just Uncle Anton's place," Max replied casually.

"But it looks like something from the future instead of the past!" she protested.

"You sound disappointed."

"Well, I am. A little," she admitted, reluctantly letting go of her *Heidi* fantasy.

Max squeezed her hand. "Don't let on to Uncle Anton that you are. He designed his home himself. He's an architect. In fact, a rather successful one before he retired. He designed buildings all over the world.''

"And I assumed he was a simple mountain man.''

"Oh, he's that, too,'' Max said. "We Kaisers try never to forget our peasant background. That's why Uncle Anton has gone back to speaking in his village dialect and rarely leaving the mountains now. I suppose he's grown a little eccentric in his old age.''

They had to climb three flights of rough timber stairs to reach the house. Susan tried not to look down the sheer rock face. Uncle Anton must have heard them trudging up, because he was waiting for them on the deck with chilled glasses of wine to reward their effort. His home might be modern, but he was dressed traditionally, in a bright blue embroidered peasant smock, black woolen knickers, white knee socks and clogs.

He greeted Susan with a cheerful *"Gruezi!"* and a kiss on each cheek. "Tell her she's even prettier than I remembered,'' Anton instructed his grand-nephew.

Max humored the old man, as always, and translated his compliment.

"Danke," Susan said, then remembered he understood English. "This is quite a place you have here, sir.''

Grunting to acknowledge her remark, Anton opened a sliding door and ushered Susan and Max inside.

It was almost the same as being outside because most of the walls were glass, with a panoramic view from all angles. Even the domed ceiling was glass, letting in the blue sky. The interior was spare, austere, without one superfluous piece of furniture to compete with the view.

As if anything could, Susan thought. A snatch of a poem floated into her head. Without thinking, she said it aloud. "'I built my soul a lordly pleasure-house.'"

The old man gaped at her. "'Wherein at ease for aye to dwell,'" he recited back, his speech crisp, his accent, for the moment, perfectly British.

"Uncle Anton, you're speaking English,'' Max remarked with a surprised laugh.

"When someone can quote my favorite poem, you're damn right I'll speak back to her in English!" Anton declared. "So you are familiar with Tennyson, Miss Barnes?"

Susan wished she could tell him that she was. She shook her head. "I must have remembered that line from my school days. It just popped out." She was sure her confession would cause Uncle Anton to go back to speaking in his dialect.

He didn't. "I'm happy my house inspires poetry in you, young lady."

"I've never seen a building that's so much a part of its surroundings."

She must have said the right thing again, because Anton went on talking to her for the next half hour or so, explaining how he'd used innovative structural techniques in his design so that the house could be constructed on such a precarious site. "Now come see how the solar power system works," he said, taking her arm.

Max intervened. "If you're going to monopolize Miss Barnes's company, at least feed her something first, Uncle Anton. And me, too. We had a long trip up here, and I thought your invitation included lunch."

His uncle gave him a glare from beneath his bushy eyebrows for interrupting his discourse, then relented. "If food is what you want, then food is what you'll get. Go sit at the table on the deck. I'll bring it out." He waved away Susan's offer to help and stomped off to the kitchen.

"You probably wish he never started speaking English now that he won't stop talking," Max said when they went outside.

"I find him fascinating," Susan replied. "I'm glad I came here with you today."

"I am, too." Max's voice grew wistful. "I almost wish we didn't have to go back to the Grand."

So did Susan. All the time she had been listening to Anton, she had been acutely aware of Max watching her, his eyes always on her when she looked his way. And much as she liked his uncle, she had longed to be alone with Max again, not for just a few hours, but for days.

She didn't tell him that, though. "But we have to go back," she said.

"Well, of course we do. I know that." No wistfulness in his voice now, only impatience. He even looked at his watch, which he hadn't done all day. "We'll return to Zürich right after lunch."

Susan sighed. It seemed she'd known just the right thing to say to Max's uncle to get him to open up to her. And yet she always ended up saying the wrong thing to Max. But that was the way it was with them. As he'd said when they first met, they'd started off on the "left" foot. And Susan doubted that they could ever fall into step together. One of them would always pull back to prevent it.

Anton came out with a wooden platter in one hand, plates and cutlery in the other, and a bottle of wine under his arm. He plunked everything onto the deck table without much ceremony. He was obviously not used to playing host. He sat down on the bench next to Susan, close enough to touch shoulders, although there was plenty of room.

"She smells like mountain meadows in the spring," he told Max in Swiss German.

Max nodded.

"She's intelligent, too. And honest and practical from what I've observed. Good head for business."

Max nodded again. He had to hand it to old Anton. He was a good judge of character.

"Too bad she isn't Swiss, or she'd make you the perfect wife," the old man added. "But because she isn't, the family will never accept her. Especially your mother. So don't lose your heart to this young woman. She's an outsider and will only bring you more problems than you already have. Your duty now, Nephew, is to run the family business. Put all else aside for the next few years. Then find yourself a good Swiss wife and raise the next generation of Kaisers."

Max made no response. He sat rigid and silent.

Susan spoke up. "Mr. Kaiser, you have broken my heart," she said, turning to the old man. "I thought I'd won you over enough to speak English in my presence."

"Oh, I will now," he told her. "I had something to clear up with Max first. A small family matter that is of no concern to you, Miss Barnes." He smiled at her.

Despite the smile, Susan thought he looked a little sad. She wondered what sort of family matter he had felt the need to discuss with Max. But as he'd said, it was no concern of hers. She smiled back at him.

"Look what I have brought us to eat!" he exclaimed, his enthusiasm sounding a little false. "A traditional Swiss meal. A *Bündner Teller*."

Susan looked at the food on the platter and admired the artful arrangement of paper-thin slices of rosy dried beef, golden chunks of rye bread, tomato wedges and little pickles.

"I dried the beef myself," Anton told her. He went on to explain how he first rubbed a piece of raw rump steak with a mixture of pepper, juniper berries, herbs and salt, and then left it to dry outside for several months. "Factories do it much faster than that, with the use of air blowers," he said disparagingly. "But for the right taste you need the spice of pure Swiss mountain air. That is the only true *Bündner Fleisch*."

He placed a sliver of it on a slice of rye and handed it to Susan.

"First a bite of that, then a nibble of tomato and pickle, and you will be tasting Switzerland, my dear," he declared.

Susan enjoyed the meal although she noticed that Max was more quiet than usual. He ate little and barely touched his wine. When Anton left to get the dessert she asked him if anything was wrong.

Max regarded her for a long moment. The sun burned into her hair, making it look more red than brown. "No, nothing's wrong," he said.

"That family matter your uncle brought up. It isn't serious, I hope."

"Only if I let it become so." He forced a smile. "My uncle is anticipating a problem that doesn't exist. Or at least it hasn't reached a serious stage yet. His advice was unnecessary."

"He seems like a very wise old man," Susan said. "If he feels the need to give you advice, perhaps you should follow it. But I don't mean to interfere. I don't even know what the problem is, after all."

"It's my uncle who's interfering," Max said gruffly.

Anton returned with a flat custard pie. He gave the first piece he sliced to Susan.

"Delicious," she declared after sampling it. "So rich."

"That's because it's made with *Briesmilch*," Anton told her. "From a cow that has just delivered a calf. I milked her myself this morning so you could have *Brieskuchen*, Miss Barnes."

"You've made me feel very welcome."

"Good. Then you will have a nice memory to bring home with you when you return to America." Anton gave his grand-nephew a pointed look. Then he pulled out his tobacco pouch and pipe.

Susan almost clapped. "So you *do* smoke one," she said.

"Miss Barnes had a stereotyped image of you as a Swiss mountain man, Uncle Anton," Max explained. "Making cheese in your hut while you yodel."

"I never mentioned yodeling," Susan objected, blushing a little.

"Don't be embarrassed," Anton told her. "Indeed, I can yodel with the best of them. So can Max. I taught him how."

"Really?" This new piece of information delighted Susan. "May I have a demonstration?"

Anton was willing, but Max shook his head. "I'm out of practice. I haven't yodeled since I was a boy." He changed the subject. "Have you been by the Kaiser Klein recently,

Uncle?" He looked at Susan. "That's what we call the family ski chalet up here."

"Yes, I went past it the other day," Anton replied. "Looks to me that it needs a new roof, or at least major repairs."

Max groaned. "I've just finished paying for major repairs at the Kaiser Grand. Do you think I could put it off for another year?"

Anton shrugged. "That's your decision to make. Go see for yourself while you're up here."

"Would you mind if we stopped by on our way back?" Max asked Susan. "It's not too far out of the way."

"I don't mind at all." She was curious to see the place, curious about anything connected with Max.

After finishing the strong, thick coffee Anton served them, they said their goodbyes. The old man kissed Susan on each cheek again, tickling her with his whiskers.

"I'm sorry to see you go," he said and sounded as if he truly meant it.

He turned to Max and spoke quickly in dialect. "Don't stray off the mountain path, Nephew. She isn't Swiss."

The Kaiser Klein, Susan soon discovered, wasn't that "small," despite its name. Three stories high, and wide enough to have twelve shuttered windows, it was made of dark timber, with a deep-hipped roof and a balcony encircling the second floor. The timber and beams were carved with illustrations of flowers and birds. When Max cut the motorcycle engine, Susan could hear the rushing of waterfalls in the background and the wind swishing through the spruce trees all around. Mighty mountains rose behind the house, as if guarding it from intruders.

Max didn't waste any time getting a ladder from a toolshed and climbing onto the roof. Susan watched from below as he scampered over its slope, somehow maintaining his balance without looking as if he was even trying. Apparently heights of any sort meant nothing to him. But of course he was Swiss.

"How does it look?" she asked when he came down.

"Not good. But not bad, either. If I had the time, I could do the work myself."

He sounded like a man who liked doing the work himself. He put away the ladder and came back to the front of the house where Susan waited, leaning against the motorcycle. She wondered if he was going to invite her inside to take a look around his family retreat.

"You know that special place I told you about," he said instead. "It's not too far from here. We could walk there in about an hour."

"Are you offering to show it to me or just making small talk?"

Max laughed. "I'm offering. But it's not an easy hike. Mostly uphill."

Susan had already walked a lot more than she usually did. And the high altitude and sun, combined with the long, exhilarating ride on the motorcycle, had taken their toll. But she wanted to experience anything Max was willing to share with her today. They probably wouldn't have a chance to be together like this, far away from a business environment, ever again. She didn't want to go straight back to the Grand. Not quite yet.

"Hey, I've been going uphill all my life," she told him, only half joking. "And nothing worth doing is easy."

Max tapped her pert nose with one finger. "Spoken like a true..." His voice trailed off. He'd almost said "Swiss."

"A true what?" Susan asked him.

He could think of no word to substitute. "You fill in the blank," he said lamely.

She shook her head and stared at him. "How I wish I could read your mind at times, Max."

At least she couldn't do that yet, although she'd managed to take over every free thought he had. But there was nothing he could do about that. Lord knows, he'd tried. Worse yet, when he was with her, he never knew what he was going to say or do next. Why had he suggested this walk? Why did he feel so compelled to take her to a place he loved? Well, he wasn't going to stand around analyzing it. He took her hand and led the way through the spruce forest.

As they walked on and on and on, Susan had to bite back asking Max how much farther they had to go. He'd warned her that it wouldn't be easy. It wasn't. He'd also warned her that it would be mostly uphill. It was. Her legs began to feel like rubber bands. Her boots, which she'd found so comfortable all day, began pinching her toes. Why had she agreed to go on this hike, anyway? What was she, crazy? Crazily in love?

They passed through the spruce grove and broke into an open area. This new, rocky terrain came as a surprise to Susan. It looked treacherous and alien. A jumble of boulders lay ahead, chalky white with bright orange lichen growing on them. There were patches of Alpine grass here and there, but mostly outcroppings of jagged rock, like the teeth of some monster. No softly molded slopes here, no gentle ringing of cowbells.

"Have we landed on another planet?" she asked Max.

"Beautiful, isn't it?"

It seemed a cold, desolate place, and she couldn't understand Max's attraction to it. But she didn't understand much about him, anyway. "This is what you wanted to show me?"

"Partly. There's more."

"More, I surmise, means more walking?"

"Just to the cliff. The view from there is the best in all of Switzerland, I think."

"Cliff?" Susan didn't like the sound of that word. "What cliff?"

Max raised his hand above his head.

She had to tilt her chin to see where he was pointing. She got dizzy just looking. She gulped.

"It's not as steep as it looks from down here," he told her.

"*Down* here? We're already above the tree line!" She selected a boulder that had less sharp edges than the rest, and sat down on it. Carefully.

"You're not tired already?" Max looked amazed that this could be possible.

"I'm not a mountain goat like you are, Max."

Laughing, he sat down beside her. "Legend has it that the Swiss are part ibex, you know. That's a wild mountain goat. We may see some on the cliff if we're lucky."

Susan figured that she'd be lucky enough if she made it up to the cliff.

"And herdsmen drank the blood of a goat to gain the surefooted swiftness of the animal," Max went on to inform her.

Susan wrinkled her nose. "Charming custom."

"These herdsmen were ferocious warriors. The rest of Europe feared the wild men from the Alps. When they invaded a country they took what they wanted without thinking twice about it."

"I thought the Swiss were so peace-loving."

"Yes, we're very civilized and rational now. Not like the good old days."

"The good old days? You sound as if you would have liked being one of those wild men."

He smiled, baring his strong teeth. "Deep down I am one, Susan. I just hide it well."

She believed him, because he didn't hide it that well. His eyes gave him away. Their blue depths seemed ruthless to her at times. She'd never seen eyes like this before and had nothing to compare them with. But she sensed that the veneer of a few centuries of civilization could be cracked very easily. If you scratched him too deeply, beware.

"And I'm tempted to take what I want right now," he told her in a low, quiet voice.

Susan's toes curled up in her boots. She sat very still and said nothing. In one swift movement he pulled her to her feet, his hand a vise around her arm.

She breathed hard and stared back at him in surprise. He could change in a flash, this man, always catching her with her guard down. She felt defenseless, alone in this bare, isolated place with him. "I want to go back, please," she managed to say.

He had startled her, maybe even frightened her, Max realized. And he was gripping her arm too tightly. Swearing to himself, he released it. "Yes, whatever you want," he said. "It's been a long day. Of course you must be exhausted."

But she wasn't now. Her heart was racing, her blood pumping. Now that he'd agreed to take her back, she didn't want to go anymore. She didn't know what she wanted. Frustrated by her own confusion, she felt like slumping back onto the rock, covering her face with her hands and crying. She stood firm and dry-eyed instead.

"Since we've already gone this far, we might as well go all the way up," she told him.

"No, we'll go back," Max insisted; he knew now why he'd brought her this far and wanted to take her higher. He wasn't some tour guide showing off mountain sights. He was a man in the deep throes of…what? Love? Lust? With Susan, it was hard to separate the two.

"I don't want to go back," she said, kicking a small stone with the tip of her boot.

"You just said that you did."

"A moment's weakness. That cliff looks tough to climb. But I want to do it. I want to see the view from up there."

"The hell with the view!" Max said. It was time he admitted the truth to both of them. "There's a ledge up there, flat and grassy and soft as a bed. It's the perfect place to make love, and that's why I want to take you there, Susan. So now that you know, let's go back."

She didn't budge. Her mind was clicking on and off. Yes, no. Stop, go. She heard a shrill whistle. It wasn't in her head. She looked around and saw a chunky little creature perched on a rock. It rested on its hind legs, staring right at her with bright, beady eyes as if it, too, was waiting for her to make up her mind.

"What's that?" she asked Max, stalling.

"A marmot. They're all around here."

She looked more closely and could make out many little brown creatures among the rocks, nibbling on the sparse grass between them as if there were no tomorrow.

"Storing up for hibernation," Max told her. "They'll sleep deep all winter on full stomachs."

"And the memories of fresh grass and sunshine in their dreams," Susan added. What would she have to remember when she left Switzerland this winter? Making love to a man she wanted with every fiber of her being? Or saying no to him and not risking a thing? She gave the rock a final kick. "Let's go," she told Max.

"Back down?"

She looked at him. She saw a craving in his eyes that cut through all her reservations. "No, up," she told him in a trembling voice.

His smile came slow, almost hesitant. He touched her cheek. "It won't be that difficult," he promised her.

But as they climbed the cliff Susan realized that he had underestimated the effort involved. For her, at least. It wasn't the climb that was so hard. It was knowing that when they reached their destination she would become one with him. It took her breath away—and gave her energy and motivation to keep climbing, too.

Chapter Nine

It was too beautiful and too scary. There were no barriers on this grassy ledge to keep her from falling thousands of feet. Susan felt faint and stepped back into the solidness of Max, standing behind her. He placed his hands on her waist to steady her.

"Does it frighten you, Susan?"

"Yes. I can't bear to look down. It makes my head swim."

"Look straight across at first to get your bearings," he advised.

She gazed across the valley and saw three majestic mountain peaks much higher than the one they were on. Glaciers of fathomless depth lay between them, a translucent blue. Now Susan knew what to compare Max's eyes with. She trembled.

Max kissed the top of her head. "You'll get used to it. Just take your time." He slipped his hand under her jacket and began massaging her back with long, strong fingers, easing away the tension in her muscles.

But Susan still couldn't make herself look down. Keeping her eyes straight ahead, she saw a herd of graceful ibex racing across the peaks beyond. "Oh, look, some of your relatives," she said.

Max made no reply. He reached around and slowly unzipped her jacket. Then he pulled her against him. She heard him sigh as his hands molded the fullness of her breasts through her thick sweater. She settled back against him. How solid he felt. But she would not look down.

They stood on the edge of the cliff for long moments, and Max's hands remained gentle and soothing, straying to her neck, kneading her shoulders, then stroking her breasts again.

"Had your fill of the view?" he finally asked her in a thick voice that gave away his impatience more than his touch had.

"Yes, it's spectacular," she said, unable to admit to not looking down.

"Good, now it's my turn," he said, pulling her back from the edge and to the center of the ledge. It was the size of a large room, carpeted in green velvet, with blue sky for walls. "Take off your sweater," he demanded.

She only hesitated for a moment before complying. The strong sun warmed her bare back and shoulders. Max unhitched the front clasp of her lace bra and drew it away from her breasts. "Yes, spectacular," he said.

Susan resisted the impulse to cover herself with her arms as he stared. The hunger she saw in his eyes excited her, and she felt her nipples harden under the light caress of the breeze. She waited, breathless, for him to caress her, too.

Max had promised himself that he would take his time with her, that he would savor every moment of their lovemaking. Their time together was too precious to be hurried. But her beauty excited him beyond measure, and he was almost afraid to touch her now, to lose control.

How proud she looked standing on this mountaintop, her eyes never leaving his, her bare breasts firm and white as snow. But she looked so vulnerable, too, her flesh so tender, her expression so trusting. He would never hurt her, he promised himself. He forgot that every other promise he'd made himself about her had been broken by bringing her here. He enfolded her nakedness in his arms and covered her mouth with his own.

She wanted to hold back something from him, even though she was ready to give herself to him. She knew that she loved him. She had tried so hard not to, and yet it had happened. Since he already had her heart, it seemed right that he should have her body, too. She loved him, but it was beyond her to trust him completely. She could never let herself do that. Then she would be defenseless. Still, she kissed him back with fervor. How could she not? His heat radiated through her, melting her.

He broke their embrace to kneel before her and untie her boots. He slipped them off, stripped away her socks, and still kneeling, unfastened her slacks and peeled them down. She stepped out of them, then he sank his fingers into her buttocks and pulled her to him. He laid his cheek against her abdomen and whispered her name.

Her knees almost buckled. She knelt beside him and shuddered. He cupped her face in his hands and stared at her, fire in his eyes. "I was a fool to think I could resist you," he said.

He pushed her down onto the grass, soft as moss beneath her bare skin. He stood and towered over her, taller than the mountains. His hair looked like gilt in the sunlight. She adored him, but still believed that she could keep a part of herself separate, unreachable even to him.

He undressed quickly, then paused to take her in again. His stomach muscles clenched at the sight of her naked beauty against the lush green. For all his love of the mountains, he had never seen anything in nature that could move him as she did now. And of all the challenges he had taken on in life, she was the only one worth winning. It took every shred of his self-control not to fall upon her and take her savagely and quickly, hard and hot, and be done with it.

Instead, he knelt beside her again and worshiped her with his hands and mouth, drawing out her sweetness. She moaned and the sound escaping her lips made him smile to himself. He would conquer her totally. She would be his completely. He wanted nothing less now.

Her body absorbed his caresses like a sponge until she thought she could stand it no more, the exquisite pain of this building pleasure filling her to the brim without release. Her hands clawed and clenched at the grass, and she rolled her head back and forth against the earth.

"Please!" she cried. She was lost now and didn't even care. She lifted her arms and reached out to him.

Even as he entered her he took his time, slowly sinking into her hot, melting core. Molten silk sheathed him inch by inch. He pulled back, then plunged deeper, and she captured him, tightening her legs around him. He became her willing prisoner, the conqueror conquered.

They moved to new heights together, climbing higher and higher. And then, when they'd reached the point of no return, they jumped off the cliff together, spinning in spirals of ecstasy. The landing was sweet, soft relief.

When Susan awoke she saw that the mountains across the valley were on fire. She sat up with a start. Then she smiled at the most beautiful sunset she had ever encountered, making the glaciers and snow peaks an orange red. With a smile still tilting her lips, she looked down at the most beautiful man she had ever encountered, his long, hard body glowing in the last blazing rays of the day. There could be no holding back with a man like this. He had not allowed it. He had broken through all her defenses. She touched his cheek.

He opened his eyes instantly and smiled back at her. "What time is it?" he asked.

She sighed. She could imagine a more romantic greeting from a man awakening after lovemaking. But not Max Kaiser, apparently. "I don't know. I'm not wearing a watch." She laughed at the absurdity of this conversation.

She wasn't wearing anything. "But it looks about half past sunset to me."

"Dammit, we shouldn't have fallen asleep," he said, leaping up. He grabbed her hand and yanked her up, too. "I hope you didn't get a chill lying on the ground for so long, Susan. Hurry and get dressed. It gets cold and dark very quickly up here."

Already the rosy glow was fading into a dull wash of gray. And Susan felt the glow within her fading fast, too, because of Max's abruptness.

She must have looked crestfallen, because he took her into his arms and pressed her head against his chest. "I'm concerned about getting you back down the cliff safely," he said, stroking her hair. "It isn't the sort of trail to take in the dark. You could easily trip on the rocks. I feel responsible for your safety, and I'm impatient with myself, not you, for staying up here so long."

That made her feel a little better. If he wasn't going to whisper sweet nothings into her ear, at least he'd expressed concern. And he was right. The trail was difficult enough in broad daylight. She didn't look forward to going down in the dark. She hurriedly dressed, keeping her back to Max. She felt shy with him now. How could this be possible after what they had shared? And yet it was. For all the intimacy, all the pleasure they had given each other, they still remained strangers. It hurt her to realize that, and it made her feel foolish, too. She had been naive to expect more from him.

"Susan?"

She turned to him. He was fully dressed, as well, and stared back at her with a serious expression. Very serious. She feared he was going to tell her something she didn't want to hear.

"You asked me to do something earlier today, and I wonder if you still want me to," he said.

What had she asked him? The only thing she could want him to do was love her as much as she loved him now, but you couldn't ask a man to do that.

"I feel the urge," he continued. "And this is the perfect spot to get the full effect of it."

"Of *what?*" she asked a little testily.

His smile came then, the shy smile she always found so endearing. "My yodeling. I feel so good now that I can't hold it back."

And he didn't. He threw back his head and produced a sound from his throat that seemed humanly impossible to Susan. Unless, of course, you were a mountain man. Its undulating trill echoed off the mountains, and Susan was sure it could be heard in the valley far below.

Her heart chimed back as she applauded his effort to express himself in this unique way. She had never made a man happy enough to yodel for her before.

"We're going to spend the night here," Max announced when they made it back to the chalet almost two hours later.

It had taken them much longer to go down the steep trail because the way had been close to invisible in the growing darkness. Max knew it by heart but had insisted that Susan go slowly.

Not that she could have managed it any other way, or without the support of his strong arm at times. They'd had to stop often for her to rest. And Max had been kind and encouraging and patient. More patient than she'd ever seen him before. But when he'd offered to carry her the rest of the way, she'd refused.

Now she felt a sense of accomplishment. She'd made it back on her own two legs. Legs that ached and quivered with fatigue. She doubted she had the energy to hang on to Max during the long trip back to Zürich. And even though he'd claimed he could take the roller coaster mountain roads blindfolded, she didn't want to travel them in the dark. She'd had plenty of that sort of excitement for one day.

So she didn't argue with him. Not that he'd given her the option. "All right, we'll stay here," she said, as if she had a choice. She felt a little thrill curl through her stomach. They would be spending the night together.

"I hope you don't mind roughing it a little," Max said, unlocking the front door. "The place has been closed up for a few months and may be a little damp and chilly. And I don't know what's been left in the larder. But we'll make do." They stepped inside and Max reached for a flashlight on a table beside the door. "Wait here. I'll go switch on the generator," he said, leaving her in the shadowy hall.

Half an hour later they were sitting at a table in the parlor, before a fire in an open tiled stove, eating smoked sausage and foie gras and sipping champagne.

"You call this roughing it and making do?" Susan asked Max, looking around the cozy room filled with carved antique furniture. The walls and ceiling were paneled in polished wood that reflected the firelight.

"We Swiss like our creature comforts," he admitted. "That's why we make such good innkeepers, I suppose. This place used to be an inn, long before skiing became popular. The English would come up here to admire the view and the quaint peasant life-style. In fact, my great-grandfather got his start here as a waiter."

"You mean Josef Kaiser? That elegant blond-bearded man in the portrait?"

"Oh, he wasn't always so elegant," Max said. "His family was very poor, and he would steal rolls to bring back to them when he waited tables here. Stale rolls, mind you, that were going to be thrown out, anyway. But the owner caught him and fired him. Thirty years later Josef had enough money to come back and buy this place. It's been a family retreat ever since."

Susan sighed. "I love success stories like that. Your great-grandfather must have been quite a guy."

"You admire self-made men, do you?"

"Self-made women, too." She took a sip of champagne.

"You being one yourself?"

"Oh, I've come pretty far on my own," she allowed and took another sip. "And I intend to go a lot farther. Who knows, one of these days I may come back and buy the Kaiser Grand from *you* if profits keep slipping." She caught herself. What a stupid thing to say. "Sorry, Max. That was the champagne talking." She pushed away her glass.

"No, that was ambitious Susan Barnes talking," he said, smiling at her. "And there's no need to apologize. You're right. Unless the situation improves, we may not be able to keep the Grand in the family." He took her hand and kissed the palm. "I couldn't think of a better person to sell out to than you if it ever comes to that."

"It won't," Susan said firmly, pulling back her hand to thump it on the table for emphasis. "You can't really believe that could happen."

"Why not? Like you said, Susan, you intend to go far in the hotel business."

"Oh, forget my remark. I wasn't serious. And I hope you're not serious when you say you might have to sell out. The situation isn't as bad as all that."

"No, of course not," he said. "Profits may be down, but the hotel is still making money."

"Not as much as it could be, though."

"Oh, Susan, let's not talk business now, please." He spread a cracker with pâté and handed it to her. "That's *verboten* here, you know. One of my great-grandfather's rules. No discussion of business at the Kaiser Klein. That's why we close down the hotel the last two weeks of December. We come here to get away from it all and appreciate nature again."

Another costly Kaiser tradition, Susan thought. But she held her tongue. Max was right. This wasn't the time to discuss business. They could do that when they returned to Zürich tomorrow. Now was the time to . . . just be together.

She slid her stockinged foot up his leg. "Okay, let's appreciate nature together," she said, then giggled.

"Miss Barnes, I do believe you're tipsy." Max seemed pleased with his observation.

"I certainly am not, Mr. Kaiser. I had only one glass of champagne."

"And at this high altitude it's gone straight to your head."

"I left my head back in Zürich," she informed him. "Or at least my good sense." For some reason she found this highly amusing and giggled again. She slid her leg higher up the inside of his leg and wiggled her toes.

Max checked his watch.

Here she was trying to seduce the man, and he was checking his damn watch! She dropped her foot with a thud and glared at him.

"I think the coals have had time enough to heat up," he said, standing up and adjusting his jeans around his groin area. "I certainly have."

Yes, Susan could see that. She changed her glare into a knowing smile.

"I turned on the stove in the sauna room after I started the generator," he told her. "I thought you would like a hot steam after our long hike."

She stood up, too, and stretched, imagining steamy delights as her breasts pushed against her sweater. "Will you do your towel performance for me again, Max?"

"Oh, I have a more interesting performance in mind. One you'll be participating in." His voice was hoarse with desire.

"Lead the way," she said. Her own voice trembled with anticipation.

He scooped her into his arms. "Better yet, I'll carry you there, lady."

Max slept with all the windows open, Susan learned later that night. The cool mountain air filled the bedroom, and she was glad of the eiderdown comforter she slept under. Max had no use for it, though. He threw off his side in his sleep, and when she touched him he still felt hot. The man was a furnace, she decided. It delighted her to know how easily she could stoke the fires. She fell asleep smiling, her nose a little cold from all the fresh air wafted in.

She had never slept better in her life, but when she awoke the next morning Max was gone. She held her breath and listened for sounds of his movements in the big rambling house. At first she heard nothing, then a steady banging above. She released her breath with a sigh. No doubt he was working on roof repairs.

She got out of bed, and the cold air raised goose bumps all over her naked body. She closed the windows and looked around for her clothes. Then she remembered that she'd left them outside the sauna-room door. Since then she hadn't had much use for clothes. She opened a painted armoire and found a rough cotton shirt hanging inside, along with ski wear. She put on the shirt. It smelled delicious. It smelled like Max.

She looked around the room, which she hadn't had much chance to do last night. It was very simple. Rough ceiling beams and whitewashed walls with posters of racing skiers decorating them. There was a shelf on one wall filled with tarnished trophies. She took one down and wiped off the dust with a fingertip to read the inscription. Maximilian Kaiser. Some German she couldn't understand. And then the date. Fifteen years ago. A boyhood trophy. Max's boyhood room. She sat down on the bed and took it in, as if it were a shrine. Then, laughing at herself, she went downstairs to hunt up some breakfast for them.

The kitchen was old-fashioned, so unlike the gleaming, state-of-the-art kitchen at the Kaiser Grand. The wooden floors were wavy, the gingham curtains faded, and when she examined the big black cast-iron stove she realized it was a wood burner. She didn't have a clue as to how to get it started. Her hopes of making coffee fading, she looked around and spotted an electric coffeemaker on the counter. It was an elaborate stainless steel contraption and boggled her as much as the wood-burning stove did. Throwing up her hands in defeat, she went out into the morning sunshine to find Max.

She walked around the big house, the dewy grass tickling her bare feet. She breathed in the mountain air, the pure coolness of it filling her lungs. She loved it up here. It was close to being in heaven.

She found Max on the east side of the house, up on the roof as she'd suspected, his tall frame silhouetted against the backdrop of the rising sun. He wore only his jeans and boots, and his broad bare back looked powerful as he stood with his hands on his narrow hips surveying his domain. Sensing her presence, he swiveled, looked down, and waved.

"Did I wake you with my hammering, Susan?"

"I'm glad you did." She shielded the sun from her eyes with one hand as she tilted back her head. "It's so beautiful here in the morning. Next time I want to get up early to see the sun rise."

It occurred to her how presumptuous that remark sounded. Why assume that he would ever bring her back here again?

"Is that my shirt you have on?" he asked her.

Had that been another presumption on her part? "Yes, I hope you don't mind."

"You look adorable in it. Every time I wear it now, it'll remind me of you. I'll never be able to part with it."

Well, that was something, Susan thought. He intended to keep the shirt she'd worn, if not her. She chastised herself for such a maudlin thought.

"I won't be much longer," he told her. "I could use a cup of coffee when I come down. Would you mind making it, *Liebling?*"

He had called her darling; it warmed her all over. How could she refuse his simple request? She went back to the kitchen, determined to make him coffee. She found a bag of beans in the well-stocked pantry, then examined the machine with narrowed eyes. Two switches, two openings, what could be so difficult about figuring it out?

* * *

When Max walked into the kitchen a short time later he found Susan standing in the middle of the room, tears streaming down her face. He'd never seen her cry before, and he was overcome with deep remorse. She was having regrets, he thought. Regrets about becoming his lover. She hadn't wanted it to happen. She'd made that clear enough. And now that it had happened, she was miserable.

He took her into his arms, but he was at a loss as to how to comfort her. If he told her he was sorry, he would be lying. He wasn't a bit sorry. He'd never enjoyed making love to a woman more. And just holding her now, pressing her against him, he wanted to make love with her again, right now, even while she was crying her poor heart out.

He sat down on a kitchen chair and pulled her into his lap. She was naked beneath the shirt and his hand slid under the fabric to mold her softness, her curves, her pliant flesh. He kissed her salty cheeks, blotting the tears with his lips. And all the time he was thinking that he must take her one last time, before she had the chance to tell him of her regrets and end what they had started on the mountaintop. He knew that was selfish. He couldn't help it. But she spoke before he could stop the words with his mouth.

"I broke it," she sobbed.

This confused him. Broke what? Her pledge to keep their relationship from becoming an intimate one?

"It was such a stupid thing to do," she said.

That put him off a little. He stopped stroking her. He thought their lovemaking had been wonderful and didn't like hearing her describe it as . . . stupid. Unwise, perhaps. Impetuous, surely. But stupid? He had never been one for romantic talk himself. Still, he felt disappointed that she could sum up what had happened between them like that.

"What will your mother think?" she asked him.

His mother? Why bring her into the discussion? It seemed a little premature to Max. Much as he adored Susan, however enchanting he found her, he had no plans for her that would involve his mother. He could think of only one that could—marriage. But Max had given little thought to a future with Susan and had little inclination to do so now.

"What's happened is no concern of my mother's," he said. Not yet, at any rate, a little voice deep within him added.

"Of course it is, Max," Susan insisted. "You'll have to tell her about it when we go back to Zürich."

He didn't see why. His private life was none of his mother's business, never had been. "That's the last thing I intend to do, Susan," he stated firmly. But he tempered his firmness by caressing her softness again.

She wasn't crying anymore. She was frowning at him. "She's bound to find out sooner or later."

"Not unless *you* tell her. And frankly, I don't see why you would want to."

Susan exhaled a deep sigh. "No, it wouldn't make her any more friendly toward me, that's for sure."

Max didn't argue that point. She was right.

"Handle it any way you wish, Max," Susan went on. "I hate to see you take the blame for it, but it's probably better that she, or anybody at the hotel for that matter, not know I was here with you." She brightened a little. "Maybe you can have it repaired or replaced before she comes here in December. I'll pay for the damages, naturally."

Now Max was totally confused. "*What* damages? What are you talking about, Susan?"

She looked confused, too. "The coffeemaker, of course. I just told you I broke it."

"And that's why you were crying?"

She nodded. "I felt so angry and frustrated. I must have put the beans where the water should have gone. And poured the water into the grinder. The sound was horrible when I turned the thing on. I unplugged it right away, but I think the damage is done."

Max started laughing and kissing her at the same time, on her ear, her nose, her forehead.

"It's not funny," she said, but was relieved that he found it so.

"How silly of you to cry over it," he said. He, too, felt relief. He hadn't been the cause of her tears, after all. She wasn't going to tell him that their intimate relationship must end just as it was beginning.

"Maybe I overreacted," she said. "But I hate doing stupid things like that."

"It doesn't matter." He unbuttoned her shirt. His shirt. He cupped one of her milky breasts. His now, too, for the taking. He kissed the pink nipple, pale as an Alpine rose. It budded for him. She shifted on his lap to better offer her treasure to his lips.

"But what did you think I was talking about?" she asked in a dreamy voice as his hand massaged her belly.

"It doesn't matter," he told her again, then filled his mouth with her and suckled.

"I just think it's better this way, Max," Susan said. She had insisted he pull over at the foot of the hill and let her off.

He stayed hunched over his motorcycle, his wide mouth turned down. "It's sneaky," he said. "I picked you up at the Grand and I should bring you back there."

"It's not sneaky, it's discreet," she told him. "A whole day and night have passed since we roared away. Now I don't want to come roaring back with you, begging the notice of every staff member." She took off her helmet and handed it to him. She took off the jacket he'd given her, too. He wouldn't take that back, though. Or look at her.

"Why are you being so difficult about this?" she asked him. "It makes perfect sense to me that we should keep our personal relationship just that—personal. Surely you don't want everyone to know we've become lovers?"

Everything she was saying made sense to him, too. In fact, she was only echoing his own feelings about the situation. He admired discretion. He valued his privacy above all else and loathed the idea of the staff gossiping about Susan and him.

Still, letting her return alone didn't sit well with him. He wanted to take her back like a gentleman should instead of dropping her off here. Then it occurred to him that a gentleman would do as she wished. Another thought followed closely. If he were *really* a gentleman, he wouldn't have given in to his desire for her in the first place. In the end he was just like his ancestors, the wild herdsmen, taking what he wanted. Well, he'd already warned her about that, hadn't he?

"Max, please don't pout," he heard Susan say.

"I wasn't pouting, I was thinking." He forced a smile. "You're right, of course. I'll leave you here and see you back at the hotel later today." He touched her cheek, revved his motor, then drove away.

Susan walked up the hill, cradling the soft leather jacket in her arms, telling herself that she had no reason to feel so dejected now. Her time in the mountains with Max had been more wonderful than she had imagined possible. He had given her a beautiful gift—the gift of sexual fulfillment. She had never experienced that before.

It astounded her that she could. He had touched something so deep in her, something she had thought unreachable. Or rather, something that she had never dared let a man have from her before. Her heart, her body—they were his now.

The idea frightened her. Lord, it frightened her so much! She recalled the horrible whirring sound of the coffee machine and how she'd imagined her heart being shredded to bits in it. That was really why she'd been crying when Max came into the kitchen. But of course she couldn't have confessed that to him. He would have thought her crazy. A man like Max wasn't afraid of anything. He relished speed, he relished heights, he relished lovemaking. He seemed attracted to strong sensations of any kind. They could be both torture and bliss, he had told her once. When? Not that long ago, really. The first day she had met him. And he had already given her the bliss. But the torture? Would he give her that, too, in the end?

No! Not if she kept control over her emotions. Not if she didn't expect anything from him but what he had already given her. And she truly didn't expect any more from him. In a few months she would be gone from his life. They both understood and accepted this. Hadn't it been the unspoken condition between them before they'd climbed to the cliff?

Propelled by the thoughts racing in her mind, Susan reached the hotel before she knew it. It rose in front of her eyes like a surprise, majestic yet welcoming, the famous Kaiser Grand. She slowed her pace and composed herself before reaching the entrance. Rolf, the doorman, was out front attentively awaiting new arrivals, as always. The gold on his well-pressed uniform gleamed. His high hat was brushed to perfection. He doffed it when he saw her approach.

"*Guten Tag,* Miss Barnes," he said, his expression blank.

"Good day, Rolf. Such a beautiful one! I couldn't resist taking a walk."

"A long one, madame?"

She knew he knew that she had been away since the day before. "Not so long," she said sharply, raising her chin.

He gave her a curt bow and opened the door for her. His face remained blank. He said nothing more.

The lobby was busy. Good, Susan thought, her mind turning to business. She loved seeing the Grand busy with guests and bustling staff. This was as it should be. A hotel as fine as this one deserved to be full and active, pulsing with life. The hum of it excited her. She loved hotels, and this one in particular. She could find fault with certain areas of management and administration, but the hotel itself was faultless.

Joseph Kaiser would have been proud, she was sure, of how his ideals of perfection and comfort and hospitality had been maintained through the century. Some hotels claimed grandness. The Kaiser Grand epitomized it. But for all its luxury, it was homey, too. It maintained the feeling of a family-run inn because it *was* family-run.

Susan appreciated the importance of this. She had tried to duplicate, or at least imitate, this feeling in the luxury hotels she had brought into the Golden Key organization, but she'd always known something was lacking. Authenticity that stemmed from old traditions. And the Grand was the real thing.

She took the curving, red-carpeted stairs up to the fourth floor rather than use the elevator. She wanted to appreciate the grandeur of this wide, open staircase, and the wonderful stained-glass windows on every landing.

She felt good again, pulsing with life, her fears and reservations about Max diminishing with each stair she climbed. She would be seeing him later that day. That kept her step buoyant and her heart, too. As long as she stayed at the Grand, she would be seeing Max. And that was enough.

When she entered her suite the scent of fresh flowers welcomed her. The sun sifted through the curtains. Everything glowed. She would have liked to have brought her grandmother to a luxurious place like this. *Call room service and order anything your heart desires, Grandma!* If only she had lived long enough for Susan to share her success with her. She had no one to share it with now.

Susan walked to the bedroom. The canopied bed was made, the little lace pillows over the chintz quilt precisely arranged by the room maid. Susan realized that Heidi must also have turned down her bed last night, as she always did. And this morning she must have seen that it hadn't been slept in. She doubted that Heidi would mention this to anyone. They had become friends during the past few weeks.

She took a long bath in the deep marble tub that was standard at the Grand, then dried herself off with fresh, fluffy towels. She rubbed her body with the fine creams the hotel supplied. It would be so easy to take all this luxury for granted. But Susan had promised herself that she never would. She constantly reminded herself that she was an employee, a temporary one at that, and not a guest.

She dressed slowly and carefully, choosing a rose blouse and a tweed suit in heather tones that made her look businesslike and pretty, too. She wanted to look both when she saw Max again. And she trembled inside when she buttoned her jacket, wondering how they would act toward each other now.

Her high heels seemed to have wings on them as she strode into his outer office. She couldn't wait to see him again. Their brief separation had filled her with longing. His secretary wasn't at her desk. Susan was glad of this. She didn't want to be announced. She wanted to enter Max's office without the interference of protocol.

She turned the door handle and walked in, her heart singing. But the song faded when she saw that Max wasn't alone. Frau Kaiser and Fritz Maier were with him.

Max sat behind his desk, dressed in a suit now, the image of perfection. His face was a mask when he looked at her. "Oh, Miss Barnes," he said in a cool, neutral voice. "Is there something you'd like to discuss with me?"

"I'm interrupting. Excuse me, Mr. Kaiser." As she addressed him by his last name, she felt a hollowness in her heart, as if it had a hole in it and all the joy was pouring out. "I just wanted to talk to you about..." Her mind drew a blank. She could have had a hundred good reasons to be here now, none of them personal. But for the life of her she couldn't think of one at the moment.

"Billing procedures?" Max supplied.

"Yes, that's it. Could you have your secretary call me when you're available? I'll be in my office." She nodded to Frau Kaiser and Fritz and went out, making sure to close the door behind her.

Chapter Ten

Unlike her lovely suite, Susan's office at the Grand was small and cramped and windowless. Max had apologized about setting her up in such dreary quarters, but office space was limited. Susan didn't mind. She had what she needed — a desk, a file cabinet, a telephone and a computer. When she became immersed in her work, she didn't notice her surroundings.

She unfolded some spreadsheets and tried to get immersed in her work now. Business as usual. She'd been foolish to be hurt by Max's impersonal attitude when she'd barged into his office, she told herself. What had she expected him to do — leap over his desk and take her into his arms while his mother and Fritz looked on? He'd behaved just the way he should have toward her. But how distant and cool his tone had been! And his eyes had been icy too. Only this morning they had . . .

Stop! Susan commanded herself. You're not in the mountains anymore. Here at the Grand things were different. Max was her boss, not her lover. *Mister* Kaiser again.

She wondered if men and women went through the formal procedure of *Duzen* to get onto a first-name basis the way she and Karin had. She almost laughed. She and Max had done a lot more than kiss each other on the cheek and shake hands!

Determined to put that out of her mind, she concentrated on the productivity tables she was working on. She was gnawing on the end of her pencil, deep in thoughts that had nothing to do with Max, when she heard a knock on her door. The figures she was studying turned into a jumble. Max!

"Come in," she said, trying to sound as cool as he had, even though her heart was pounding.

It went back to a normal beat when Fritz entered. "I came to tell you that the coast is clear, Susan," he said in a conspiratorial whisper.

"Is this a weather report, Fritz?"

He smiled coyly. "You can go back to Max's office, my pet. He's alone now. You looked so terribly disappointed when you walked in earlier and found him with Frau Kaiser and me."

Susan said nothing but promised herself that she would hide her feelings better in the future.

"I looked all over the hotel for you yesterday. Where were you?" Fritz asked her.

"That's my affair."

"Apt choice of words, Susan."

She willed back a blush. "What's that supposed to mean?"

"Why, not a thing, my *Liebling*."

"Don't call me that," she said, unable to stand hearing the endearment from his lips after hearing it from Max's. "And please go away now. I have work to do."

He perched on the edge of her desk instead, like a plump pigeon. She wished she could shoo him away.

"Wouldn't you like to know what Max and his mother and I were discussing?" he asked her.

"Not from you. If Mr. Kaiser thinks I should know, he'll tell me."

"Oh? Does he tell you everything now, Susan?" When she didn't answer, Fritz's smile stretched. "It's no secret that the two of you went off together yesterday morning. This hotel is like a small village. Word gets around very quickly."

"You're so tedious Fritz," Susan said, trying to sound bored. "We went to visit Max's uncle, that's all."

Fritz frowned at this piece of information. "Uncle Anton doesn't usually care to have visitors. Was there something special he wanted to talk about with you and Max?"

Susan wondered why Fritz looked so worried. Because he did, it was her turn to smile coyly. "Nothing that has to do with you."

"Anything pertaining to the Grand has to do with me. I'm a major shareholder." Fritz looked at Susan with menace in his eyes. "If you spoke against me to the old man, my angel, I will find a way to make you pay for it dearly."

Susan's smile faded. Why was he threatening her? Because he felt threatened himself? She'd apparently fallen into a game with Fritz without knowing its rules, and his paranoia frightened her a little.

Her telephone rang; she ignored it and stared back at Fritz. He picked up the receiver and handed it to her.

"Susan?" Max's deep voice came over the line.

She didn't let on who it was in front of Fritz. "Yes, this is Miss Barnes."

Max laughed. "I miss touching you already, Miss Barnes. Can you meet me in the gardens under the willow tree? We can discuss...billing procedures."

"That could be arranged," she said stiffly.

"Oh, there's someone there with you now," Max guessed.

"That's right."

"Could you be free in ten minutes? I'm aching for you. I have to hold you for a moment."

That made her want to smile, but she didn't. Fritz was watching her carefully. "Yes, that would be convenient."

Max laughed again. "How cool you are. You would make a good undercover agent."

She'd once thought the same about him. "Thank you for calling," she said and hung up. She glared at Fritz. "And our conversation is over, too, I believe."

"For the moment," Fritz said.

"Then would you please remove your bulk from my desk top? You're sitting on a spreadsheet." She considered jabbing him with the point of her pencil, imagining him deflating like a balloon.

He stood up before she could give in to the impulse and left her office without another word.

Max felt a little ridiculous as he waited under the willow tree. What had made him arrange this tryst with Susan in the middle of a busy day? A *tryst*. He smiled and shook his head. That sounded so romantic and old-fashioned. And when he saw Susan coming toward him, her hair in a knot at the base of her neck, she looked romantic and old-fashioned to him, too. She was a modern career woman, he knew, proud of her independence and accomplishments, but now he knew how tender and shy and vulnerable she could be, and he felt a great need to protect her. But from what? Himself?

Pushing that thought aside, he hurried to her and took her into his arms, inhaling her delicious scent. It seemed like days since they'd been alone together in the mountains instead of hours. Time had lost all meaning. What was happening to him?

"You look almost as beautiful with your clothes on as off," he told her. He had meant to say something sweet and loving, but this was the best he could do.

She didn't seem to want to hear sweet words, however. She broke from his hug and nervously looked around her. "I've never had a secret rendezvous before," she said, not sounding too pleased about it. "I thought only foolish women who got involved with married men had to resort to that."

So much for romance, Max thought. "This isn't secret, just private," he said. "But from now on, if you prefer, we'll meet in my office. Or yours. Or the damn lobby!"

"No, I'd rather meet in a more private place," she said grudgingly. "Fritz has already guessed that we're...you know."

"Lovers?" Max couldn't understand why Susan was reluctant to put it into words. "Let him guess whatever he wants. The hell with him."

"Max, he frightened me a little today."

"What?" He felt his face tighten with anger. "Did he try something with you?"

"No, not that. I could handle that." She went on to relate the conversation about Uncle Anton.

Max didn't take it seriously and tried to reassure Susan. "Fritz is always worried about people talking against him. He's very insecure about his position at the Grand because he isn't a Kaiser. I think that's one of the reasons he married my aunt, to be related at least through marriage. He's just a bag of wind, though. Forget what he said to you."

"I wish I didn't have to deal with him."

"Then you won't have to anymore." Max put his arm around Susan and led her to the bench. "From now on I'll be the intermediary. If you need information from Fritz, ask me and I'll get it for you."

"No, that's not very efficient. Or professional on my part to hide behind you, Max. Don't start treating me specially because we're..."

"Lovers," Max supplied again. He tilted her chin to look into her eyes. "Lovers," he repeated softly. "Why are you so shy about saying it?"

Susan couldn't answer him. She couldn't tell him that she longed to hear him say he loved her; then they truly would be lovers instead of just two people in a sexual relationship. But perhaps it was enough that she loved him with all her heart. That made their relationship important, at least to her.

She lowered her eyes. Penetrating as his gaze was, he still could not read her heart.

"I should go back to my desk now, Max. I'm in the middle of formulating productivity tables."

"And what are those?" He seemed more interested in kissing her neck than finding out.

"Well, it's a little complicated to explain." Especially when his hot kisses were sending shivers through her. "It's a way of measuring sales against labor costs in specific areas, such as room service."

"Hmm," Max said.

"I hope to complete them by the end of the week. Then we can discuss ways to achieve higher levels of performance from the staff."

Max stopped kissing her. "I think their levels of performance are fine. Guests always remark on how attentive the staff is."

"Well, I should hope so. The ratio of employees to guests at the Grand is higher than in any hotel I know of. But there's always room for improvement."

"I don't intend to overwork my employees just to make bigger profits, Miss Barnes."

Susan stiffened. "Who said anything about overworking them? You're rejecting my suggestions before you even know what they are. You always do that."

"That's not true."

"It is! You're as closed to change as the rest of your family. Well, it's time to join the twentieth century, Mr. Kaiser, and stop dwelling on past glories." With that she got up from the bench and stomped off.

He didn't go chasing after her. He wasn't used to a woman putting him in his place like that. So he sat on the bench, brooding.

A few hours later he went to Susan's office, ready to make peace with her. He supposed he would have to make peace with her if he wanted to make love to her, and he wanted that more than anything. When he walked in she looked up from her work but didn't say anything, not even hello. He cleared his throat.

"Let's have dinner together tonight."

"I'm not especially hungry," she said.

Dammit, neither was he. For dinner, anyway. He closed the door. "At my place," he added.

"That's supposed to make the invitation irresistible?"

She gave him her tough look—chin up, narrowed eyes, her full bottom lip pushed out a little. Maybe she thought it made her look tough, but it didn't fool him.

"No, this is supposed to." He had her out of her chair and in a clinch in less than a second.

His kiss had no gentleness in it, no patience, only need and demand. He guessed she would resist at first and he was ready for it, never lessening his grip on her as she struggled, never lessening the demand of his mouth. He knew her now. He knew what she wanted. She wanted him. She couldn't fool him about that, either. He felt her softening, responding. Only then did he release her. He looked at her face, satisfied.

"Go up and change into warm clothes. It's cold out. I'll wait for you in the lobby."

"No," she said.

What did she want him to do? Plead with her? That disappointed him. They'd had a minor business disagreement, and now she was making it personal. He had thought she could keep the two separate.

"You go ahead without me," she continued. "I'll take a cab to your place. Give me the address."

So she wasn't pouting. She was just being discreet. He jotted down his address on her desk pad. "Don't take too long getting there."

She got that defiant look on her face again. He'd thought he had kissed it away. "You forgot to say please, Mr. Kaiser," she reminded him.

His smile came slowly, a little abashed. He knew he could be overbearing at times. "Please come, Susan. I want you so much." And then he gave her another kiss for good measure, more gentle this time but no less persuasive, he hoped.

"That's better," she said softly. "I'll be there in less than an hour, Max."

When he left her office Susan sighed, knowing that she was lost. She would have gone with him anyway, without the please, perhaps even without the gentleness. She had followed him up to a mountaintop, and she would follow him anywhere now . . . if he asked her.

Max snuggled close to Susan in his bed. She lay in a dazed state of contentment, amazed that each time they made love she responded more intensely. It was almost too much for her, this fiery passion between them. It rocked her to the core, and the power of it made her fearful. There were no limitations to her love, but there were limitations to her time with Max. Like her position at the Grand, her role in Max's life was only a temporary one.

"What are you thinking about, Susan?" he asked, lazily stroking her arm. "Not productivity charts, I hope."

"Hardly!"

"Good. I was worried that you were thinking of ways to improve my performance level."

She raised herself on her elbow and smiled at him. "It doesn't need improving, as you well know."

He pushed her down again and rolled on top of her. "Weren't you the one who said there's *always* room for improvement?"

"Max! You're insatiable."

"I can't get enough of you."

"But we just—"

He silenced her protest with his mouth, although it hadn't really been a protest. The trouble was, she had become insatiable, too. She opened her mouth to him, she opened her legs. When he entered her she tilted herself toward him, and he filled her completely. He filled her body and her heart and her mind, and she couldn't think anymore. She didn't want to.

Later, much later, he got up and made her hot chocolate. He brought the steaming cup back to the bed. She sat up, pulled the white cotton sheet over herself, and took it from him. She leaned her back against the wall as she drank. His narrow bed had no headboard.

His apartment consisted of three small rooms on the top floor of a town house in the oldest section of Zürich. He had the same simple taste in decor and furnishings as his old uncle, but the view from Max's long windows was of a cobbled square and a stone church instead of Anton's mountain vistas. She had asked him when she arrived why the place was so stark, and he'd answered that he got enough of luxurious surroundings at the Grand every day. She had liked that response. At heart, she believed, he truly was a simple mountain man.

He stood before her now, a little smile playing on his lips as he watched her drink the hot chocolate. Bars of moonlight, beaming through the shutter slats, ran across his naked body. She loved the long, lean shape of him, all sinewy muscles and hard, smooth flesh. She felt so small and soft in his arms. Her curves fitted so perfectly against him, as if they were two pieces in a puzzle, the only two that could match.

"What are you smiling at?" she asked him, wondering if he was thinking the same thing.

"The way you drink cocoa, holding the mug in both hands and taking those tiny sips," he said fondly. "Savoring the taste and making it last."

"A habit from childhood," she told him. "If I liked something, I wanted to make it last for as long as possible. Not just food. A box of crayons, a pair of new shoes, a good book and especially..."

"Especially what, Susan?"

"I was going to say people. My relationships with them, I mean. But I had no control over that part of my life. Those relationships never lasted. I would always get displaced."

Max frowned. "Displaced? I don't understand."

Of course he didn't, Susan thought. From birth he'd had a secure place in the world. "I grew up in foster homes since I was eleven," she explained, trying to sound indifferent about it. "Some were good, some were bad, but none of them were permanent."

Max sat on the bed beside her. "You're an orphan?"

She almost laughed. He made it sound so melodramatic, the poor little Match Girl shivering in a snowstorm. But she had never lacked shelter or gone hungry. Her deprivations had been much more subtle.

"My father was killed in Vietnam before I was born," she told Max. "And my mother was killed in the line of duty when I was four. She was a policewoman. My grandmother told me always to remember that both my parents were heroes because it would make me strong and brave."

Max bent to kiss her hand, still tightly wrapped around the warm mug. "You are, I believe," he said. "Like that statue I showed you in the park. The woman warrior, ready to do battle."

"Oh, I don't know if I'm all that brave," Susan replied. "But I have had to rely on my own inner strength at times." She took another sip of chocolate. "My grandmother raised me after I lost my mother. She was a widow, and we didn't have too much in the way of material wealth, but we had a good life together for seven years. Then she developed emphysema and eventually died of heart failure. And I became a ward of the state."

"Weren't there other relatives to take you in, Susan?"

"I don't come from a big, close family like yours, Max."

"But surely someone?"

Susan sighed. She had wanted to skip over that part of her history. It still pained her to remember.

"There was one aunt who took me in for a while," she told him reluctantly. "She was divorced, raising four small boys on her own, and it was a financial strain for her to have me as an additional mouth to feed. But I was old enough to help her out with the housework and caring for my little cousins." She smiled at the memory of them. "I adored those little monkeys. I used to think how nice it would be to have a big family of my own one day. I still do."

"Really?" Max looked at her closely. "I thought all you cared about was your career."

"One doesn't necessarily discount the other. Back in America, anyway, women manage to have both. But I'm not so sure that's the case here in Switzerland."

"We're getting off the subject," Max said.

That had been Susan's intention.

Max persisted. "Why didn't you stay on with your aunt?"

Susan shrugged. "Oh, the situation changed. She remarried." She pulled the sheet tighter around her. "Let's talk about you for a change instead of me, okay? Tell me about your childhood, Max. I imagine it was wonderful. I bet you learned to ski before you learned to walk."

"Just about," he said. But he wasn't going to be distracted. "Your aunt remarried. Then what happened?"

"He was a very good provider," Susan replied stiffly. "He paid the rent on time and only drank at night."

"So he drank. What else, Susan?" Max's voice was tense now. She could hear an edge of anger. "Did he like little girls with big, innocent eyes?"

Susan nodded.

Max muttered a curse that caught in his throat. "Did he rape you?"

"No, but he tried to." She kept her voice monotone, devoid of emotion. "My aunt had gone out for the evening. I'd put the boys to bed and was washing the dinner dishes. He'd been drinking and watching me all night. I sensed something awful would happen but didn't know what exactly, until he attacked me from behind. It was horrible! I grabbed a knife from the water and stabbed him with it."

"You killed him!" Max stared at Susan. There was amazement in his expression. And something else, too. Admiration. "You *are* like that statue of the woman warrior."

She shook her head. "I didn't kill him, Max. It was only a dull little kitchen knife, not a sword. It didn't even pierce his skin. But I scared him plenty. When he ran out the back door, I called the police, afraid he would come back.''

"Good. He was arrested, at least," Max said. "And eventually sent to prison for what he tried to do to you, I hope."

"No," Susan replied wearily. "No charges against him were ever filed. My aunt accused me of lying—and worse. That shattered me then, but now I can understand it better. She needed that man. She didn't need me. In the end *I* was the one who was taken away. For my own protection, the social worker who became involved in the case said. At least she believed me, thank God. I never had to see that man again. But I never saw my little cousins again, either."

The wistfulness in her voice seeped into Max's heart. He took the empty mug from her hands and put it aside. He wrapped his arms around her. "My poor darling Susan," he said, wanting to comfort her and somehow make her forget the pains of her past.

But she wrenched herself away from his hold. "Don't pity me, Max! I can't bear pity from you."

She seemed to change before his very eyes, vulnerable one moment, now defiant. She leaped from the bed, all energy and self-will.

"It's getting late," she said. "I'd better get back to the hotel."

"Don't be ridiculous. You're spending the night here."

"Don't *you* be ridiculous! I have no intention of facing your poker-faced doorman again tomorrow morning after another night away. Or having the room maid discover I didn't sleep in my own bed again."

"Yes, appearances must be kept up," Max said in a scoffing tone to hide his hurt. He stood up, too. "Miss Barnes has her precious reputation to uphold."

She had her back to him, searching around the moonlit room for her clothes, and swiveled to face him, heavy breasts swaying from the sudden action, eyes flashing in the dimness. Her tousled hair fell over her bare shoulders, and Max thought that she looked ready to pounce on him.

"You're damn right I do, mister. My reputation is one of my assets in this business, along with my brains. And if you cared even a little about me, you would understand that. But of course you can't understand because you're a man, and a Kaiser to boot. You've always had everything given to you. You take it for granted. But I had nothing to start with in life, and I will not risk what I've worked so hard to get. Not for you. Not for any man."

How fierce she could look, Max thought. He was drawn to her fierceness as much as her vulnerability, and was excited by it, even though her words had stung him deeply.

She glanced down and saw his rising excitement and laughed harshly. "That's all you want from me. That's all you care about, isn't it?"

He couldn't deny it. He had wanted to make love to her from the first moment he'd laid eyes on her. And when she had given of herself so willingly, so generously on the cliff, he had taken what he wanted. Seeing her cry, he had wanted her. When she acted tough, he wanted her. When she flung hurtful words at him, he wanted her still. He wanted to possess every aspect of this woman, sink into her flesh, her changing moods, her very essence. Yes, that was all he cared about. But that was everything! Why couldn't she understand that? The fact that she couldn't understand hurt him more than her mere words ever would. His sexuality was his very essence.

They stared at each other, two naked people who had been lovers only a short time before. And now a chasm of silence and misunderstanding seemed to separate them.

Max was the one to break the silence, if not the misunderstanding. "Very well, then. I'll call you a cab," he said with cool politeness. He plucked his robe from the hook on the door, slipped it on and walked out of the room.

Susan's shoulders slumped; heavy misery replaced anger. So this was all his passion amounted to in the end. Coldness and rejection. *Very well, then. I'll call you a cab.* The superior Max Kaiser would not tolerate criticism or anger from her. Fine. She could not tolerate pity from him, either. She hurriedly dressed and found him in the living room, gazing out the long window. On the lookout for the cab, no doubt, anxious to get rid of her.

"I'll wait in the square," she told him. She didn't want to lose the shaky grip she had on her composure in front of him again.

He turned to her, and she saw a plea in his eyes that she hadn't expected. "It's still early, Susan. And if you feel it's worth your time, I'd like to share a little of my past with you, too. Stay and talk to me for just a while longer, will you, please?"

How could she refuse such a request? She joined him at the window. He put his arm around her, and they gazed into the night. The square was empty. The full moon was high. She waited for him to speak, resting her head on his shoulder. If he wanted to share anything with her, anything at all, she would listen. All she wanted from him was to know him completely.

Chapter Eleven

"I do care about you, Susan. Very much," he began. "And I try not to take anything in life for granted now. I admit that I used to. I thought I was invincible. I was one of those hotshot skiers who took too many risks. Even when I wasn't competing. Just for the hell of it."

"What made you change?" Susan asked softly when he paused.

"One night I went skiing alone during an ice storm and lost control on a cliff I shouldn't have attempted to go down in the first place. I went right over the edge. But instead of falling thousands of feet, I landed on a ledge."

She raised her head from his shoulder to look at him. "The ledge where we first made love?"

He laughed softly at her wide-eyed expression. "That's right, Susan. I told you it was a special place, didn't I? I almost died there a few years ago." He saw the question in her eyes. "And yes, you're the only woman I ever brought there, although I've been back many times myself to remember that long night I lay in the snow, both legs broken, convinced I would die.''

She shivered inwardly. ''Why do you want to remember that, Max?''

''Because something important happened to me there. The moon was like it is now, big and full, and as I gazed up at it, unable to move, I thought how empty my life had become. Races, medals, money, women whose faces and bodies I could only vaguely recall. None of that mattered. I realized that I would die without making myself *matter* in the world I was leaving behind. And my vanity evaporated in the cold dark chill of that night.''

Susan buried her face against his chest, feeling the soft cashmere of his robe and his hard, hot flesh. She breathed him in, the scent of vibrant, living male.

He stroked her hair abstractedly and continued. ''But don't think that I was willing to give up my life, unimportant as I realized it was, without a struggle. I crawled in the deep snow as best as I could, dragging my legs behind me, determined to get down that cliff on my belly. But you know the terrain, Susan, you know how impossible that would have been to do. And the cold and the pain got to me before I made much progress. I didn't pass out exactly. I just closed my eyes and fell asleep. So easy. So peaceful. It was rather pleasant, in fact.''

She pressed harder against him. ''Oh, Max, how did you manage to survive?''

''I was saved, Susan. I was awakened by this whirring sound. And I remember being irritated that angel wings made such a loud noise.'' He laughed his sharp laugh. ''Why I assumed I was being taken to heaven, I'll never know. Anyway, I opened my eyes and saw this image in the sky. A big red helicopter hovering above me, silhouetted by the full moon. A rope ladder dropped from it. Men climbed down from it and landed on the cliff. Moon men, I thought. I heard one tell the other that I was still alive before I passed out, and I was happy to hear it. When I awoke in a hospital bed I knew what I wanted to do with the rest of my life.''

"What they did," Susan said. "Save people."

"Yes, that's all."

"But that's everything, Max."

"It was," he said, continuing to stroke her hair. "Now there's you, too. I haven't fitted you into the scheme of things yet, but I hope to, Susan Barnes."

She said nothing, although she had the same hope. If she'd loved him before, it was nothing to the way she felt now. She stood on tiptoe to kiss him, holding back nothing from him now. They were both survivors, and it seemed to her that they were meant to come together. Clutching his robe, she sank to the floor, pulling him down with her. He never got around to calling a taxi for her.

"Don't look as if it's the end of the world," Max said, reaching across his desk to touch Susan's cheek.

His secretary came in, and he lowered his hand. She gave Max some papers to sign, and while he was checking them over, Susan tried to resign herself to the news he'd just dropped so casually, as if it were nothing. Nothing! He would be away for two weeks, serving in the reserve militia of the Swiss army. Two precious weeks that she wouldn't be able to share with him.

His secretary left them alone again. "I don't understand why a country that's been neutral for five hundred years has an army," she told Max.

He smiled. "We say in Switzerland, 'In every country there is an army. Here it is better to have our own than another one.' Neutrality means not attacking outside our borders, Susan. But we sure as hell are prepared to keep invaders out if they attempt to cross them."

She sighed. "But how can you just walk out on..." She almost said "me," but stopped herself just in time. "On your duties at the Grand, Max?"

"I also have to do my military duty. Every Swiss male does. That's an accepted part of life here."

So she would have to accept it, too, Susan thought. As if she had a choice in the matter! "Who are you going to leave in charge here while you're away?"

"Fritz Maier."

Susan had been afraid of that. She didn't look forward to taking orders from that little gnome.

Max picked up the chunk of amethyst crystal he now kept on his desk. He weighed it in his palm as he looked at Susan. "You would be a better choice, of course," he said. "But it wouldn't look right if I put you in charge, Susan. For one thing you're not a permanent employee here."

"And for another I'm your temporary mistress," she added.

He arched an eyebrow. "That's not the way I would describe our relationship."

She wished she hadn't, either. She was still upset about his departure. Her time here was too short for her to be separated from Max that long. And they had been getting along so well together lately, spending every free moment they had in each other's company, taking long walks through Zürich, short rides into the beautiful countryside, and spending blissful hours in Max's narrow bed.

She hadn't spent the whole night with him again, though, and they'd never made love in her suite. Those were the two rules she still clung to for the sake of propriety, although she doubted they were fooling any of the staff. She would have had to walk around wearing sunglasses day and night to hide the love light she knew poured out of her eyes whenever she looked at Max. And for all his natural reserve, his regard for her—she dared not call it love—showed through in many little ways—a possessive touch, a lingering smile, a way of looking at her in a crowded room as if she alone existed.

But how *would* he describe their relationship? she wondered. He'd never put his feelings for her into words. At times he worshiped her body with his, with supreme gentleness. At other times he took her with a wildness that could have been selfish if it hadn't pleased her so much, too. She looked at him now, this man of contradictions that she could not resolve, and waited for him to say more.

But of course he didn't. Not about his feelings for her, anyway. He put down the amethyst and asked her about the progress she'd made in assessing the hotel. He now accepted her suggestions for improvement more readily. And Susan had learned to accept why certain things could never be changed.

"I've been studying the figures Fritz gave me," she said, in answer to Max's question. "Everything seems to be in order. There were high expenditures over the last few years."

"Yes, my brother had some major renovations done. At least we won't have those expenses this year."

"Or such a sizable salary for the general manager," Susan said. "Yours is only a quarter of what your brother's was. Why's that? You're doing the same job now."

Max smiled. "Gerhard had a different life-style. You know how simple mine is, Susan. So why take more than I need?"

Susan hoped the family appreciated his personal economy. "I've also studied occupancy rates for the last five years," she went on. "They're down, but I think that can be blamed on the present world economy. Lots of luxury hotels are feeling the effects."

"Karin came up with some interesting promotional programs to deal with that problem," Max said, sounding both surprised and proud that she had. "You should ask her to tell you about them."

Susan knew all about them already. She'd helped Karin refine her ideas and make them more practical. She didn't bother mentioning that to Max. She was glad he'd seen the light and allowed his sister to become involved in the business.

Max leaned back in his chair and regarded Susan. "So what *is* the problem?" he asked her.

"I know occupancy rates are down and expenditures are high," he went on. "But are those the major reasons profits are so much lower?"

"No, I don't think so," she replied. "Those two factors only account for a small percentage of the loss, and I still can't put my finger on a major problem. I've explored so many different areas, and although I can find minor faults with the way things are done around here, I've reached the conclusion that the Grand is a smooth-running operation supported by a devoted staff. In fact, if I were assessing this hotel for Golden Key, I would advise Tony Armanto that it was a good investment."

"All right," Max said. "Let's pretend for a moment that Armanto did buy the Grand. What would he do to make it more profitable?"

"Put in a more hard-nosed general manager, for one thing," Susan said flatly. "One who only cared about the bottom line."

Max laughed sharply. "And what else?"

"There would be a complete overhaul of personnel, with no regard to loyalty or length of service." She tried to keep her tone cool, dispassionate. "The hotel's bed capacity would be increased by renovating all the rooms, making them one third smaller. The gardens would become a parking lot, the salons turned into nightclubs or cheaper restaurants for additional revenue sources, and guests would be considered as 'units' rather than people. Oh, and Lady Stilton's dog would have to go. No pets allowed at Golden Key lodgings. The Grand would lose much of its unique character in order to conform to the chain-management way of doing things."

"And Josef Kaiser would turn in his grave!" Max exclaimed, looking slightly horrified. "I expect you to come up with better solutions than that, Miss Barnes."

"I intend to. I don't want that to happen to the Grand any more than you do, Mr. Kaiser. Luckily, we were only pretending. Since the hotel is family-owned, it can't be taken over. I'm just going to have to work harder to discover why it's losing money. None of the studies I've done so far account for such a loss. Yet the books balance.'' She stood up, shaking her head, and headed for the door.

"Wait, Susan. What about tonight?"

Ah, so they were back to being personal, were they? She turned to him, trying to keep her expression aloof. "Tonight? I plan to work."

"Well, how late?" he asked, shifting impatiently in his chair.

"I really don't know," she replied. She did know what he wanted, though. A rendezvous at his place. And because she wanted it, too, she had trouble maintaining her cool demeanor.

"I was hoping you could have dinner with me here at the hotel," he said, surprising her. He had a way of doing that. They usually met at a little bistro near his place, where the food was simple but good and the service fast.

"Why here, Max?"

"Why not? The Grand offers the best dining experience in Zürich, doesn't it?" He grinned. "At least that's what our brochure claims."

She smiled back but hesitated. "I don't know if that's such a good idea, Max." His mother usually came down to the dining room for her evening meal, and Susan didn't want to be under the cold, disapproving eye of Frau Kaiser.

"I think it's a splendid idea," he said. "Besides, you can't refuse me."

Susan knew that well enough. But she stuck out her chin, nonetheless. "Why not?"

"Because, my stubborn one, it's my birthday. So you have to go along with my request."

His birthday! The day suddenly became very special for Susan, too. "All right, Max. I'll meet you in the dining room. What time?"

"Everybody is coming at eight."

"Who's 'everybody'?" Susan waited for an explanation.

Max gave it offhandedly. "Well, my mother, my sister, my aunt and Fritz. You know, the family."

Susan certainly hadn't known that when she'd agreed. But she didn't consider backing out. The fact that Max wanted to include her in his family birthday celebration made her heart blossom. "I'll be there, Max," she said.

By later that evening, however, Susan's blossoming heart had wilted considerably. As she stepped out of Max's bathroom, wearing Max's robe, she began to talk about the birthday celebration. "Did you notice that your mother didn't eat a thing?"

"No, I didn't."

"Well, did you notice that she didn't say one word to me all during dinner? It was pretty obvious that she didn't think I belonged at a family celebration."

Max sighed wearily. "*I* wanted you to be there. My mother's opinions don't affect the way I conduct my personal life. Anyway, I think she was in a bad mood because John Morgan went back to the States yesterday. They'd become very dear friends during his stay here, and she feels the loss of his company now."

Susan knew John had left. She'd even given him a lucky silver charm to help ease his fear of flying when they'd said goodbye. But she didn't know that he and Frau Kaiser had become "very dear friends." She'd assumed John had delayed his return home because of his interest in local botanical sites and his deep reluctance to board another plane. Then she recalled how he and Frau Kaiser had hit it off during his first visit to the Grand. How ironic, she thought, that she had been the one to bring them together, considering how much Frau Kaiser seemed to dislike her.

"I'm sorry your mother misses John," she said sincerely.

"Yes, he was good for her. He brought her out of her depression, at least temporarily. But I don't want to talk about family now, Susan. We had enough of them for one evening, don't you think?"

She certainly did and nodded.

Max patted the bed. "Come here, then. We'll celebrate my birthday privately now."

"I wish I had known about it sooner, Max. I didn't have a chance to buy you a present."

"I don't need or want anything." He regarded her, eyes glittering. "Yes, I do." He patted the bed again. "Come here, my sweet Susan."

He didn't have to ask her a third time.

"Will you stop looking so glum?" Karin urged Susan.

She made an attempt at a smile and failed. Max had left that morning for his annual military service. Now she and Karin were sitting in the elegant Kronenhalle bar in Zürich, after spending the afternoon at the museum a few blocks away. Karin had suggested the outing to cheer Susan up.

"It's not as if Max has gone off to war," Karin told her. "They do practice maneuvers in the mountains, like pretending boulders are enemy tanks. He'll be back before you know it. Two weeks isn't so long."

Easy for her to say, Susan thought. Karin's time at the Grand wasn't limited, but Susan would be gone in January.

A white-coated barman came to take their order.

"Oh, just mineral water, please," Susan requested dully.

Karin contradicted. "No, bring us two Bloody Marys. My friend here needs something to lift her spirits."

Susan didn't have the heart to argue with her. The image of Max, so tall and proud in his tailored green army uniform with gold stripes on the shoulders, was vivid in her mind.

Karin took out a pack of cigarettes and offered one to Susan.

"No, thanks. I gave up smoking three years ago."

"Really? I should, too. Was it hard to do?"

"At first. But then I didn't miss it at all." Once she gave up Max, she would miss him for the rest of her life, Susan knew.

But why dwell on that? They hadn't parted forever... yet. The barman brought their drinks to the table, and she and Karin raised their glasses and said, *"Zum Wohl!"*

Susan nibbled dejectedly on her celery stick as Karin chattered on. "I never smoke at the hotel," she said. "Mother doesn't approve of it, and she has her little spies everywhere. She knows everything that goes on without ever leaving her room."

"She doesn't go out much, does she?"

"No, but when John Morgan was here, they toured botanical gardens together, and I thought he'd managed to cure her of her reclusive ways. But she's back to them again." Karin inhaled smoke contemplatively. "Maybe she's mourning the loss of his company along with the loss of my brother Gerhard now. It would probably have been better if she'd never met Mr. Morgan."

"Oh, I don't agree," Susan said, coming out of her lethargy a little. "He made her happy, and even if it was short-term, surely it was a worthwhile experience to have known him." She caught herself, surprised at her own words. She would never have spoken like that before knowing Max.

"I suppose," Karin said. "But it isn't easy to part with someone you care about." She stubbed out her cigarette. "Believe me, I know. I fell in love with the wrong man once, and it took me a long time to get over it."

"What was wrong with him?" Susan asked her.

"Nothing at all! He was the kindest, most wonderful boy. I met him when I traveled abroad during my student days. The trouble was that he wasn't Swiss. Mother put a stop to our romance. She can be very persuasive."

"But if you truly loved him, Karin, how could your mother persuade you to give him up?"

Karin shrugged. "Perhaps I didn't love him enough to go against my family's wishes. I was raised to believe that family ties are more important than anything else. I couldn't break them. It was as simple as that."

Yes, how simple, Susan thought grimly, *if* you were a Kaiser.

Karin gave her a hard elbow jab in the arm. "Look who just walked in," she said in a shocked whisper.

Following the direction of Karin's wide eyes, Susan glanced over her shoulder and saw Fritz Maier in the company of a young blond woman in a mink coat. Fritz was helping her off with her coat, nuzzling and kissing her neck in the process.

"What a jerk!" Karin said. "I've heard rumors of him cheating on Aunt Berta, and now here's the proof of it."

Fritz and the woman took a table at the back of the room without observing Susan and Karin. They did, indeed, have eyes only for each other.

"Let's get out of here before I throw up," Karin said.

Susan thought that a good idea. They left money on the table for their drinks, hurried into their coats, and departed. Karin took Susan's arm as they walked up Rämistrasse.

"What should I do, Susan? Should I tell Aunt Berta I saw Fritz with his mistress?"

It was one thing to advise Karin about promotional ideas, quite another to advise her about matters pertaining to the Kaiser family, Susan thought, especially since she wasn't a member of it. And much though she despised Fritz for cheating on his wife, she didn't like the idea of such a kindhearted woman as Berta being hurt by the news.

"Oh, Karin, it's not up to me to counsel you. Call Max and ask him what to do."

"I can't call Max. Unless there's a dire family emergency, he can't be reached. Besides, he would probably tell me to mind my own business."

"Then maybe you should."

"But it *is* my business! Aunt Berta is family. I need a little time to think it over before I say anything, though."

"Well, I won't say anything to anybody," Susan assured her.

"Oh, I know you won't. You know your place."

Karin said this with such nonchalant disregard for Susan's feelings that she was stunned for a moment. And then she laughed hollowly. "Yes, Miss Kaiser. I know my place."

Max's sister stopped in her tracks. "Oh, Susan, I didn't mean that the way it sounded."

Susan stopped, too. "Then how did you mean it?"

Karin shifted uncomfortably in her beautiful fur coat. "I don't know. I'm upset."

Susan clutched the collar of her own simple cloth coat, feeling the chill of the November wind. And feeling a deeper chill, too. But Karin looked close to tears, and Susan felt sympathy toward her. Hadn't they pledged to be friends for life? "It doesn't matter," she said. "Forget it."

So Karin did, hooking arms with Susan again. "Aunt Berta should never have married Fritz in the first place," she said as they walked on. "He was only a paid employee of the Grand, with no fortune of his own. A mere nobody!"

Susan uttered another hollow laugh, but so softly that Karin didn't even hear her.

Ten left. Susan sat in bed, the box of chocolates on her lap, and counted them once more. Max would be back in five days. That meant she could have two every evening until he returned. For some reason she felt it important that the chocolates he'd given her the day she arrived at the

Grand should last until then. She chose carefully, selecting a dome-shaped one, guessing it contained a strawberry filling. She bit into it. Wrong. Mocha. But that was almost as good. She closed her eyes to better savor the taste.

A knock on the door interrupted this small pleasure. Susan got up, stuck her feet into her slippers and went to answer it, sure it was Heidi coming to turn down the bed for her. Susan had told her time and again that it wasn't necessary; she could very well do it for herself since she wasn't even a paying guest. But Heidi always insisted that it was her duty as a room maid. Susan knew that the girl looked forward to a cozy chat with her in the evening. And Susan looked forward to it, too. So she opened the door with a big smile on her face. It faded immediately.

"Frau Kaiser!"

"Do forgive me, Miss Barnes, if I'm interrupting you from something."

"No, not at all. I was just . . . uh . . ." Indulging in chocolates and memories of intimate moments I have shared with your son. Oh, if she only dared say that! But of course she didn't. "I was just relaxing. Please come in."

"Thank you." Frau Kaiser, dressed in a fine suit and exquisite leather pumps, stepped into the room and looked Susan over with cold eyes, clearly taking in the sweatshirt, cutoff jeans and fuzzy slippers with bunny ears attached to them.

Susan decided, there and then, that she would burn the entire outfit the first chance she got. Then she decided—the hell with it! What was she supposed to wear alone in her rooms, a fancy designer peignoir? Well, that wasn't her style.

"A lovely suite, isn't this?" Frau Kaiser said, looking around, not missing a thing.

Let her look, Susan thought. Not only did she have nothing to hide, she was also very neat. "Yes, I've been very comfortable here," she replied politely.

"Oh, I'm sure, Miss Barnes. These tower suites are the finest accommodations the Grand has to offer. My son gave you one only because none of them was occupied at the time of your arrival, you know."

"Yes, I know." Now Susan thought she understood why Frau Kaiser had come. "But you've suddenly had reservation requests for all four. No problem. I'll move out tomorrow morning."

"Good. I was hoping that wouldn't be a problem for you, Miss Barnes. But the truth is we have no requests to occupy them at the moment. It's a rather slow time at the Grand, as you must know. So I thought it would be a good time to give all the tower suites a fresh coat of paint."

"Fine," Susan said, although it didn't make much sense to her. Why not do one at a time, leaving the other three free? But she didn't want to argue with Frau Kaiser. "I'll still move out tomorrow morning."

"Yes, you'll have to. That's when the painters are coming. Of course a room maid will pack up all your belongings and bring them down to another room for you. It's much smaller than this suite and doesn't have a view. But it's very comfortable, as all accommodations here are."

"That's fine," Susan said. "It doesn't really matter that much to me where I stay."

Frau Kaiser smiled tightly. "I'm happy to hear it doesn't matter, Miss Barnes. I would hate to offend you. Good night."

"Good night, Frau Kaiser."

The moment Susan closed the door after the older woman, she kicked it. Since her bunny slipper didn't give much protection, she stubbed her big toe in the process. She hardly felt the pain. She was already too hurt. Lord help her, she was being displaced again. She thought she had left that horrid empty feeling behind long ago, but she felt it now as she went back to the bedroom.

She took out her suitcases from their storage area behind the armoire and threw them onto the bed. She began packing. She didn't need a room maid to help her. She'd done her own packing many times before. And like those many times, she wept as she did so. How stupid of her to have thought she had put those old feelings of rejection behind her! They would always be there, closer to the surface than she wanted to admit.

Oh, stop being such a baby, she chided herself, wiping her eyes with the back of her hand. So what if Frau Kaiser was kicking her out of her suite? No big deal. It wasn't as if she'd become especially attached to the place, the way she had to foster families in the past. She didn't belong in such luxury, anyway. And it had been made very clear to her that Frau Kaiser knew that, too.

Max wasn't prepared for the trouble that greeted him when he entered the Grand five days later. He had stopped at his flat only briefly, to change into civilian clothes and shave with hot water for the first time in two weeks, then hurried to the hotel, eager to see Susan. He went directly to her office. She wasn't there. He looked around the lobby for her, then went up to her suite. He found a painter in it, but no Susan.

"Why are you here?" he asked the man.

The painter waved his brush. The answer was obvious. Max looked around impatiently. Drop cloths covered everything. Not a trace of Susan anywhere. What was going on?

He went to his mother's suite on the fourth floor, hoping to find out. Her personal maid opened the door and informed him that Frau Kaiser was in Herr Maier's office. So Max went there. He flung the door open without knocking and walked in.

His mother pressed her hand to her heart when he entered. "Thank God you're back, my son," she said.

"What's wrong?" He looked from her to Fritz.

Fritz shook his head and tugged at his goatee. "Max, I have bad news, I'm afraid."

Max felt the world crack open. Or was it his heart? He felt the blood drain from his face. Icy fear filled his veins. *Something had happened to Susan!* He stood frozen, numb, unable to speak.

Chapter Twelve

"Perhaps you should tell Max, Frau Kaiser."

"No, Fritz. You were there when it happened. I really had nothing to do with it."

Max found his voice. It ripped from his throat in a roar. *"Tell me what?"*

Frau Kaiser looked taken aback. "Really, Maximilian, there's no reason to shout."

He ignored her and turned toward Fritz. "Where is she? Where is Susan?"

"In her office, I presume."

"I saw her from my balcony a short while ago," Frau Kaiser said. "She was taking a walk through my gardens."

"You mean she's all right?" Warmth began returning to Max's veins.

"Miss Barnes is perfectly fine," Frau Kaiser said irritably. "We have a much more important matter to discuss with you."

"Actually, she had a lot to do with it," Fritz said. "If Susan hadn't discovered that those bottles of wine were missing, Chef Duprés would still be with us." A sly little smile crept to his lips for an instant, then he looked serious again.

"Still with us? What's all this about?" Max demanded.

"Chef Duprés has gone," his mother finally informed him. "He left the hotel in an outrage less than half an hour ago."

Max sat down, in control now that he knew Susan was alive and well and still at the Grand. He could handle anything else. "All right, let's start from the beginning," he said calmly. "Why was Chef Duprés in an outrage?"

"Because I had no choice but to ask him for an accounting," Fritz replied.

"Of what?" Max prodded as patiently as he could.

"There are a number of expensive bottles of wine missing from our cellar and unaccounted for, according to Susan Barnes." Fritz picked up a paper from his desk and read from it. "A 1961 Château Lafite, for one. A '70 d'Yquem. A '53 Margaux. Even a '49 Latour."

"The Latour!" Frau Kaiser cried. "Gerhard's pride and joy!"

Max took the sheet of paper from Fritz and recognized Susan's neat, precise handwriting. The missing wines she had listed accounted for thousands of francs' worth of inventory. Some bottles were irreplaceable. His brother Gerhard had devoted much time and energy and money into acquiring these priceless wines for the Grand. They were too expensive for all but a rare guest to request on occasion, but Gerhard had felt they added to the Grand's prestige.

"Why did Miss Barnes become involved in taking a wine inventory?" Max asked Fritz.

"I asked her to. I thought she might as well do something useful while she was here."

Max ignored that disparaging remark—for the moment. First he wanted to get to the bottom of the problem at hand. "So then you showed Chef Duprés this list, Fritz?"

"Who else? The only other two people who have a key to that area of the wine cellar are you and I, Max. When the sommelier gets a request for a vintage that is priced over five hundred francs, Duprés personally goes down to get it."

"That's true. But surely Chef Duprés had an explanation for these missing bottles."

"None whatsoever! His face became all red, and he said he would not tolerate being suspected of thievery."

Frau Kaiser shook her head sadly. "Alain Duprés has been with us for twenty years. Losing him will do great harm to our reputation. He's part of the reason people come here. And I still can't believe he would steal from the Grand."

"Well, I didn't collect the evidence against him," Fritz said. "Susan Barnes did. And I proceeded on the assumption that her findings were accurate."

"I have no doubt that they were," Max said. "Miss Barnes is extremely thorough and exacting in her work."

He felt a sudden infusion of warmth and looked toward the doorway to see Susan standing there, her face serious but her eyes glowing as she looked at him. She stepped into the room, bringing in the fresh scent of the outdoors with her.

"Excuse me, but the door was open and I heard my name mentioned as I was on the way to my office," she said, unbuttoning her coat. "Has something happened that I should know about?"

Max rose and came to her. How beautiful she looked to him, her cheeks a delicate pink from her walk. He restrained the impulse to swoop her into his arms and kiss her and politely helped her take off her coat instead.

"Welcome back," she said softly.

"Thank you, Miss Barnes." He held her coat against his chest and absently stroked the cloth as he stared at her.

Susan stared back at Max, unable to contain her expression of joy. She had missed him so much. She fervently wished that this first meeting after their separation had taken place in private.

Frau Kaiser cleared her throat. "What has happened, Miss Barnes, is that our chef has left because you accused him of stealing."

"What?" Susan tore her eyes from Max and looked at Frau Kaiser, confused. "But I made no accusations! I merely reported my findings to Fritz."

"It amounts to the same thing."

"Now wait a moment, Mother," Max said. "You're making it sound as if Miss Barnes is the guilty party rather than Duprés. It's thanks to her that we discovered this loss."

"How horrible it would be, though, if Miss Barnes is mistaken," Frau Kaiser replied.

"But surely she can't be," Fritz said. "She assured me she checked and rechecked her findings." He turned to Susan, his sly smile returning. "Didn't you, Susan?"

"Yes! I suggest we go down to the wine cellar now, and I'll show you how I discovered the wines were missing." She wanted to clear up all doubt.

"There's no reason for me to go. I believe you," Fritz said. "Otherwise I wouldn't have confronted Duprés."

"I'll come with you, Miss Barnes," Max said, plucking the list from the desk. "And once I see for myself that the wines aren't there, it will settle the matter."

Susan looked at him gratefully. He obviously had full confidence in her. And now that he had come back, everything would be all right.

They took a special service elevator to the basement, and the moment the doors slid closed, Max had Susan in his arms. His kisses were wild and hungry, taking her breath away.

"I dreamed about you all night, I thought about you all day," he told her between kisses.

The elevator doors opened. They didn't get out. The doors closed again and he resumed kissing her, pressing her against the wall, pressing against her. "I want you so much. I want you now," he murmured.

He had kissed away most of her good sense but not all of it. "Max, we can't!" she gasped. "Not here in the service elevator. Someone will want to use it any minute now."

And sure enough, it began to rise. They straightened their clothes, smoothed down their hair, and had some semblance of propriety when it stopped on the third floor. A maintenance worker stepped in. He got off on the first floor. They continued down again. The worker had reminded Max of something.

"Why are your rooms being repainted, Susan? Didn't you like the colors?"

"That was your mother's idea, not mine."

"But that suite was just painted a few months ago."

"Well, maybe *she* didn't like the colors." Susan changed the subject to a more pressing one. "When I reported the missing wines to Fritz last night, I had no idea he would question Chef Duprés. I assumed he would wait for you to return and handle the situation."

"Well, he should have. But Fritz never misses a chance to play big boss."

This time, when the elevator stopped they got out and walked down a long basement hall to the wine cellar.

Max paused at the metal door. "This is really a waste of time, Susan. I trust your findings and was only humoring my mother. Let's go back to my place right now." He cupped her face in his palms. "We have a lot of catching up to do." His blue eyes glittered with desire as he looked at her.

How tempted she was. But she remained adamant. "No, Max. You told your mother you would check this out personally, and you must. I want you to."

Max sighed and dropped his hands. "Very well."

So now he was humoring her, Susan thought. But that was all right. It was important to her that Max see for himself that she hadn't been mistaken.

They entered the cellar, which was in actuality a modern, well-lit storage area kept at a constant temperature of 13° Celsius—about 56° Fahrenheit. Spirits and tobacco products were also stored here, and the man in charge, on duty until midnight, kept precise records of whatever was taken upstairs to more convenient locations, such as the kitchen and bar. He saw Max and Susan from his glass-enclosed office and stepped out to greet them.

"Miss Barnes and I have been working together all week," he told Max.

"And thanks to Mr. Müller's excellent stock records, we accounted for everything without any problems," Susan said.

Mr. Müller beamed. "It was a pleasure to help you, Miss Barnes. I only wish I could have helped you with the rare wines, too, but that's not my department." He looked at Max rather accusingly. "She spent many long hours in that cold little back room, taking inventory all by herself."

"I found the work fascinating," Susan said.

But Max felt a spurt of anger that Fritz had assigned Susan such a time-consuming task. And what was all this about his mother having her suite painted? He was getting the impression that Susan had been treated like Cinderella during his absence. Frowning, he followed her down a corridor lined with racks of red wines on one side, whites on the other. She took a sharp turn past the champagnes, knowing the area well now, and stopped at another door, this one of thick, old wood.

"Oh, I don't have the key anymore," she told Max. "I gave it back to Fritz."

"I have mine," Max said. He unlocked the door and pushed it open. It squeaked on its hinges.

Susan switched on the overhead light. A large chart hung on the wall, designating the location of every wine in the room by its rack slot number.

"That was a great help," Susan said, pointing to the chart. "But I didn't rely on it. I went to the source."

She took a heavy, leather-bound book off the shelf, placed it on the scarred table, and opened it. It contained handwritten listings of all the wines in the room. The handwriting varied. Many Kaisers from the past had logged their additions and withdrawals there.

"It's sort of like a family history, isn't it?" Susan said. She turned the pages carefully. "Look at these entries, Max. All dated around the turn of the century. Your great-grandfather Josef, made them. See, here are his initials. How wonderful!"

"Yes, wonderful," Max agreed, but he was staring at Susan's bent neck, so white and smooth under the light. And then he was kissing it.

She laughed. "Max, pay attention."

"I am, Susan. You're lovely."

"I don't mean pay attention to *me*. Look at the book." She turned a few more pages and began explaining her method of taking inventory. "Now here's a listing of all the Sauternes that should be here. I located every single bottle in the exact location that was designated on the chart. Except for one. The 1970 Château d'Yquem."

"One of the most expensive."

"Absurdly so!" Susan said. "Why anyone would pay that much for a bottle of wine, I'll never understand." She shrugged and turned to the racks. "Anyway, it should have been in this slot, but instead I discovered a less expensive Sauterne." She pulled out the bottle and handed it to Max. "See for yourself."

"You're right. But I knew you would be."

"Well, I'm sorry I am," she said with a sigh. "For all his puffed-up arrogance and temperament, I really liked Chef Duprés. He took great pride in his work, and I admire that."

"Yes, I had great respect and admiration for him, too. I was even considering offering him stocks in the Grand. He would have been the only one who wasn't family to become a shareholder, but I thought he deserved it, since he'd done so much to enhance the hotel's reputation." Max shook his head regretfully. "And all this time he was stealing from us. It's hard for me to accept that."

"I can understand why. He didn't seem the type to betray your trust," Susan said. "To tell you the truth, when I first discovered the missing wines I thought that—"

"Fritz Maier had taken them," Max guessed.

Susan nodded. "But that was so unfair of me. And stupid, too, since he's the one who ordered me to take this inventory in the first place."

"It could only have been Duprés, I'm afraid. No one else can enter this room except for Fritz and me." Max put back the bottle, but the label on the one lying next to it caught his eye. He pulled it out. "Susan," he said in a very quiet voice, "here's the '70 d'Yquem."

"No, that can't be!"

He showed her the bottle. "It was just in the wrong slot, that's all."

"But Max, I took *every* bottle out and checked it!"

"This must have been your only mistake," he said, quickly replacing the bottle, as if to hide the fact that she had made an error.

"I don't see how that's possible. Do you have my list, Max?"

He took it out of his inside jacket pocket and gave it to her.

She had to blink a few times to see it clearly, she was so discombobulated. "Okay," she said, taking a deep breath. "Let's look for the '53 Margaux together."

Max was the one who located that one, too. "Again, the wrong slot," he said, his voice bleak now. "Three down from where it should have been according to the chart."

"Forget the chart! I didn't go by the chart! I told you that I took every bottle out and checked each label." But she felt a sense of dread rise to the surface of her skin and at the roots of her hair.

In the end they located all the missing bottles, none of them in their correct niches. At each new discovery Max remained tight-lipped, silent. Susan knew he was waiting for an explanation, but she had none. She looked at him, feeling utterly desolate.

"Fritz should never have asked you to take this inventory," he finally said. "You're not a wine expert, and labels can be very confusing."

Susan couldn't allow him to make excuses for her. "I accepted the assignment. And I'm the one who's responsible in the end."

He wrapped his arm around her to comfort her. "It's not the end of the world, Susan."

It almost felt like it to her. "I swear those wines weren't here when I looked for them," she told him.

He shook his head and sighed deeply. "It's cold and lonely down here, and perhaps you gave up checking each bottle and ended up relying on the chart to make the project easier."

"I didn't!" she protested. "How many times do I have to tell you that, Max?" Once should have been enough, she thought. "You don't believe me, do you?"

His wide mouth drooped wearily. "I believe that your intentions were good. But we all make mistakes, Susan. Lord knows, I've made plenty myself."

Her heart sank like a stone; she was sure he thought she was one of those mistakes.

"I'm going to Chef Duprés's home right now," he said. "Since I wasn't the one who questioned his integrity, he may listen to me when I ask him to come back to the Grand."

"I'll go with you. I should be the one to beg him to come back, Max."

"No, you've already done—" He didn't finish his sentence.

Susan completed it for him. "Enough damage," she said flatly.

He didn't contradict her. But he took her icy hand. And when he spoke his voice was gentle. "Don't worry. Everything will be all right again."

She wanted to believe him. But she was hurt that he didn't believe her. Now that he had lost his trust in her, could things ever be all right between them again?

"I don't understand how it could have happened, Frau Kaiser," Susan said.

She had taken it upon herself to tell Max's mother about finding the missing wines while he went to talk to Duprés. The maid had ushered her into Frau Kaiser's bedroom, where she held court from a chaise lounge, dressed in a gray satin robe and silver slippers, a book on her lap, an orange cat at her feet.

"I knew it," Frau Kaiser replied. "I knew Alain Duprés was innocent and you were wrong, Miss Barnes. If I had the authority to do it, I would dismiss you immediately. You have proven to be most incompetent."

Susan's cheeks heated. But she held her tongue. How could she refute the claim that she was incompetent? The wines were there, and the valued chef was gone.

"I do give you credit, though, for coming here and admitting your mistake to me personally," Frau Kaiser added in a less severe tone. "That couldn't have been easy for you to do."

Easy? Susan found it agonizing. "I thought you deserved to know about it immediately. And I'm sure Max— Mr. Kaiser, that is—will be able to convince Chef Duprés to come back to the Grand."

"Let's hope so. The kitchen is in an uproar. One of the *sous-chefs* is also threatening to leave. Things ran so smoothly before you came here, Miss Barnes."

Susan didn't think it was the best time to remind Frau Kaiser that however smoothly things might have been going, profits had been steadily slipping.

"Well, you'll be gone soon enough," Max's mother continued. "Back to where you came from. Far away from here." She looked at Susan with cold, piercing eyes. "You do accept that, don't you? You don't expect my son to ask you to stay longer?"

"I don't expect anything from him," Susan replied stiffly.

"Nor should you. Maximilian has never thought of you as anything but a temporary...employee. He assured me of that."

"Did he?" Susan's voice was small and tight. "When?"

"Why does that matter? My son never changes his mind."

Her words hung heavily in the air, and Susan dully heard a telephone ringing in the background. The maid came in and announced that Mr. Kaiser was calling. Frau Kaiser reached for the phone by her chaise lounge.

"Miss Barnes is here with me now, Maximilian," she said in English. "She admitted her dreadful error to me. Have you persuaded Chef Duprés to return to us?" She listened a moment. "Yes, of course you must follow him there. I'll explain the situation to Miss Barnes. Good luck, my son." She hung up and gave Susan a stony look. "Chef Duprés left for his country home in France before Maximilian had a chance to talk to him."

"That's too bad. I gather Max is going there now?"

"He phoned from the airport. He won't be back until tomorrow. This is all so upsetting."

She reached for her cat, and the book on her lap slipped to the floor.

Susan picked it up for her. It was a book about ornamental plants by John Morgan. She made no comment when she handed it back to Frau Kaiser, but she had noticed that a letter with his name and address in the upper left-hand corner was being used as a bookmark.

"Thank you," Frau Kaiser said. "You may go now, Miss Barnes."

Nodding as brusquely as she had been dismissed, Susan left and went directly to Fritz's office. She didn't relish eating another helping of crow but felt obligated to admit her mistake to him, too. She quickly told him everything as she stood before his desk, sure he would give her an even harder time than Frau Kaiser had. But he was surprisingly sympathetic.

"Poor Susan, you must feel terrible," he said, coming around his desk to pat her shoulder.

"I can't figure out how I could have been mistaken." She was so despondent she hardly noticed that his avuncular pats were becoming more like caresses. "Max doesn't believe me, but I examined every single bottle in that room. And the ones I listed as missing were *not* there!"

"I believe you," Fritz said, fondling her shoulders.

"You do?" She looked at him, stunned. He was the last person she had expected to.

"Of course. That's why I didn't go down to the cellar and personally check your findings. I had full confidence that you were correct. And I still do, Susan."

"Even though the wines were there when Max and I looked? How can that be explained?"

"Well, here's a theory. Duprés heard that you were taking inventory. So last night, when no one was around, he returned the bottles he had stolen."

"If only Max had considered that possibility rather than assume I'd done sloppy work!"

"Perhaps Max *did* consider it," Fritz said.

"No, he's chasing after Duprés right now, determined to convince him to come back. Max wouldn't want him back if he thought he was a thief."

"Don't be so sure, Susan. Duprés is one of the best chefs in Europe. He adds so much to the prestige of the Grand that Max may be willing to overlook a little pilfering. After all, Duprés did return the wine, and it's doubtful that he'll dare steal any more. So Max would prefer to forget it ever happened."

She shook her head. "That wouldn't be right."

"Listen to me, Susan," Fritz said, stroking her back. "People like the Kaisers don't think in such terms as right and wrong. All they care about is what's best for their family and their hotel. And it's really in the Grand's best interest for Max to take Chef Duprés back and pretend you were the one at fault. The chef is indispensable." He paused. "But you, sad to say, are not."

Susan shook her head more vehemently. "Max wouldn't use me as a scapegoat."

"Don't be so naive, Susan! His allegiance is to his family and the hotel, not to *you*."

She felt a shiver run up her back and realized that Fritz's hand was crawling all over it. She moved away from him, instinctively repulsed by both his words and his touch. She would not let Fritz persuade her that Max would act with such cold disregard toward her. Yet Fritz Maier had managed to plant a seed of doubt in her heart. And she loathed him for it. She hurried out of his office, as if fleeing from a conversation with the devil.

Susan heard the telephone ringing as she unlocked the door to her room. Max! Please let it be Max, she prayed. She desperately needed to hear his voice now. Then she remembered that he was on a plane to France.

It turned out to be a voice from the past—the rather recent past. "Hi, Susan. It's Tony Armanto."

"Tony! You sound like you're right here in Zürich instead of thousands of miles away."

"Actually, I am in Zürich. I arrived yesterday." He chuckled at her response of stunned silence. "Don't worry. I didn't come chasing after you, Susan. I'm here for business reasons, not romantic ones."

Susan hoped her sigh of relief didn't travel over the wire. "What sort of business, if I may ask?"

"Oh, you can ask. But I don't have to answer. Would you like to have dinner with me tonight? Or maybe you don't have time for your old friends now that you're a big-deal consultant."

"Oh, Tony, I've never felt less like a big deal than I do now. And of course I have time for an old friend like you. Come to the Grand for dinner."

"No, let's meet someplace else."

Susan wouldn't hear of it. She insisted, and he finally gave in.

"I would like to see the Kaiser Grand for myself," he admitted.

When Tony arrived at the hotel that evening, Susan gave him a tour of the lobby and reception rooms before they went into the dining room. If he was impressed, he didn't show it. But that was Tony's way, Susan knew. A short, wiry man in his mid-fifties, with graying temples and a mischievous grin, he didn't give away much. Susan had learned a lot working for him. He'd been her mentor and a bit of a father figure, too, until he'd turned their easy relationship into a complicated one by declaring his love for her.

"Slow night," he said, looking around the half-empty dining room. They had been seated at an isolated corner table at Tony's request.

"Well, it's not the tourist season," Susan said defensively. In a way, she was glad it was slow, considering that Duprés wasn't there to supervise in the kitchen. She didn't mention that the chef had quit. That was Grand private business.

She was also glad Frau Kaiser hadn't come down to dinner this evening. She would enjoy Tony's company more without the older woman's disapproving presence.

"Let's get one thing clear right off," Tony said, as they waited for their aperitifs. "I still love you, kiddo. But I'm not *in* love with you anymore, if you know the difference."

Susan certainly did. "That's one of the things I admire about you, Tony. You always get right to the point."

"No sense beating around the bush. In fact, the best thing that could have happened to me was your leaving Golden Key, Susan."

She forced a laugh. "There's such a thing as being too frank, however."

"Hey, I don't mean that in a derogatory way. You did damn good work for me, and I miss your input, believe me.

But after you stepped out of the picture I was able to look at other women again. I started dating a great lady, and the attraction is mutual."

"I'm happy for you, Tony." And she sincerely was. At the same time, her vanity suffered a bit. It hadn't taken Tony very long to get over her and direct his affections elsewhere. Well, at least he missed her input. "So how are things at Golden Key?" she asked. "Did you follow my recommendations and buy the Princess?"

"You bet. She's a beaut of a hotel, Susan. A real jewel in the crown. But we're going to have to polish her up a bit and pare down overhead to make her fit in with the rest of them."

"Just don't lose too much of her unique character in the process," Susan cautioned. They talked shop for a while. And by the time the first course was served, Tony had brought the conversation around to the Kaiser Grand, prodding Susan for inside information.

She wouldn't give it to him, though. "Tony, I can't answer questions like that," she said, laying down her soup-spoon. "I'm not working for you anymore, remember. I'm a consultant *here* now."

"Okay, okay." He put up both palms to signify he'd given up. "Just making small talk."

Susan knew better. Tony never wasted time with frivolous questions. She narrowed her eyes. "I've invited the wolf to dinner, haven't I? You're interested in acquiring the Grand."

He gave her his impish grin. "See my big sharp teeth, Susan. The better to gobble up this hotel."

"Well, forget it. It's been family-owned for a hundred years, and all the shareholders are determined to keep it that way."

"Not all of them." Tony pushed away his soup bowl, folded his hands on the table, and lowered his voice. "In fact, I was approached by one of them recently. For the right price, this particular shareholder would be happy to sell out."

"Who approached you, Tony?" Susan demanded.

"I'm not about to reveal that. But I will tell you this much. I've put out feelers and know that other shareholders would be willing to sell, too. Dividends have been disappointing recently. If the situation at the Grand doesn't improve soon, I think I can get controlling interest in it."

"No way," Susan said adamantly, then remembered where she was and spoke more softly. "Max Kaiser would never sell out. And neither would his mother or uncle."

"So?" Tony crunched a bread stick. "There are lots of other relatives out there whose shares don't amount to much individually, but added up would give me control."

"The Golden Key style of management wouldn't work here," Susan told him. "You need a very special type of person to run a hotel like this."

He pointed his bread stick at her. "Would you like to be that person? Help me get the Grand, and the job is yours."

She took a long, deep sip of water before speaking again. "I don't know whether I should be flattered or insulted."

"I just offered you the job of a lifetime. Why be insulted by that?"

"Because you're asking me to work against the man who's currently employing me, Tony!"

"Don't be naive. To survive in this world, you had better take the best deal you can get. What has Kaiser offered you except a short-term consulting job?"

"Nothing," Susan admitted. She'd been called naive twice in one day and was beginning to wonder if the accusation were true.

"Well, what's your answer, Susan? You've always wanted to be the general manager of a hotel like this one. And I think you could do a damn good job for me."

She knew she could, too. But she also knew that she could never go against Max. "I'm not going to help you, Tony. The Grand should stay in the family."

"Why should it matter to you if it does or not? You're not a Kaiser."

"No," she said. Hadn't she been reminded of that all day? "But I've grown very attached to this place and would hate to see it change too much."

"I'm disappointed in you, kiddo. I thought you would jump at the chance of running it."

Susan leaned her elbows on the table, intense now. She knew what she had to do. "Listen to me, Tony. The Grand can't be run like your other hotels. It's labor-intensive and very personal. Leave it alone. There are plenty of other hotels out there for you to add to your empire."

"Yeah, but this one would be the biggest jewel of all." He looked around the elegant dining room.

"It won't *work* for you. Only the Kaisers can make it work. You used to trust my recommendations. And what I recommend now is that you walk away from this one. You don't need it, Tony!"

He didn't say anything for a long, tense moment. Then he nodded. "You're right, Susan. I need the Grand like a hole in the head. Swiss regulations concerning foreign investors are damn complicated. I'm better off staying on my side of the pond. I know what I'm doing in America. Besides, I don't trust that shareholder who approached me. He seems like a snake in the grass."

"Or a skunk," Susan said. "You're referring to Fritz Maier, aren't you?"

"I'm not gonna name any names, kiddo. Now that I've decided to drop this deal, I don't want to get into any legal hassles. But whoever it was promised me that other shareholders would sell out when they saw that the Grand was getting into deeper and deeper trouble. He even hinted that he would cause a little of it himself."

Like getting Chef Duprés to quit, Susan thought. It all became clear to her now. Max wasn't using her as a scapegoat. Fritz was! He was the one who'd taken and then replaced the valuable wines, hoping to get rid of her and Duprés at the same time. And what else had Maier been doing to cause trouble? She was determined to find out.

"What a fierce expression you have, Susan," Tony remarked. "Aren't you pleased that I've decided to follow your advice and leave the Grand alone?"

"Yes, I'm very pleased, Tony," she said. "But now I have to catch a little rodent, and that's not going to be easy."

Tony laughed. He had a loud laugh, and Susan saw a number of diners turn to look in their direction. "Well, if anybody can do it, you can. Let's order champagne and drink to your success at the Kaiser Grand."

So they did. They didn't discuss Grand business anymore, though. Now that Tony had decided to back off, he wasn't interested. They shared a pleasant meal talking about other Golden Key projects. Susan wanted to charge the dinner on her account, but Tony wouldn't let her. He paid for it with his credit card. She walked him to the entrance, kissed him goodbye on the cheek, and waved as he went off in a cab. She noticed Rolf the doorman taking it all in, but what did she care? She bade him a cheery goodnight and went up to her room.

Chapter Thirteen

Max and Susan were back in the little room where the special wines were stored, but it wasn't chilly there now. It was as warm as a sauna as Max gazed at her with love in his eyes. He told Susan that he had complete faith in her and knew, without a shadow of a doubt, that she hadn't made a mistake. How good that made her feel! She tilted back her head to receive a kiss from him and then . . .

And then the telephone rang, bringing Susan out of her dream. She reached for it groggily, knocking over the travel alarm clock on the bed table in the process. She picked up the clock from the floor, squinting at the luminous dials as she answered. It was two in the morning.

"Susan, did I wake you?" Max's deep voice came over the line, filling her with longing.

"That doesn't matter," she told him. "I'm so glad you called."

"I tried to reach you earlier this evening but you were out. Where were you?" he demanded.

"At dinner, probably. Where are *you* now?" She could hear loud music and raucous laughter in the background.

"I don't know for sure. Some French nightclub or other. Alain Duprés and I have been bar-jumping all evening."

He meant barhopping, Susan assumed, but didn't bother to correct him. "Has he agreed to come back?"

"Yes! That's why we're out celebrating. Once I managed to calm Alain down and explain how you misread those wine labels, he was very understanding about it."

"But I didn't misread..." Susan sighed. "Oh, never mind about that now." Max sounded as if he had been doing quite a bit of celebrating, and the music in the background was getting louder. It wasn't the best time to reason with him. "Anyway, I appreciate your calling to tell me the good news."

"I thought you'd want to hear as soon as possible. But that's not the only reason I called, Susan. I want to tell you something else. Something even more important, at least to me."

There was a long pause, and all Susan heard was background noise. "What, Max?"

"Well, maybe this isn't the best time. I should say it to you face-to-face and sober. Goodbye, Susan. See you tomorrow."

And then he hung up, impossible man. Would he always keep her dangling like this, not knowing where she stood with him? Had he been about to tell her that he loved her? That hope kept Susan awake for the rest of the night.

Max sat on a platform in the Grand's sauna, elbows on his knees, face sunk into the pillows of his palms. He'd never been much of a drinking man and thanks to his night out with Alain Duprés, he was suffering from a horrible hangover. Thanks to the information that had recently come his way, he was suffering even more from a combination of confusion, injured pride and sense of loss and betrayal. He didn't want to face Susan until he'd sorted everything out, but his head was throbbing too much to allow him to think clearly.

Dammit, somebody was coming into the sauna now. He should have locked the door. He lowered his hands to watch as it slowly opened. He almost laughed when Susan walked in, a towel around her. But none of this was the least bit funny.

"I hoped you would be here," Susan said.

When Max's secretary had told her that he was back at the hotel, she'd gone looking for him. And now she had found him. Her lips tilted up at the sight of him naked. She decided to tease him a moment before she took off her towel, too. She was still a little put out with him for not believing her about the missing wines, but she was willing to forgive him. How could she not? She loved the man.

But why was he staring at her like that, as if the sight of her gave him pain? Then she recalled his 2:00 a.m. phone call and decided that he really was in pain.

"Poor Max," she said, reaching out to stroke his hair. "You did too much celebrating last night, didn't you?"

He flicked back his head to avoid her touch, making it throb all the more. He glared at her as she looked back in surprise, her hand still reaching out, touching nothing but steamy air. She lowered her hand.

"What's wrong, Max?"

"Go away. I need to be alone. I'll talk to you in my office later."

"No, I need to know now. What's happened? Did Duprés change his mind about returning?"

"Hate to disappoint you, but he's back, Miss Barnes. Your little trick only worked temporarily."

"My trick? I don't understand."

Max couldn't bear the deceitful innocence in her big eyes as she stood before him, holding her towel so modestly in place. It was her eyes that he'd been captured by first. What a fool he had been! "Get out of here," he said again.

She didn't budge. Hot though it was in the small room, she was frozen in place by his frigid stare. "I won't leave until you tell me what you're talking about."

"But you already know what I'm just beginning to figure out." His voice was empty of emotion. "You came to the Grand as Tony Armanto's little spy. You reported to him that the hotel was in a weak position at the moment. You even attempted to make it a little weaker by trying to get rid of our chef with incriminating evidence. And now Armanto is here, ready to move in and take over."

Susan said nothing. The hurt she felt was almost suffocating. She could barely breathe, let alone speak. The heat swirled around her.

Max smiled. The cruelty of it sliced through her heart. "You're beginning to sweat, Miss Barnes. Didn't you expect me to catch on eventually? I admit I was slow in doing so. It's always a good idea to sleep with the boss. Sex is a great diversion, and you diverted me plenty. When it comes to that sort of manipulation, you're very good at it. Congratulations."

Silently she began to cry. The tears rolled down her damp cheeks.

"You really are amazing," Max told her. "Not only can you act in bed, you can cry on cue."

"Stop, Max," she warned, finding her voice. But she knew hers had no anger in it, only misery. "Stop, before you destroy everything we've shared together."

"That's exactly what I want to do!" he said with searing emotion. Then he took a deep, shaky breath and continued in a flat tone. "I'm almost inclined to believe you're really hurt when you look at me that way. But I know too much now. One of the shareholders Armanto offered to buy out put family loyalty before greed and tipped me off today. But you wouldn't understand loyalty, would you?" he said scornfully. "And then a staff member reported to me that you had dinner with Armanto here last night. Right here! You even toasted your success in taking over the

Grand in front of everyone. That was pretty low, Miss Barnes, even for you."

"Oh, Max, be reasonable! Why would I bring Armanto here if we were plotting against you?"

"Because you don't give a damn if I know now. Armanto has managed to acquire enough shares of the hotel for a complete takeover, hasn't he?"

"No! He's given up the idea."

"At least you admit that was his plan. And what did he offer you in return for helping him? Probably the top position here as general manager."

"Yes, but I turned him down, Max."

"The ambitious Miss Barnes turns down such an offer? Don't make me laugh." He didn't laugh, though. He pressed his fingertips against his temples.

"Listen, Max, I only found out about Tony's interest in buying the Grand last night. And I talked him out of it."

"You talked him out of it?" Max repeated in audible disbelief. "You're so brazen you can lie to me even now that I'm on to you." He got up slowly and towered over her. "You have no shame, Miss Barnes." He yanked the towel off her. He threw it to the floor and looked her over slowly, contemptuously.

Painful though she found it, Susan didn't cower under his scornful gaze. She stood her ground.

"How can you believe this of me?" she asked him in a choked voice.

"How can I *not*, Susan?" For a moment his expression softened. "What else can I think when all the evidence is shoved into my face?" His face grew hard again. "And you're the one who did the shoving by bringing Armanto here last night! Is he your lover, too? I heard rumors about you and him before I hired you. But I discounted them until now."

"And if you believe them now, you're a fool, Max Kaiser. I didn't make you one. You did that all by yourself."

She turned. He grabbed her arm and twisted her around to face him. "Not so fast," he said. "I want to get my fill of you before you go. One last time. Even a fool like me deserves that much, doesn't he?'' He yanked her closer.

Now she was breathing hard, wanting and hating him at the same time. ''What were you going to tell me when you called last night, Max?'' Three words, she knew, would end this steamy nightmare.

I love you, Max thought. That was what he'd been going to tell her. At least he had kept hold of a shred of dignity by not blabbing it over the phone to her last night.

''I was going to tell you that your services are no longer needed, Miss Barnes.'' He released her. He could never take her in anger. The marks his hard fingers had left in her soft flesh horrified him. ''Get out!'' he ordered once more.

She picked up her towel with a certain amount of dignity, wrapped it around her, and left him alone.

She'd left him in hell, Max thought as he poured water onto the hot coals and steam rose into his face. He found it astounding that he still wanted Susan. And that he could still care for her. He wished that he hadn't seen her until he'd regained more control of his emotions. He would have been able to deal with her better then, after he'd had more time to accept that she'd been plotting against him all this time.

The shock of it had sent him reeling. But it shouldn't have been a shock. He knew how ambitious she was. He'd even admired her for it! She'd mentioned more than once how important success was to her. And he remembered one intense moment when she'd told him that she wouldn't give up what she'd worked so hard to get in life for him or any man. He recalled that she'd reminded him of a fierce woman warrior, but hadn't remembered then that warriors let nothing stand in their way and showed no mercy.

Of course, she'd had a rough life, Max thought, pacing the small room, his body glistening with sweat. Susan hadn't had the advantages growing up that he'd had—the main one being a solid, stable family. Perhaps she'd never had the opportunity to learn about ethics, morals, right and wrong. But he had seen such goodness in her eyes; he had sensed such a purity of spirit. Or did his consuming sexual desire for her make him *want* to see, to feel, those qualities in her?

Max picked up the bucket beside the stove and poured cold water over his head. He had to review all the evidence against her. She had made a mistake about the wines, and she *never* made mistakes. Family members had been approached by her old boss about selling their shares. How would Armanto have even known whom to contact if Susan hadn't given him a list of shareholders? Their names weren't listed publicly because it was a privately owned business. And then she had even brought Armanto to the Grand so he could look the place over.

That took amazing gall, but so did everything else Susan had done. She'd once told him, Max recalled, precisely what Armanto would do when he took over the Grand. She'd sat in his office, so sweet and sincere, and said the first thing he would do was put in a more hard-nosed general manager who only cared about the bottom line. A manager like Susan Barnes! She'd been licking her pretty chops over that happening, right in front of his eyes. And he had been too blinded by her charms to even see. How she must have been laughing at him all the time!

That was what hurt. Even more than losing the Grand, that was what hurt Max. He gazed into the steam, head throbbing, heart aching, and wondered how he could have been so wrong about her. Then, with a searing flash of insight, he realized he hadn't been wrong about her. He had to trust his heart, and the evidence against her be damned. Susan hadn't betrayed him. He had betrayed *himself* by thinking she had.

Susan packed her suitcases, dry-eyed this time. *Your services are no longer needed, Miss Barnes.* A cold, heartless man, that was Max Kaiser. Hadn't she sensed the coldness in him the first day she'd met him? But even then she had also felt his compelling attraction. And if she had been smart, she would have taken the next flight back to the

States. Instead, she had stupidly thought she could control her feelings toward him. But love was something you couldn't control. She knew that now, a lesson learned the hard way. She remembered a time when she'd objectively observed others falling in love with the wrong person. How could you let that happen to yourself? she'd wondered.

Well, it had happened to her now. Thank God, it was over. Max had ended it with his accusations. He had wiped out all the love in her heart in one fell swoop. She slammed shut her suitcases. She slammed shut her heart, too. And she promised herself no one would be allowed entry into it ever again.

The knock came softly. She ignored it.

"Susan, please let me in."

She ignored Max's voice, too. She didn't need to hear any more hateful words from him. She'd heard enough.

He came in, anyway. She'd forgotten he had a master key to all the rooms. He came in and leaned against the door, haggard and silent, staring at her with those impenetrable blue eyes of his.

Susan realized with a terrifying certainty that she still loved him. Still! And more alarming than that was the knowledge that she would always love him, even years from now, with an ocean separating them.

"Please don't go, Susan," he said.

Her smile felt so bitter, so strained, that she thought it would crack her face. Remember how tough you are, she reminded herself. "You didn't say 'please' when you ordered me to leave less than an hour ago, Mr. Kaiser."

"I wasn't thinking clearly then. I really did need some time alone to sort everything out. Instead, you caught me in the middle, and I said things to you that I no longer believe are true. It just took me a little more time to reach that conclusion."

"Time enough for me to pack." She pointed to her suitcases. "Luckily, I travel light." No need to mention how heavy her heart was. No need at all. "I'll take a cab to the airport. But before I go, I want you to know one thing, Mr.

Kaiser." How proud she was of her steady voice. "Tony Armanto has given up the idea of buying the Grand." She didn't want him to worry about that. But she couldn't resist putting in a dig. "He decided it wasn't worth his time and effort."

If she'd made a direct hit with her last remark, Max gave no sign of it. He seemed numb. "I no longer think you were in collusion with him, Susan."

"Why not?" She raised her chin defiantly. "You made a very good case against me. I was even seen breaking bread with the enemy last night. What more damning evidence do you need than that? Surely you don't think that I'd simply invited an old friend to have dinner with me and had no idea of his takeover plans?"

"Yes, that's what I do think now. Susan, please don't look at me with such cold disregard. I can't stand it."

She was apparently a better actress than she'd thought. "Oh, excuse me, Mr. Kaiser. Would you prefer I looked at you the way you looked at me a while ago? With pure contempt?"

He swallowed hard and said something that was clearly extremely difficult for him to say. "I'm sorry. I was wrong."

"What makes you say that now? How have I suddenly been absolved of such heinous crimes?"

He absorbed her sarcasm without blinking. "My heart absolved you," he answered softly.

Damn the man! He'd said just the right thing to bring tears to her eyes. But she wasn't going to let him see tears, only rage. She blinked back the tears and released the rage. "You hurt me so much, Max! How could you hurt me like that if you cared for me even a little bit? I can never forgive you for distrusting me."

"Never, Susan?" He closed his eyes a moment, still leaning against the door, as if he needed it for support. "Would you forgive me if I went down on my knees now and begged you? Just ask me to and I will."

She was so tempted to make him do just that, so tempted to humiliate the proud Max Kaiser the way he had humiliated her when he'd pulled off her towel in the sauna. But she couldn't make herself do it. Knowing that he had given her the power to do it was enough.

"I don't need that from you, Max," she said, and couldn't keep the gentleness out of her voice. "I need time."

"Then I'll give you that," he said. "I'll give you anything you want. Only please don't leave now."

"Why should I stay?"

What a simple question, Max thought. Yet it would have been much easier to go onto his knees in front of her instead of trying to answer the question to her satisfaction. To tell her he loved her would sound absurd at this moment, after all the hurtful things he'd told her only a short time ago. She would probably laugh in his face. But he believed that time really did heal all wounds, and that she would eventually forgive him. To make her stay he would have to appeal to her sense of responsibility.

"You have a job to do here," he said. "I need your help more than ever, Susan. Armanto made it clear how vulnerable the Grand is to an outside takeover, and I still need some solutions as to how to make it more profitable, so that won't happen."

She looked at her packed bags and back to him. Even if he believed in her innocence now, others might not if she left so suddenly. Frau Kaiser, for one. Running away would make her look guilty, and she didn't want nasty rumors following her when she departed from the Grand. "All right," she said. "I signed a contract with you, and I'll stay to fulfill it." Her tone was brisk and businesslike.

"That's all I ask," he said with relief. But he made it clear he wanted more when he tried to take her into his arms.

Susan backed away, slamming her calves against the side of the bed. "Please don't touch me," she said. "I told you, Max. I need time."

He had no choice but to accept that. He had no choice, even though it had been two weeks and two days since they'd made love. He bowed like the gentleman he'd always thought he was—until he treated her so badly in the sauna. No wonder she wanted no part of him now. He nodded and left her room.

Susan snapped open her suitcases and began unpacking. She had meant what she'd told Max. She was a long way from forgiving him. A long way. But she would stick it out here until the bitter end. She had a job to do and it was a big one. She was going to nail Fritz Maier.

But to do that she needed proof, solid proof. Tony hadn't supplied her with any concrete facts, only intimations.

And she wasn't about to accuse Fritz of anything with only circumstantial evidence. In the first place, he might be able to worm his way out of it. She would have to keep her suspicions to herself until she'd hooked him, well and good. She'd seen Max let him off the hook before because he was "family," and she wasn't going to let that happen again.

In the second place, she could be wrong about Fritz. She didn't think so, but there was a slight possibility. And if she were wrong, how horrible it would be to accuse an innocent person.

She shuddered, remembering how that felt. Oh, Max, she sighed, hugging the nightgown she was holding against her chest. How could you have done that to me?

Max came into Susan's office and placed a silver-wrapped package upon her computer. She turned her attention from the figures on the screen and stared at it suspiciously.

"What's this?" she asked him.

"An early Christmas present."

She said nothing and turned her eyes back to the column of figures on the screen. She had to hand it to Fritz. He kept meticulous records of hotel expenditures.

"Well, aren't you going to open it?" Max asked, trying not to sound impatient. He should have worn a hat, he thought, so he could stand with it in hand.

"I'll wait until Christmas," she said.

"But I won't be around for Christmas. I volunteer to do rescue missions during the holiday season. I have helicopter duty all that week. The ski trails are at their busiest then."

Susan finally looked at him. "Be careful," she said.

"Where will you go for Christmas?" he asked in a light, conversational tone, although he was burning to know.

"Oh, I'll probably stick around here."

"But you know that the Grand closes up and the family goes to the Kaiser Klein. You're invited there, too, of course."

"Oh, really? That's news to me."

"But didn't my mother ask you to—?" Max bit off his question. Obviously his mother hadn't followed his suggestion. "*I'm* inviting you, Susan."

"But you're not even going to be there."

"That should be all the more reason for you to go," he joked. But it was too close to the truth to be funny.

"I think I get enough of the Kaiser clan during working hours," she said. "And I would feel out of place celebrating Christmas with your family."

Max took a deep breath. "I do not want you staying alone here, Susan. The only other people who'll be around are the caretaker and his wife. It'll be much too lonely for you."

"Then I'll go to Rome. Or Paris. Or Vienna. I haven't seen a bit of Europe since I've been here."

"You'll never get reservations anywhere at this late date. I want you to go to the Klein, and that's final."

She gave him the cold smile that she had mastered in front of the mirror, just for him. "You can't give me orders on how to spend my free time, Mr. Kaiser."

He didn't want to argue with her. He wanted to make up with her. He ached for her. He yearned for her. "Please open my present now," he said. "That's not an order. Just a request."

She snatched it off the computer and tore off the beautiful ribbon and paper, not being the least bit gracious about it. But when she opened the long velvet box she gasped. It was the platinum gold necklace with amethyst stones they had seen in the window together. The one with the five-figure price tag. "Good heavens, Max!"

He adored seeing her flush like that. It reminded him of how she looked after they'd made love. It had been so long since they had. Days of misery for him. "I knew you'd like it," he said. "Remember that night we walked together down Bahnhofstrasse and—?"

"Yes, I remember that night," she said testily. She remembered the passion of the kiss they'd shared that night,too. She shoved the box back at him without taking out the necklace. "I can't accept a gift like this from you."

Gift, in German, meant poison, and Max wondered if Susan knew that. She was certainly acting as if he'd just given her something poisonous. "Why can't you accept it?"

"It's too expensive! What are you trying to do? *Buy* my forgiveness? Well, it's not for sale, Mr. Kaiser."

That did it. Max closed the box and marched out of her office with it.

Karin came knocking on Susan's door that night. "I come as Max's emissary," she said.

Susan let her in. Karin laughed at her bunny slippers, then kicked off her own shoes and made herself comfortable on Susan's bed.

"I don't know what the problem is between you and my brother, only that there is one," she said, fluffing up a pillow to lean against. "He's very concerned about you spending Christmas alone here and sent me to entreat you to come to the Kaiser Klein."

The idea of going there was unbearable to Susan. It would only remind her of the blissful time she and Max had shared there when they'd first become lovers. But she wasn't about to tell Karin that. "Oh, I've made plans to spend that time in Vienna," she lied, just to settle the matter once and for all. "An old friend from college lives there and will be putting me up. I'm really looking forward to it," she added for good measure. "There's nothing like getting together with old friends during the holidays."

"Are we still friends?" Karin asked, looking uncomfortable. "I said something horrible to you a few weeks ago, Susan. About knowing your place. That must have sounded dreadful."

"Forget about it," Susan told her. "I have." And she really had. Too much had happened since then that had hurt a lot more.

"No, I can't forget about it, because I really think your place is here at the Grand, Susan. We could make such a great team running this place, Max, you and me." Karin's eyes, almost as blue as her brother's, lighted up at the thought.

Susan couldn't disagree. It *would* be a great team—a combination of tradition, new ideas and practicality.

"I really think running the Grand is too big a job for just one person," Karin went on. "Especially if that person has higher aspirations. Max isn't a born hotelier like my father was. He sees his life beyond the limits of the Grand. So you and I could help him here, Susan, while he goes off and saves lives and the like."

Karin had struck a chord too deep in Susan's heart. She tried not to show it. "I thought only Kaisers ran the Grand," she said dryly. "And I don't qualify."

"A mere technicality," Karin said, waving her hand. "All you have to do is marry Max, and you would be a Kaiser, too."

Susan's laugh was dry, too. "A marriage of convenience, you mean."

"No, dear friend. A marriage of love. Don't you think I can see how you and Max feel about each other? Or did, anyway. What *is* the problem between you now?"

Susan didn't answer.

Karin didn't press. "Mind if I smoke?" she asked.

Although she did, Susan handed her an ashtray.

"Well, keep in mind what I said," Karin told her, lighting up. "Being Max's wife *is* your place, and I would love to have you as my sister-in-law."

Susan looked away, hoping the pain she felt wasn't visible.

Apparently it wasn't because Karin continued to chatter away. "And speaking of in-laws, there's one we could all do without. But I've decided to wait until after Christmas to tell Aunt Berta about Fritz and his mistress. Why ruin the holidays for her? I even learned the hussy's name. *Sheba!* Sheba, of all things. And Fritz keeps her in high style. Buys her the best of everything. Well, Sheba's life of luxury will come to a sudden end once Fritz loses his job here. I wonder how long she'll stick with him after that?" Karin stubbed out her cigarette and got up from the bed. "Once Aunt Berta finds out, I suspect that Fritz's days in the Kaiser clan are numbered."

A moment later, Karin's expression turned glum. "I've never seen Max so unhappy, Susan. I don't know, maybe he deserves to be, but I hate seeing him like this. If you can make him feel better before he goes off on those rescue missions, I wish you would. I mean, they're dangerous, and if anything happened to him . . ."

"Dangerous!" Susan exclaimed, paling.

Karin nodded and left her with that thought.

Chapter Fourteen

Everyone on the Grand staff was in a jolly mood the day before the hotel closed for the holiday season. Everyone but Susan, that is. And when she walked into Max's office she saw that he wasn't exactly the personification of Santa Claus himself. He stood up when she entered, his expression desolate.

"I found a message on my desk that you wanted to see me," she said.

"Yes, of course I wanted to see you. I was hoping that we could part as friends today."

"Not as enemies, anyway." She stuck out her hand.

He took it between both of his. The warmth of his touch passed up her arm and into her heart.

"How much more time do you need before you can find it in your heart to forgive me, *Liebling?*" he beseeched her.

Oh, he was pulling out all the stops now by calling her that, Susan thought. If expensive necklaces don't work, try a little sweet talk together with a soulful expression. And the truth was, that did work a lot better. She sighed.

"I don't know how much more time I need," she told him honestly. She wanted to forgive him, but a part of her couldn't. Not yet. It wasn't that she wanted to punish him or make him suffer. But she wasn't ready to trust him the way she once had. And Max seemed to understand that. He seemed to understand that he had done a great deal of damage to her heart, and she still felt a need to protect it from further hurt.

"Karin tells me you're going to visit a friend in Vienna for the holidays," he said, attempting to sound casual.

"Yes, I'm leaving tomorrow." Susan made an effort to pull back her hand but he wouldn't let go.

"Is this a female friend?" he asked her.

Her intention had never been to make him jealous. She didn't play games like that. She didn't play games at all. "Oh, yes. A woman I've known for a long time."

Max released her hand, seemingly satisfied with that much, anyway. "Then have a happy Christmas, Susan."

"You too, Max."

They both almost smiled at the impossibility of either of them having that.

"And you'll come back here after the holidays, won't you?" Max asked her. The muscles around his eyes were tense. There were deep shadows beneath them.

She nodded. "My contract with the Grand doesn't end until mid-January."

"That can be extended."

"No, I don't think so. By then I'll have a full report for you, with concrete suggestions for improvements. So there'll be no reason for me not to... move on."

"Do you have another consultation assignment lined up?"

"Not yet. But I will." She looked away. She didn't want to talk about the future with him. She noticed his duffel bag in the corner of the office.

He followed her gaze. "I'm going directly to the heliport as soon as I clear my desk and say goodbye to the staff," he said.

Susan bit her lip, then spoke. "These rescue missions—how dangerous are they?"

Max shrugged. "Not very, if you know what you're doing. I only take calculated risks, Susan."

He had told her that once before and it still made her uneasy. "God keep you safe, Max," she said and walked away without looking back.

But later she saw him in the lobby, shaking hands with staff members, wishing them a good holiday. She went to his office and wrote a short note on his scratch pad. Only three words. *I forgive you.* She wanted to put his mind at ease so he could better concentrate on flying. She folded the note and stuck it into his duffel bag. And she felt much better when she hurried away because the moment she had written the note she'd realized that she really had finally forgiven him—even though she still longed to hear him speak three other short words to her.

Well, this is a nice way to spend Christmas Eve, Susan thought grimly. Breaking and entering. She jimmied the lock on Fritz's office door with a screwdriver, trying not to make too much noise in the process. She didn't want to alert the caretaker, but there wasn't much chance of that. Mr. Schulz and his wife were in their apartment in a far-off wing of the hotel. She'd even had the audacity to ask Mr. Schulz to lend her the screwdriver, telling him she needed it to fix her hair dryer. Since that was personal rather than hotel property, he hadn't offered to fix it for her.

She wedged the tool between the door and the frame, scarring it. She couldn't believe she was actually doing this. If she didn't find the evidence she needed, she would have a lot of explaining to do. Oh, well. Nothing ventured, nothing gained. Fritz was with the family at the Kaiser Klein, nobody else was around, and she couldn't pass up this opportunity to confirm her suspicions that the two-faced financial comptroller was keeping double books. The accounts Fritz had turned over to Susan just didn't make sense, even though they balanced perfectly. She'd pored over them for the last three days, trying to discover what was missing. And she'd come to the conclusion that the only way she could do that was by going straight to the source.

The lock clicked. She turned the handle and went inside, closing the door firmly behind her. She turned on the lights and went straight to Fritz's file cabinet. It would probably take all night to go through the files. So what? She had all night. But the metal cabinet was locked, too. Damn! She didn't know how she could manage to pry it open.

She had another idea. An even better one, she hoped. She sat down behind Fritz's desk and switched on his computer. All the computers in the hotel were on the same system, but she was sure Fritz had a hidden file in his that nobody could access without knowing the password. And only Fritz knew that. But Susan had a hunch. She wiped her sweaty hands against her skirt and placed her fingers on the keyboard. She typed carefully, holding her breath all the while. *Sheba*. Eureka! Numbers filled the screen. Numbers much different from the ones Fritz had given her.

Max's family was already gathered around the table for Christmas Eve dinner when he walked into the Kaiser Klein dining room. They always ate at eight sharp, but he was a few minutes late because he'd called the Grand to check up on things before coming to the table. Mr. Schulz had given him some surprising news. Susan wasn't in Vienna, after all. She was at the hotel. And all this time Max had assumed that he couldn't get in touch with her.

"Better late than never," his mother said, when Max took his place at the head of the table. "I'm so pleased that you could make it to dinner this evening, my son. You should always put family duties before others."

Max smiled at her wearily. He'd taken a break from his rescue duties to be with them, and knew his mother was sincerely pleased that he had, but she still somehow managed to make it sound like a reprimand. As always, he took it in stride.

He looked around the table at the people he loved. His mother, of course. His sister Karin, who was proving to be a valuable addition to the Grand staff. His dear Aunt Berta. And Great-uncle Anton, who had always given him such wise counsel.

No, not always. Max had made up his mind to disregard the last piece of advice Uncle Anton had given him, because the one other person he loved—the one he now loved most, in fact—wasn't present this evening and should have been. Yes, Susan Barnes should have been part of this family gathering. And he fervently hoped that next year she would be.

He had carried the note she'd left in his duffel bag close to his heart during all his rescue missions this week. She'd forgiven him! And Max knew that the reason she had was because she loved him. Only one matter remained to be settled between them now. He intended to drive to the Grand and settle it right after dinner.

Max noticed that there was one family member missing this evening—one whom he didn't even like, much less love.

"Where's Fritz?" he asked.

Aunt Berta raised her head high. "I ordered him out earlier today. He can either go to hell or to his mistress, and they are one and the same as far as I'm concerned."

"Fritz has a mistress?" This was news to Max. "How did you find out about it, Aunt Berta?"

"I told her," Karin said. "I was going to wait until after the holidays, but I couldn't bear seeing that hypocrite here, acting like the lord of the manor."

"I had my suspicions, anyway," Berta said. "I will begin divorce proceedings immediately. And frankly, it will be a relief to be rid of him. As a husband Fritz was... disappointing, to say the least. But until now I couldn't bear to admit I made a terrible mistake when I married him."

Max had his own suspicions concerning Fritz. But he hadn't wanted to confront the man until he could verify that he'd been embezzling from the Grand. After all, Fritz had been a devoted employee for many years. Both his father and his brother had trusted him. But Max didn't. And now he would call for a full-scale investigation.

It could result, Max knew, in an ugly scandal, but since Aunt Berta was divorcing Fritz, he wasn't concerned about that anymore. And Berta didn't seem particularly upset about it, either, Max thought, as he watched her take a large serving of the goose being passed around. He smiled. Perhaps Fritz's goose was cooked, too.

Frau Kaiser cleared her throat. "I, too, have some news, Maximilian," she declared. "But not as shocking as Berta's, I trust. My dear friend John Morgan has asked me to visit him in America, and I've decided to accept his kind invitation."

"What?" Karin's eyes widened. "You hardly ever leave the Grand and now you're going off to America, Mother? Surely you're joking."

But Frau Kaiser never joked. "I'm quite serious. I have isolated myself for too long. I will always mourn my losses, but as John pointed out to me when he was here, life is for the living. We're very compatible, he and I."

"How long will you be gone?" Max asked her.

"That depends," Frau Kaiser answered vaguely. "John and I will see where our friendship leads."

"I hope it leads to happiness, Mother," Max said, and saw Karin nod in agreement.

"If no one else has an announcement, I suggest we eat," Great-uncle Anton said gruffly, his knife and fork poised.

Max rose. "I do have an announcement," he declared. Now that his mind was made up, it seemed a good time to make his intentions known to all of them. "I am going to ask Susan Barnes to be my wife. She may not accept. We've had a recent breach in our relationship. But she's forgiven me for that, and I believe she loves me as much as I love her. I hope you all wish me well in winning her hand in marriage.''

"I certainly do, Max!" Karin said.

"Lovely young lady, Miss Barnes," Aunt Berta said mildly.

"She isn't Swiss!" Great-uncle Anton objected, pounding his fist on the table. All the wineglasses trembled. Then he sighed. "She is lovely, though, Nephew. And if I were a little younger, I might be inclined to give you a little competition in winning her over."

Frau Kaiser said nothing. She stood up, stared at Max for a long moment, then left the table, one hand pressed to her heart.

Susan leaned back in Fritz's chair and rubbed her tired eyes. It had taken her many hours to untangle his web of deceit and figure it all out. But she'd eventually established that the Grand's profits were much higher than Fritz had reported them to be. For the last few years he'd not only been skimming, he'd been digging deep. His embezzlement amounted to millions. Susan assumed he'd been stashing the money in some secret bank account. And by God, the Grand would get it back now that she had the proof. She made a copy of the file and slipped the disk into her skirt pocket. Her Christmas present to Max and his family, she thought with satisfaction.

She heard footsteps outside the door, and her heart began to pound. But what did it matter if the caretaker discovered she had broken into the office? Her action had proved to be warranted.

"Mr. Schulz, is that you?" she called.

The door opened. Fritz Maier walked in. "Guess again, Susan." He closed the door softly behind him. "I told Mr. Schulz and his wife to take the evening off. They've gone to visit family. So we're all alone. Isn't that lovely?''

How calm Fritz seemed, Susan thought. That frightened her more than if he had shown anger at finding her here in his office. She knew she was in big trouble, and her mind raced over ways to get out of it. Fritz wasn't a tall man, but he was burly. She didn't think she could overpower him. She spotted a heavy paperweight on the desk, heavy enough to crack a man's skull. But the idea of actually doing that to someone was abhorrent to her. Besides, Fritz had made no menacing moves. Yet.

He shook a finger at her. "It's not nice to break into people's offices, Susan."

"Well, it didn't do me much good," she bluffed. "I didn't find anything interesting."

"That's too bad," he said. He took some keys out of his pocket and tossed them to her. "Go open my file cabinet. Everything you need to know is inside."

Was this a trick? But he was blocking the way out, so she had no choice but to follow his orders. She got up and unlocked the cabinet. He moved right behind her when she did. But he didn't touch her. He yanked open the top drawer and reached in. He pulled out a little gun and pointed it at her. And he laughed.

"You really *are* naive, my lamb," he said. "Now go sit down again. And if you try to run away, I'll shoot you."

She did as she was told and attempted to reason with him. "Fritz, you can't kill me. You'll never get away with it."

"Why not? I came upon a burglar in my office. I shot before seeing who it was. And oh, dear me, much to my chagrin, I turned on the light and discovered it was none other than Miss Barnes!" He clucked his tongue. "Such a pity. I'll be so upset when the police come. But they'll look at all the evidence and conclude I made a justifiable mistake."

Max loved traveling on his motorcycle at night. The roads were clearer, and he could drive faster. He couldn't wait to reach the Grand and be with Susan. It was close to eleven and he was almost in Zürich. They would be sharing Christmas Day together, after all. They would be sharing the rest of their lives together if she said yes. With every mile he covered Max prayed that she would.

"Why would you want to kill me, Fritz? I've found nothing that could hurt you."

His eyes moved to the blank computer screen. Thank God, Susan thought, that she had exited from his secret file after making a copy of it. She felt the disk rubbing against her skin through her skirt pocket. If he searches me, I'm dead, she thought. She tasted panic on her tongue, a sharp, metallic taste.

"I don't *want* to kill you," he told her, still as calm as could be. "In fact, I've always been attracted to you, Susan. And I could sense that you felt the same about me from the first moment we met."

Good Lord, he really was crazy, Susan thought. "You're right, Fritz," she said. "I find you very attractive and exciting." The words almost choked her, but she managed to get them out. If she could just get him to put down the gun!

"And what about Max, my pet?" Fritz asked. "Are you still attracted to him, too?"

"That's over," she said. "He fired me because of the mistake I made about the missing wines."

"Sorry about that, Susan. I'm the one responsible for that little episode." Fritz seemed to think for a moment and frowned. "But if Max fired you, why are you in my office now?"

Good question. And Susan feared she couldn't come up with an answer to save her life. Well, she *had* to, because it really might save her life. "I'm spying for Tony Armanto," she said.

"Why? He told me he was no longer interested in acquiring the Grand."

"He's changed his mind again," Susan said quickly. "And now that you know, he'll pay you any price you want for your shares."

Fritz looked crestfallen. "Too late. Berta is divorcing me, and I'll lose control of those shares. She became enraged when she found out I had a mistress."

Act sympathetic, Susan told herself. Make him think you're his friend now. "She found out about Sheba? What a shame, Fritz!"

In the next instant she knew what a dreadful slip she had made. She saw the click in Fritz's little black eyes. He raised his little black gun. "So you know about Sheba, do you?"

Susan shrugged, still trying to bluff her way out. "So what if I do? I don't care if you have a mistress, Fritz. I didn't tell Berta. Live and let live, that's my policy."

Fritz glanced at the computer screen again. "But I don't think I *can* let you live now, my pet. If you know my mistress's name, you know an entry code to a certain file. When I came here tonight to delete the file, I noticed a light in my office. So I dismissed Schulz and came back to deal with the intruder. I had a hunch it was you."

"What code? I don't know what you're talking about."

"Susan, my dove, you know *everything*."

She knew bluffing wasn't going to work anymore. "It doesn't matter if I do. Wipe out the records, and then there won't be any proof." Now the disk seemed to be burning a hole in her pocket.

"I should wipe you out, too," Fritz said, and then laughed. "That's American gangster talk, isn't it?"

Max had expected to find Susan in her room. He was disappointed when he didn't. Had she gone out for the evening? He went back to the dimly lit lobby. It occurred to him that she could be in her office. It would be just like Susan to work on Christmas Eve. He headed for that area and noticed a crack of light under the door of Fritz's office.

"Susan, are you in there?" he called. He turned the knob and spotted the jimmied lock. The hairs on the back of his neck stood up. He froze.

"Yes, she's in here, Max," he heard Fritz Maier say. "And I have a gun pointed right at her. I suggest you come in very slowly."

Max followed the suggestion. Susan, pale and wide-eyed with terror, was sitting in a chair behind the desk. And Fritz really did have a gun pointed at her.

"Don't move any closer," Fritz warned him. "Don't move at all."

"Stay calm, Fritz," Max said. "Don't do anything crazy."

"But I'm as calm as can be," he replied, turning his attention—and the gun—toward Max.

Good, Max thought, let him keep the gun on me instead of Susan. "What the hell is going on, Fritz?"

"Shh," Fritz said, raising a finger to his lips. "I'm trying to think things out." After a moment he sighed. "And the only solution I can come up with is to kill both of you. Your bodies won't be found until tomorrow. That will give me enough time to get out of the country. Luckily, I have enough money in a numbered account to keep me quite comfortable wherever I choose to go." He smiled at Max. "Kaiser money."

The important thing to do, Max thought, was to keep him talking. When the time was right, he would overtake Fritz. He hoped Susan had sense enough to dive under the desk when he pounced. He didn't want her getting hit by a stray bullet. Max supposed he could possibly get shot in the process, but he was much bigger and stronger than Fritz, and chances were good that he could avoid being killed. It was a calculated risk that he was most willing to take to save Susan. He had no doubt that Fritz truly intended to murder them. He could see it in the man's eyes.

"Kaiser money?" he inquired.

"Oh, yes. Millions, dear Max. I've been stealing from the Grand for years. And enjoying every minute of it. I hate you Kaisers, you know. So privileged. So superior. I devoted the best years of my life to the Grand and got nothing in return."

"Sounds to me like you got plenty. Why do you hate us so much? What did we ever do to you?"

"You made me feel inferior. But I would have given back all the money I embezzled if the family had decided to make me general manager instead of you. Because they didn't, I decided to destroy this hotel. But alas, that plan failed. So now I'll have to be satisfied with just destroying you, Max."

"Fine. Take your revenge out on me, and let Susan go."

"I can't!"

"Yes, you can," Max said. He didn't dare take his eyes from Fritz to look at Susan. He was dealing with a man consumed by insane jealousy. "Tie her up and make your escape. There's no reason to kill her. She's not a Kaiser."

"But she'll end up dying in the fire, anyway, Max. She'll suffer less with a quick bullet." Fritz's smile was benevolent. "You see, I've just decided to set fire to the hotel before I leave it for good. I can't imagine why that happy thought didn't occur to me sooner." Fritz watched Max carefully. "Let me see you suffer, Max. Think how your family will suffer, too. You'll be dead, and they'll be left with nothing."

Max saw a flash of movement behind Fritz. It happened so suddenly he had no time to even blink. Susan smashed something against the back of Fritz's head and he fell to the floor in a heap.

"Oh, God, I hope I didn't kill him!" she exclaimed, dropping the heavy paperweight.

But Fritz wasn't even unconscious. He moaned as Max grabbed the gun from his hand.

Max smiled at Susan. "Poor Fritz didn't know he was up against a woman warrior, did he, my love?"

Susan was exhausted. After the police had come to arrest Fritz, she and Max had had to answer questions for hours. They'd just arrived at his flat, and now they stood before the long window in his bedroom to watch the sun come up. It tinted the stone church in the square a rosy pink.

Max wrapped his arm around Susan's waist. "That church is called the Sankt Peterskirche," he said. "Generations of Kaisers have been married in it. And I would like to be married in it, too. Would you have any objections to that, Susan?"

Well, she knew an indirect marriage proposal when she heard one. But she wasn't going to settle for anything less than the real thing.

"What do my objections have to do with it, Max?"

"You would be the bride. I'm asking you to marry me, Susan."

Good for him, she thought. He'd come right out with it. But she needed to hear more than that. She turned to look him straight in the eye. "Why, Max?"

"Why?" Her question seemed to stun him. "There's only one reason. I love you."

Finally! Susan breathed a sigh of relief. "I love you, too, Max," she told him.

"Then it's settled," he said.

Not quite. She shook her head. "I don't want a marriage filled with family problems."

"What problems? Karin already thinks of you as a sister. Uncle Anton has reconciled himself to the fact that you're not Swiss only because he finds you as irresistible as I do. And Aunt Berta couldn't care less."

"You haven't mentioned one major family member yet, Max. What about your mother?"

"Ah, yes. My mother." Max smiled. "When I announced my intention to ask you to marry me, she left the room without a word. And she came back with this." Max patted the pockets of his jacket. He located what he was searching for and pulled it out—a little jewelry box. "She gave this to me before I left the Kaiser Klein last night."

Susan took the box and opened it—to discover an exquisite cameo framed in diamonds. Although it was far more elegant, it reminded Susan of the cameo her grandmother had left her. The one that had been stolen from her long ago.

"It's a Kaiser tradition for the women in the family to pass this brooch down from one generation to the other," Max explained, as she stared at the cameo. "All good wishes go with it."

"And your mother wants *me* to have this?" Susan asked Max, amazed.

"Yes. It means she welcomes you into the family, Susan. But even if she hadn't, it wouldn't have made any difference to me. I still would have asked you to marry me. You come first in my heart and always will."

Susan believed him. But she also knew that life would go much more smoothly, now that Frau Kaiser had made her this peace offering.

Max watched her pin the brooch on her blouse. "Does that mean you accept my proposal?"

"I need to think about it a little longer," she teased.

"I'm not a patient man, Susan."

To prove it he picked her up and threw her onto the bed. He took off all his clothes and stood before her naked, mighty and vulnerable at the same time.

"I'm going to stand here until you make up your mind," he said.

So she said yes.

*   *   *   *   *

BIG SUMMER READ

Summer Reading At Its Best

In July, Harlequin and Silhouette bring readers the Big Summer Read Program. Heat up your summer with these four exciting new novels by top Harlequin and Silhouette authors.

SOMEWHERE IN TIME by Barbara Bretton
YESTERDAY COMES TOMORROW by Rebecca Flanders
A DAY IN APRIL by Mary Lynn Baxter
LOVE CHILD by Patricia Coughlin

From time travel to fame and fortune, this program offers something for everyone.

Available at your favorite retail outlet.

BSR

Linda Lael Miller

the author of bestselling historical and
contemporary novels,
presents her readers with

Beyond the Threshold

two stories linked
by centuries, and by love....

There and Now

The story of Elisabeth McCartney, a woman looking for a love
never to be found in the 1990s. Then, with the mystery of her
Aunt Verity's necklace, she found her true love—Dr. Jonathan
Fortner, a country doctor in nineteenth-century Washington....
There and Now, #754, available in July 1992.

Here and Then

Desperate to find her cousin, Elisabeth, Rue Claridge searched
for her in this century . . . and the last. She found Elisabeth, all
right. And also found U.S. Marshal Farley Haynes—a nineteenth-
century man with a vision for the future....
Here and Then, #762, available in August 1992.   SELLM-1

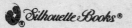